PAUSE BETWEEN ACTS

Mavis Cheek

SIMON AND SCHUSTER
New York   London   Toronto   Sydney   Tokyo

Simon and Schuster
Simon & Schuster Building
Rockefeller Center
1230 Avenue of the Americas
New York, New York 10020

*This book is a work of fiction. Names, characters, places and incidents are either the
product of the author's imagination or are used fictitiously. Any resemblance to actual
events or locales or persons, living or dead, is entirely coincidental.*

Originally published in Great Britain by
The Bodley Head Ltd.
SIMON AND SCHUSTER and colophon are registered trademarks
of Simon & Schuster Inc.
Designed by Deirdre C. Amthor
Manufactured in the United States of America
1 3 5 7 9 10 8 6 4 2
Library of Congress Cataloging in Publication Data
Cheek, Mavis.
Pause between acts/Mavis Cheek.

p.   cm.
ISBN 0-671-66730-0
I. Title.
PR6053.H4334P3   1988   88-18290
823'.914—dc19   CIP

Grateful acknowledgment is made to the following:

Excerpt in "Tulips" from *The Collected Poems of Sylvia Plath*, edited by Ted
Hughes. Copyright © 1962 by Ted Hughes. Reprinted by permission of Harper
& Row, Publishers, Inc.

From "Fidelity," from *The Complete Poems of D. H. Lawrence*, edited by Vivian
da Sola Pinto and F. Warren Roberts. Copyright © 1964, 1971 by Angelo Ravagli
and C. M. Weekley, executors of the estate of Frieda Lawrence Ravagli. All rights
reserved. Reprinted by permission of Viking Penguin Inc.

Excerpts from "Rhapsody on a Windy Night," "Gerontion," and "The Waste
Land" in *Collected Poems 1909–1962*, by T. S. Eliot. Copyright 1936 by Harcourt
Brace Jovanovich, Inc. Copyright © 1963, 1964 by T. S. Eliot. Reprinted by
permission of the publisher.

For my daughter, Bella

*For their friendship, encouragement
and the gift of time, special thanks
to my female friends,
without whom . . .*

PART ONE

Chapter One

I suppose it all began three years ago when Jack left me. That had a kind of theatricality. I was just putting the fairy lights on the tree – far too early but it was our first married Christmas and the trees had looked so fresh and green in the market – when he rang from Durham.

I think I knew as soon as he said he was extending his visit, though I soldiered on saying things like – Oh well – it doesn't matter – and deliberately not asking why. It wasn't that unusual since Jack made films for television and such a life is not bound by rigid schedules. So I continued to chat, twisting a piece of tinsel around my finger, looking through the window at the fresh snow on the road, asking what the weather was like up there and weren't they cold in the cathedral (they were filming in it) and he said yes, he was, but the whole thing was proving a marvellous spiritual experience.

A bloody marvellous spiritual experience it must have been because – as he told me in a firm this-is-the-way-it-is voice – he had fallen in love. There, surrounded by all that Romanesque glory, hearing the choir's soaring songs, watching the night sky dim that great, stained window, he had in his uplifted state turned to find – not me – but a pale-faced sub-editor with big boobs, Irish eyes a-smiling and a penchant for her attractive, successful superior.

She won. By the time he rang me hers was the victory – the battle was over. I can't remember exactly how the telephone conversation changed, nor how he managed to suddenly be saying that – actually – he wouldn't be coming home at all. Nor do I recall very much of what I said except the strangely inapposite 'Oh dear – and I've bought the tree – what a shame ...'

I only remember that when he rang off my internal pain was lessened somewhat by my external one. I had wound the tinsel so tight that its cord had cut into my finger. Red drops on the white carpet. It only needed holly or laurel to complete the festivities.

Poor tree and poor me. By the time I came round from the state of agony all the needles had turned a crisp brown so they

9

fell at a touch. It leaned groggily on its manufactured stump –
rootless, lifeless, rather like me.

I went to see him at her flat. I took a dozen red carnations
with a card on them that said, I still love you. I didn't want all the
doors to be closed when he wanted to come back. I'd put an
elastoplast over my wound as I had on my finger and in time I
knew it would mend. This could only be a frivolous encounter.
This could not last. He had been silly. I would forgive him –
eventually. In the meantime I would behave myself. Be composed. There was little danger of being anything else since I felt
utterly composed. Dead, as I said, like the tree. I parked my
Morris Minor – yes, yes, a Morris Minor sort of a person – in
the road adjacent to hers – and got out feeling OK in a dead sort
of way. A little walk in the frosty air would bring some colour
into my cheeks – an attractive phenomenon which might take
care of the fact that I hadn't had a clue what to wear. What does
one wear for one's first meeting with a miscreant husband?
Shops are full of signs in dress departments saying Sports Gear,
After Eight Chic, Cocktail Hour – but none, so far as I know,
put up a sign saying Cuckolded Wife Wear ...

Imaginatively I wore jeans and a jumper. This is how I am,
Jack – This is how I was, Jack. Look. Look, I am not going over
the top – I am exactly the person I was when you went away.

On reflection I wish I had worn a velvet G-string and thigh-
high boots. He'd have hated it, being a surprisingly pedestrian
love-maker. But at least I'd have gone out in style. And the
sharp coldness of the afternoon would have brought a glow to
more than one pair of cheeks. But no. Joan Battram, *née* Ellis,
was ever one to dream about lifting off. So the jumper and jeans
made their inexorable journey towards their doom.

She lived, of course, in Notting Hill. All thrusting and thriving
and cosmopolitan, with a hundred names to every front door
and rooms without net curtains full of pot plants and esoteric
posters. I had lived here once – so had Jack though in a better
part of the same area. It was the life we both eschewed when we
got married and bought the house in Chiswick less than a year
ago. Chiswick had milkmen who whistled and came regularly
each morning – real stability. Notting Hill sold its milk in
cartons and nobody knew your name. The area felt quite alien to
me now as I stomped through the slush to her hallowed portals.

I was no longer of that transient, singular life. In the nine months of our marriage I had taken to security like a duck to water; liked our neighbours Geraldine and Fred, liked making plans for home improvements – even liked gardening; Notting Hill no longer suited me. But when Jack opened the door, I could see it still suited him. He looked, quite simply, marvellous. All glowing and about ten years younger, he was forty and looked thirty, I was thirty and felt ninety. Nine hundred and ninety when he ushered me in and I saw that she was there as well. Being a well-bred sort of a person I hadn't liked to say, when we made the arrangement, that I wanted to see him alone. I had assumed it would be so. A wrong assumption. I gave him the flowers and there was a surreal moment – more theatre – when he handed them to her, Lizzie was her name, assuming I had brought them for her. She read the card, coughed delicately, and handed them back to him. He read the card and looked at me with eyes of pity. I'd lost.

They went on to reiterate how incontestably I had lost, sitting close to each other on the hessian settee, she mostly silent, nodding occasionally and once or twice saying in her dulcet Irish tones that she was sorry, so very sorry. No doubt she meant it. I remained very well behaved throughout, accepting everything with intelligent eyes and mute mouth, giving up listening after a while to look at them as they spoke to me so earnestly. They made a beautiful couple. Jack tall, long legged, powerful shoulders and slim hips – all the clichés; dark greying hair cut close to his head, Mr Smoothie face, a refugee from a lavish American soap opera. Except he wasn't really like that, he just looked it. She was a typically Gaelic beauty with a mass of black curly hair, large dark eyes and that creamy slightly freckled skin. Small boned but rounded, infinitely touchable, and with the blessing of a generous bosom that made war on her soft woolly jumper. Mine was a pair of cherry pips by comparison. I wished she would go for a moment instead of sitting there so close to him. But the little banshee knew better than to leave us alone. I looked into his eyes trying to communicate but he would have none of it and blinked and looked away finding a sudden interest in the towering houseplants that crowded about the room. I began to listen to what he was saying – after all, that was what I had come for. It was all practicalities, addressed mostly to the cheese plant or the variegated ivy. I nearly leaned across the

11

small divide between us to prod him and say 'excuse me, I'm over here' but – what the hell – it didn't matter whether he spoke to the foliage or to me – the messages were the same. Jack was in love with his Lizzie, Jack was no longer in love with his Joan. It was no fault of mine – just a matter of chemistry – and he would make sure that I suffered as little as possible. Like an animal about to be put down, I wanted to say, but I controlled it just in time because I realised it was a remark of borderline hysteria. Irish was looking down at her hands throughout, calm as a nun. So I just listened.

The house, of course, would be mine. And if I didn't mind, Mind?, would I arrange for Jack's personal effects (like a death, then?) and his technical equipment and anything else that I thought it correct for him to have, to be packed and sent on to an address he would give me.

'Not here then?' I said brightly.

Heavy scrutinisation of a jasmine frond and then, 'Er – no – we're moving to Fulham. I've sold the boat.' He gave a little deprecating shrug. 'It's only a little house ... But it's what we can afford. I didn't want you suffering, you see' (that word again). 'The mortgage on Chiswick will be paid off for you. My solicitor is seeing to that ...'

His solicitor?

So that really was it then? I looked at the carnations forlorn and forgotten on the arm of the settee. What was it Sylvia Plath wrote about red flowers? Red flowers – not carnations but tulips – but still the same redness. I suddenly understood the lines but would have preferred to remain in academic ignorance.

'The tulips are too red in the first place, they hurt me ...
Their redness talks to my wound, it corresponds ...
They concentrate my attention, that was happy
Playing and resting without committing itself ...'

Bloody poetry condensing pain.

I got up, stiff from tension and the stupidity of her taste in low level chairs. My palms were sweaty, I felt sick and faint. They stood up, seeming a long way off, I heard Irish say 'Are you all right?' What a crapulous question. I remembered a television news reporter interviewing a young woman whose husband had been blown to pieces by a bomb. 'And how do you feel now?' he asked. It would have been to her eternal credit if she had said 'Oh fine, just fine. I'm going to have a cup of tea and then nip

12

down to the Palais for a folk dance ...'

'Fine. I'm fine' I said as they began to take their proper perspective in the room again. 'Just a bit warm in here ...' 'Yes' she said 'I keep the heating on high for the plants.' 'I can see they respond.' And then, No – I was damned if I was going to get into conversation.

Somehow I got out. Jack put a piece of paper into my hand as I stood on the step and my heart gave a sturdy leap. But it wasn't a note of assignation or personal for your eyes only comment – it was the forwarding address and the date from when they would take up residence. Of course it was.

'OK?' he asked gingerly.

Fine, just fine. I'm going to have a cup of tea and then nip down to the Palais for a ...

The coldness restored me. I walked around for half an hour or so thinking about it. I saw it in its simplest terms. The old, old story. He had fallen in love with a pair of adoring grey eyes and fifteen years fewer than his own. Simple. Where he had gone wrong, the fool, was to spice it up with so much theatricality. He had always loved drama, always wanted to make films about plays and players – worlds within worlds he called it when he did the Royal Shakespeare Company. And now he was living his own little one act piece. He should have just kept quiet about her. Not told me, let it run its course so that when the lovers' frisson died amid the early morning grumpiness and rings around the bath, he hadn't lost everything. His job would have made a perfect cover for an extra-marital affair – he could easily have run us both together, but no – not Mr Jack 'call me Schlesinger' Battram – too ordinary.

And of course, by the time some of their more irritating habits had eroded the Tristan and Isolde bit – which was less than six months later – I didn't give a damn for him, nor for anyone much. I was perfectly at one with myself, cold as marble, and quite content to remain like that forever. I'd have given that news interviewer a run for his money.

The suspicions I had been scarcely allowing to surface came to a head about a week after this visit to their plant strewn love nest. I collected a little phial from the doctor's surgery, did my little pee, and got the result a couple of days later. I was pregnant.

It didn't seem worth telling anybody, apart from the necessary discussion with my GP, because I had no intention of having the

13

child. I was booked into a clinic for a Wednesday and came out on the following Friday as a single entity again. It had all been like a turkey line and the wonderful story I had composed to while away the time was never required. I had imagined a caring starched white nurse bending low over my pillow with her sympathetic cool hands placed on my brow while I told her that my husband had died, mysteriously, in the African bush and I had no will to bear his child alone. As it was I was dealt with by a pinched untidy staff nurse who looked as if she had been weaned on lime juice and would have had us all arrested if she could. The small ward was redolent with guilt, shame, remorse and low vulgar wit. The only bright spot was a Scots girl called Annie who was on the game and having her third abortion and who, in between filling in her puzzle magazines, said she reckoned it was safer than taking the pill.

'What do you do for a living?' she asked me.

'Nothing' I said.

'No' she replied in a desultory manner. 'Neither do I – much. Most of them just want to talk about their mothers nowadays.'

She was flicking through a magazine as she spoke, then she suddenly stopped, folded the page back and said 'Don't mind me saying this but you'd look better with your hair done this way.' She threw the magazine onto my bed. Up from its page glared a high cheekboned model, flaring her nostrils and giving venom to the camera. The hair was cut like a Chinese waitress's, a hard edged black helmet.

'Go on' said Annie. 'It'd suit you. Honest.'

'But I've got fair hair' I said critically.

'Doesn't matter. That long curly look's right out now. Anyway you can always grow it back ...'

'Maybe' I said non-committally – but I knew I would do it. And up yours, Jack, I thought, for all those nights long ago when you used to twine it around your hands and pull me to you.

Kim, my hairdresser, balked at first. She ran her fingers through the hair she had so carefully nurtured and stared at me in the mirror.

'Definitely not' she said. 'It won't suit you. It's perfect for you the way it is.'

I met her eyes in the mirror. 'All perfection must be flawed, Kim' I said 'or we should all be God.'

14

Clearly she thought I had become a little unhinged – well, perhaps I had – but she argued no more and the scissors went to work and when it was done she said, grudgingly, that it didn't look too bad after all. It didn't. Annie of the magazine had been right. It looked rather good. Just not like me. A stranger sitting there staring into my eyes. A new haircut for a new life, was it? Hardly. More a shriving of the old to meet a new kind of death. A somewhat over dramatic view of things but then everything that had happened since Christmas had a kind of theatricality about it. I moved through my life feeling as if I was a one-woman play, and also the audience for it. The problem was it was somebody else's script. The woman in the mirror's.

Chapter Two

I didn't particularly want anyone to know what had happened to the other woman, the one with long curling tresses. Not because of shame or sorrow but because she was gone. I pulled up the drawbridge against her and that was that. I wasn't hiding my emotions – there simply were none – and there was nothing I wanted to communicate or discuss. At Easter I finished at the big fashionable comprehensive and gave up vocational teaching. Instead, because there were bills to pay and an income required despite Jack's guilt ridden gift of the house, I began a mornings only job locally. All I had to do, said the breezy headmistress, was give the eleven to thirteen year olds a flavour of literature before they began the serious stuff of exams. Breezy as she, I accepted the task. It was satisfactorily useless; I neither sought to inspire, nor did I inspire, and being a reasonably middle class area the children were, on the whole, well behaved. Occasionally when we were reading round the class I would hear the dull, flat stumbling tones of a child speaking the lines of a favourite text, Henry wooing Katherine in his broken French, Ozymandias, – and there would be an automatic rising in my throat to say 'Stop – you must sing and soar with it' – but I never did. If I no longer had the thrill, how could they? It says something for the quality and greatness of the works in the syllabus that, despite everything, the class did moderately well. I received no criticism either from the rest of the staff or the head; if I was barely

15

swimming, at least I was afloat and Shakespeare and Shelley and their kin were sturdy enough to keep it so.

I managed to avoid most of the staffroom intimacies through being only part-time. I finished at twelve fifteen every day so I never got caught up with the pub lunches, nor the early evening drinks when the danger of friendships would have been at its most acute. I practised a kind of autism with my peers, sitting in the most hidden corner of the staffroom and shrinking into a book if I passed them in the corridors, and though I could never demean those who suffer truly from being autistic, I understood a little of how it can be comforting to make no contact with fellow human beings. I just wanted to stay in my own private world which no-one could penetrate and therefore could cause no more hurt.

I once overheard a conversation between two of the women which summed up what they had come to think. Rhoda Grant, a fiery redhead who taught history and who generally spoke her mind, and Margery Drew who taught needlework and home economics – a bright bouncy woman of about my own age who was both beautifully dressed and substantially overweight, spin-offs from her profession, I suppose. She had been particularly friendly – offering theatre tickets, inviting me to supper at her flat, trying to persuade me to lunch with them now that the benign warmth of early summer offered the treat of a riverside pub. Her overtures had been the hardest of all the friendliness to overcome but as my involuntary eavesdropping made clear, even with her I had won, for to Rhoda Grant's acid suggestion that I was, quite simply, 'stuck up' Margery replied 'I'm afraid you're probably right – though – I don't know – there seems something vulnerable about her – I would have liked to get through ...'

'Oh, come on, Marge – you've practically worked your knickers off trying to be friendly! She can't even be bothered to rub two words together. She's just snotty-nosed – that's all ...'

'I wondered if she was still grieving – you know – if one of her parents had died – or her husband even. I mean – she's married but you never see or hear anything about the husband.'

'She's divorced, that's why.'

'Did she tell you?'

'No – I asked Pimmy.'

Pimmy was the school secretary, an owlish spinster of indeterminate years who was less wise than curious.

'Well then – that's probably it, she's probably grieving over it – losing a husband – that kind of thing ...'

Rhoda snorted. 'Good God, Marge – you can tell you've never been married! Nobody grieves over losing a husband, they're euphoric about it.'

'Oh Rhoda – you are awful.'

'Not at all – I just speak plain. Anyway, whatever's going on with that cold fish you're better forgetting all about her. If she doesn't want to be friendly then there's no way you can make her.'

'Perhaps she needs more time ...'

'Oh come on, Marge – she's been here nearly two months and no-one's had one decent conversation with her. Just leave well alone.' Silently I willed Marge to take Rhoda's advice.

'... she can stay in her own little private world – whatever it is ...'

'I suppose so' said the reluctant Margery. 'And being part-time doesn't help. She never joins in anything.'

'Just as well. It's bad enough seeing her sitting so prim and prissy in the staffroom without having to put up with it outside school.'

Margery sighed. 'Well, I suppose you're right. I give up. I shan't bother to waste my time any more.'

None of what they said upset me, which was curious. I was far more concerned that they should not discover my overhearing. Partly for their own protection, but also because I found the whole thing fascinating with its strange duality of my being both audience and player again.

They began to move away and I heard Rhoda say *sotto voce* 'There's one person who won't give up so easily.'

'Who's that?'

The whisper was just audible. 'Robin Carstone of course. He's got a real thing about her. Perches on her chair like a bird of prey ready to swoop. You must have noticed!'

'No!' Margery sounded shocked. 'I thought he was engaged to that nice girl – what's her name – Barbara or something – the one at Belmont Infants'. You're inventing it ...'

Rhoda gave a low-pitched throaty chuckle full of innuendo. I found myself envying its wonderful lewdness.

17

'I'm not. He's been showing a marked interest in her – syllabus – just recently ...' She gave another laugh. 'But I don't think it's her books he's really after ...'

'But he's maths and games – what would he want with the English syllabus?'

'Oh Marge – you are a goose. Perhaps he's thinking about a different sort of games – '

'Well' she said doubtfully 'he *is* very athletic ...'

Rhoda exploded with rich and raunchy laughter. 'Athletic is right. Have you seen him in those short shorts cycling in? Very muscular those thighs ... got to be careful negotiating that cross bar though ...'

And then the bell rang, which was a pity as the experience had been riveting, though it told me nothing I did not already know, especially about Robin Carstone of the bicycle and the muscular thighs.

It seemed that the more I retreated, the more interested he became, and his overtures which had been fairly tentative and unexplicit in the first month or so had begun to take on a new intensity during the past few weeks. I could see exactly what was happening, but I was quite powerless to stop it. The cooler and more remote I remained, the more intriguing he found me. He had even gone so far as suggesting, with some embarrassment, that I had become a 'woman of mystery' which nearly choked me at the time since it was such an uncharacteristic phrase for him to use and so funnily pathetic when he followed it up with an invitation to 'take in a film'. But I had no way out of appearing mysterious. I *was* remote. As distant from my fellow humans as Atalanta from a twentieth-century typist. Events had made me as old as time and produced a chasm between me and ordinary mortals – not from snobbishness as Rhoda would have it but from the metamorphosis of my inner self so that even if I had the wish to cross the chasm, I could not. I was in the world, but not of it. And I neither wanted to change it, nor did I have the power to. The remoteness was quite without artifice; it was not something I put on with my clothes when I got up each morning – it was just there. Irreversible. And, such being the way of Sod's Law, it had brought in its protective wake an aura of attraction. Robin Carstone, poor soul, had developed the hots for me. Atalanta looked down from her mountain Arcadia at the beautiful mortal toiling up the lower slopes and felt – well – nothing very much ...

Ah yes. Sex. I had been nearly half a year without so much as a peck on the cheek but it wasn't until Robin Carstone placed his essentially masculine buttocks on the arm of my chair so that I could feel their warmth pressing against me, that I knew it moved me not. I neither resented nor enjoyed the intimacy of it. The drawbridge was already up and now I knew that the walls of the citadel were complete. For six months previously his combination of handsome vigour and interest in me would have had me drooling at the knees. He was one of those men who combine a kind of innocence (perhaps I mean vulnerability) with a healthy outdoorish animalism. The sort who needed to be taught the variations of sex but, once aware of them, would embrace them with unselfconscious appetite. A man hungry for experience and eaten up with unfulfilled desires that no amount of rugged activity and cold showers could subdue. I recognised the type from my first day in the staffroom when he had practically leapt over an armchair to stand by my side and then spent the entire introduction of himself addressing my breasts. Not in a nasty way, not lasciviously, but like a hopeful dog who, given the chance, would learn his tricks and repeat them often. Whoever Barbara was she had much to give him, and much to gain, if she played her cards right. She had only to run her fingers through his healthy Nordic crewcut, or brush her lips across his perfect pectorals, and they would be in Paradise together. She hadn't got there with him yet. Whatever the current state of their sex life it had not set Robin alight. If it had, he wouldn't have been so interested in me.

Retrospectively it seems easy to say that I should have done this or that to dissuade him, but at the time I could only watch it all taking place, unable to alter the passive course that was ultimately leading him on. Rhoda was right. If my cold withdrawal had worked with the rest of the staff it was to have the opposite effect on him. The woman of mystery was like a red rag to a bull and he kept on charging it daily. Literature became the driving force and Robin Carstone began an ostentatious interest in my syllabus. One morning, shortly after the overheard conversation between Rhoda and Margery, I arrived a little early and so I parked and sat for a moment looking at the school. It was one of those freakishly hot late May days; the trees were heavy with blossom, the sky cloudless, and you could be forgiven for thinking that the world was not such a bad place after all.

19

The school looked back at me with distinct reproach. Wasn't it about time, those redbrick Victorian walls seemed to say, that I did more than turn up for my morning sessions, teach, and go home again? Perhaps, I muttered, perhaps. And then Robin Carstone hove into view on his bicycle, braking desperately when he caught sight of my car and swinging his brawny sweat-soaked thighs off his impossibly angled saddle. I very nearly caught his chin in my window as I wound it up.

'Hi' he said. 'How are you this morning?'

'Fine thanks.' I heaved my bag of books from the car and locked it. He settled his bicycle and then unstrapped the books and classroom clothes from the back of it. He always showered and changed before morning assembly.

'Couldn't be anything else on a day like this' he said. He carried his books under one arm and trailed his shirt and trousers over his shoulder. I could see a couple of the sixth-form girls staring at him.

'You remind me of James Bond' I said.

He shot me a look of hope and pleasure so that I immediately wished I hadn't.

'Do I? Why?'

'It doesn't matter. It was just a thought.'

I speeded up. He accelerated so that we were suddenly whizzing through the playground, avoiding groups of children like a pair of players in a pinball machine.

'Come on' he said as we entered the building. 'You can't say something like that and not explain. Why James Bond?'

'It is just something I've remembered from one of those films. *Dr No* I think. Where he emerges from a wetsuit in full evening dress and goes into a party – '

He looked puzzled. I pointed at his bare knees.

'Like you every morning arriving like this and emerging in your smart school clothes.' I smiled. The thought was quite funny really.

He returned the smile. 'I remember. Do you like James Bond then?'

'Not specially' I said. 'Though I think Ian Fleming has a good crisp style ...'

'Who?'

I laughed. 'Fleming – the chap who wrote them.'

'You've got a lovely smile when you choose to use it.'

I looked at my watch. 'You'll be late' I said and stepped past him. A shadow of irritation crossed his normally open face and he said 'Well who do you read then if not this Fleming? What do you like?'

'D. H. Lawrence' I called from a safe distance now. It was the first name that came into my head.

Later that morning he came over to me in the staffroom.

'I don't know much about D. H. Lawrence' he said. 'Can you lend me something?'

'I don't lend my books. But the library will have them all.' I went on marking books until he retreated.

The following day, a Friday, he began again. 'I went to the library. You were right. They had masses of stuff on him. I picked out one – I wondered if you'd have a look at it with me?'

'Sorry' I said. 'No time now.'

'Ah' he said. 'Of course. Have a good weekend. Going anywhere?'

I shook my head, keeping it well buried in the worksheets I was preparing. I didn't want any inroads on my perfect isolation. It was a complete and happy thing. I had the weekend before me.

Chapter Three

When May decides to give its sun it seems peculiarly generous, the heat twice as impressive as it would be in July or August. Up until now my normal weekday pattern was to get home, have lunch, and then go to bed for a couple of hours, curling up under the duvet for a peaceful and totally unnecessary sleep. That left the evenings free to read or watch television or just potter. Looking back it amazes me how easily I filled my time. I was not lonely, I did not sit at home in the dark twisting a handkerchief to shreds and chanting witch-like threats against the rest of humanity. My home had become like a precious second skin under which I invited no-one, nor needed anyone, to slide. In the five months that I had been living alone I had adapted perfectly to the process. Without rancour on my part – though I cannot speak for theirs – I had turned my friends away and saw no-one. I knew when I left the house that when I returned it would all be exactly as I had left it. Order out of chaos. Crumbs on the kitchen table would be exactly as they were when I left, the angle of a chair remained unchanged unless I did something to it; a neat living room would still be neat for there was no other hand to alter it. You could say this is a description of loneliness but for me it was only a description of being alone. I had become like an eccentric old lady, very set in my ways and wanting nothing to disturb the bland peace of my existence.

But in this sudden bright warm weather curling up under a duvet seemed, even to me, an unseductive proposition. So I hunted about for a sun lounger and took it out into the garden. It was the first time that I had set foot out there that year and, not surprisingly, it was a wilderness of neglect.

When we first came to view the house we had stood together at the window of the upstairs back room and looked down on our garden and the two that flanked it. The plots were large for Chiswick and each one terminated in a massive sycamore tree that, although barely budding with leaf at the time, would make an effective natural screen from the houses we backed on to later in the year. Our garden was very basic – a large square piece of grass with ribbon flower borders running its length and breadth – utterly predictable. For years the house had been let to a series of tenants whose aim, judging by the dearth of growing things, had been to remove anything that required upkeep. It was barren. But the garden to the left was wonderful, not at all fussy or regimented, no straight rows ready for the bedding plants but one great sweep of lawn leading down to the sycamore out of which had been cut great curving islands for shrubs and flowers. Later as the season moved into summer I saw the garden full of colour – geraniums of classical red, shocking pink, fiery orange, lilacs, weigela, hibiscus, all interspersed with bird-sown poppies and snapdragons – and at the end, half shaded by the massive tree, a complicated structure of canes for the runner beans was built so that they could grow and twine and hide the meticulously tended compost heap beyond. It was a garden that had been planned over long and happy years and like all successful man made structures it retained a naturalness of form that belied the initial work and planning. And at the top, immediately outside the house and accessible for the kitchen and the french windows, they had built a small bowery patio.

22

'*Le Grand Meaulnes*' I had said to Jack, stunned by all its perfection and its effect on me.

'Not quite' he said, kissing me. 'For you will not lose it as you grow older – it will always be here ...'

And of course I had believed that. Recognising the longevity and maturity behind the garden next door I had believed that one day ours would reflect the same.

Well – we had managed the patio. That was the first move towards introducing our own vision of the future. We had worked on it throughout the summer and finished it by the autumn. Next year, we had promised ourselves, we would begin on the rest. But of course, we did not.

The other garden we had looked down on from that upstairs back room, the one to our right, could not have been more of a contrast. It was laid out like a cemetery, rigid straight pathways dividing it into rows of carefully ordered plots in which each plant or shrub appeared to have been placed with exact measurement. The only wildness that remained was the magnificent sweep of the sycamore tree which seemed to stare down at the sterile checkerboard with eloquent disdain. And throughout the year, as the garden to our left continually sprouted and massed with colour and led our eyes a vibrant dance, so the one to our right gave up its little blots of isolated colour in unimaginative rows of french marigolds and well pruned roses. Nothing trailed or spread there and woe betide any bird flying by and bombing this precision with an alien seed.

This garden was owned by Maud and Reginald Montgomery and of the two sets of neighbours, these were the ones we met first, just a day or two after we moved in. They were very quick off the mark, leaving a little calling card and a printed invitation to drinks the following evening. Oddly enough I had been rather thrilled by this. It compounded all the fun I was having playing at being married, playing at keeping house and going to meet the neighbours. So in we went.

Reginald Montgomery was the perfect caricature of an ex-army and now retired civil servant, the compound form of the two stereotypes, only I doubt if such stereotypes really exist. Except at twenty-eight Milton Road Chiswick. He was bald with a little fringe of sandy hair at the back of his head, cut ever so neatly. His face was ruddy, his moustache bristly and clipped – a sort of microcosm of him – and he had a portly stomach

23

buttoned tightly into a double-breasted suit. When I first saw him I nearly laughed out loud because he looked as if he had just come out of a 'fifties Rattigan. Speaking to him was worse. He was the kind of man to whom it would appear ill-bred to have an original thought. Things were as they were, Britain was best, and running a close joint second came bridge and De Souza. His wife, Maud, was no less a pastiche. She could have been anything between a slightly-too-much-gin fifty or a very well preserved seventy. A Kensington lady blown slightly off course to land here in Chiswick but with her Queen Elizabeth hairstyle still absolutely intact and all her prejudices quite unruffled by the flight. As Jack said afterwards, put them in a play and the critics would never wear it.

They took to him immediately, especially since he admitted to being one of the Suffolk Battrams (which was a lie) and only worked for the BBC; Channel Four was apparently second only to the Soviet Union in its ghastliness. Me they were more chary of. Maud expended considerable effort in discovering my maiden name and I refused to be drawn – ironical really since I scarcely ever used my married name. I think if she had discovered it and asked me if I was one of the Dumbarton, or Walton-on-the-Naze, or any other damn place Ellises I would probably have spat in her eye and left. So it was just as well she gave up. When I admitted to teaching in a comprehensive – albeit a rather fashionable one – she was horribly astonished. So far as they were concerned such places were institutions for the ill-birthed and socially subnormal and Maud Montgomery gave me a little eye-screw of sympathy for being such a brave girl. Her attitude could not have been more sympathetic had I admitted to being home on leave from a leper colony.

Fortunately the conversation became a little more generalised after that. Lying through my teeth I congratulated them on their delightful garden which I could see beyond the french windows. In the twilight it wanted only the tombstones to complete its deadness.

'Very keen we are' said Reginald. 'Founder members of the Residents' Association, you know. Standards, eh? Soon knock yours into shape, I expect?'

'Yes' I said, glad to be on uncontroversial ground, 'I want to. The people at number twenty-four have got a lovely garden – I'd like ours to be a bit like that ...'

He pursed his lips and rocked on his heels and his pale eyes seemed to be popping out of his head. Mrs Montgomery cocked her teeny-weeny finger to one side of her teeny-weeny sherry glass and said 'My dear – you must take my advice and don't get involved with them at all. They are absolutely Bohemian. Dreadful people. Won't join the Residents' and they have some terribly loud friends. Theatricals, you know … I should avoid the Durrells if I were you …'

I remember once when I was teaching at the original place and we took a party of fifth formers to Amsterdam. On the night of our arrival the master in charge, a thoroughly nice history don who had never quite made it from Hobbes and Locke to Fisher and Thomson, stood on the steps of our hotel and addressed the small party. 'You have two hours before you must be back here,' he told them. 'I suggest you use the time wisely. To your right you will find all that is wholesome and cultivated in the city; to your left are the seedier and corrupted places which I hope you will avoid …'

Naturally the entire group trooped off to the right, turned a corner round the block, and set off hot foot in the left hand direction …

Similarly with the Montgomerys' introduction to Fred and Geraldine Durrell. After such an accolade on the Montgomerys' part I knew that I was going to like them. Even if it meant, as it clearly did, that it would isolate us from everyone else. We refused to join the Residents' Association – Jack said 'on principle' and although the Montgomerys were clearly confused by this they responded to the suggestion of morality it gave.

'Pity' said Reginald at the door. 'We've got Lady Wilton from number sixteen' pause for genuflexion 'chairing it.'

'Bully for Lady Wilton' said Jack so that I nearly expired from suppressed laughter.

'Yes – isn't it' said Maud. 'So nice to have met you. Goodbye.'

They must have realised pretty soon after that that we had gone, quite literally, over to the other side. We never returned their invitation and eventually even the curtly polite nods that we gave each other ceased.

Geraldine and Fred Durrell were delightful as friends and made marvellous neighbours. He was a big jolly man, always looking slightly crumpled, more like a genial country vicar than the retired GP he was. Like Reginald he was bald with a shiny dome of a head that he kept protected out of doors with a series of hats. He had a loud infectious laugh, was a voracious reader, a good talker, and apart from the odd side-swipe at the Montgomerys and their like I never heard him say a bad word about anybody. He admitted to having occasional dark moments of deep discontent but overcame these by either going off fishing, or walking for a weekend in some remote part of England. Geraldine was as small as Fred was large. A pretty, bird-like creature still girlish and fluttery despite her grey curls. She had been an actress – good, she said, but not distinguished because she had been far too lazy and unambitious to get very far, though she still loved the theatre and kept up with it. Jack said that she knew far more than her fluttery ways suggested and than within the theatrical world she was remembered and respected still. She and Fred always reminded me of Burns and Allen.

We spent some really enjoyable times together – ad hoc lunches in their beautiful garden, visits to the theatre; I got to know them particularly well as Jack was away from home so much and they seemed to keep a loose watch over me. We didn't live in each others' houses by any means but in the nicest neighbourly way, they were always there. Their one child, Portia, was married and lived in America so I suppose I made up a little for that – and since my parents lived in Edinburgh I suppose they became my surrogates too. Which made it all the more difficult when Jack left me. The rest of the world I could deal with – they were easy to drop – but with Fred and Geraldine it seemed a particularly cruel thing to do.

It was easier than it might have been because they had gone to spend Christmas with Portia when it all happened. And by the time they came back in mid-January I had sort of sealed up the gaps. I rang them, rather than called, and told them flatly and unemotionally that Jack and I were no longer living together, that he had left me for another woman and that for the time being I was not feeling very sociable. I wished them a happy new year and put down the phone. After that there had been one or two gentle overtures which I politely and coolly refused. I certainly did not want to venture into their chillingly cosy world again – that house with all its family snapshots and pictures of Fred with his fishing rods and Geraldine in her monstrous hat at Ascot, Portia smiling with the grandchildren, their annual jaunt

26

to Italy. There were too many reminders of happy duality, too much dusty clutter of fully lived lives to interest me any more. They accepted it and if we met in the street or coincided by our front doors there was just the barest enquiry from them, though somewhat tinged by anxiety, and the barest response from me, and it did not prove too difficult to continue my introvert ways.

Now, stretched out on the lounger in the sun, I could hear the two of them on their own patio next door. Presumably they were having lunch. That brought back a lot of memories of how it used to be last year, how Geraldine would pop her head over the hedge and invite us to stop our navvying and join them for whatever it might be – one of Fred's cocktails, or lunch or any permutation of conviviality. Quite often if Jack was away they would call me over and I would sit with them: it had been easy and natural then. It could never be like that now. So I just lay, silent, secure in the knowledge that they would leave it to me to make the first move towards resuming our old acquaintance, and knowing also that I had no intention of doing so.

Despite the neglect this year, or perhaps because of it, the things we had planted to decorate the little patio were flourishing. The sun had already brought the honeysuckle on so that the pink spikes were unfurling softly with their scent, and the rose which had been so frail and vulnerable looking when we planted it last summer had now taken the wall of the house as its own and climbed and budded as if it had always belonged. Noticing these things gave me neither happiness nor unhappiness – they were just there, in the sun, like me. Neither the scent of the honeysuckle nor the creamy yellowness of the rose had been part of last summer's experience; they were the new order of things. Mine, singular. As such I was perfectly content to be surrounded by them. I turned on my stomach, opened my book, and began to read.

I can recommend *Tristram Shandy* to anyone who wishes to remain uninvolved with the realities of the Universe. Laurence Sterne's characters are so completely bound up in their own world that they have no intention or interest in making inroads into ours. It is therefore perfect escapism yet written with such a fine hand, such exquisite skill in the use of language, that it uplifts at the same time. I did toy with the idea, at the beginning of my single state, of reading writers like Susan Howatch or Catherine Cookson who provide escapism on a massive scale.

Never having read any I thought with hunger of the shelves and shelves of their books that awaited me. My mother read both authors avidly; friends were always confessing to taking them on holiday. I had only ever resisted them because I knew what an undisciplined creature I was. Once embarked on reading such stuff I should probably never go back to anything that required a little effort or a lot of concentration to understand. And it was terribly important that I read – and read – yet the subject matter had to be such that it would not tempt me out of my ice-cold state into the fire of being bitter or angry or in need of somebody else. No Erica Jong, nor Marilyn French, nor Fay Weldon for me. But I tried one of these 'holiday' books and it was as unsatisfying as a steak and kidney pudding with all the meat left out. I had to look elsewhere and the best alternatives proved to be those books which created such a tight world of their own that yours as the reader simply could not penetrate. Jane Austen of course, Arnold Bennett naturally, E. M. Forster, Barbara Pym and now, currently, Laurence Sterne. Books had initially been my insurance policy against thinking. Now they and my silent house were the prop and stay of my days. I lost the sounds of Fred and Geraldine's desultory talk next door, forgot the picturesque patio and the wilderness behind me and buried my senses in the world of Shandy Hall.

I suppose I read for an hour or more and then because the sun warmed on into the afternoon, I fell asleep, resting my cheek on the book and feeling very lazy and untroubled as I drifted off.

When I awoke I felt a kind of panic – not quite sure where I was, all sticky and wet eyed and heavy from lying still for so long. The patio was almost all in shadow so I judged it to be between four and five though I had slept so deeply that it could have been later or earlier. I felt hungry and dry mouthed and irritated, as if I have been woken before I was ready. I moved my wrist to look at my watch and was just squinting at it – half past four or half past five? I couldn't be sure – when I heard the distinct and unusual sound of my own doorbell. If I had been in any state other than just awakened I would have ignored it – I often did – not that it rang very much unless a meter reader called or a charity collector, for I had long since absolved myself from friends who dropped in – but since I was still half asleep and partially Pavlovian in my response, I stumbled bare-footed into the kitchen up the passage to the hall, and had opened the door before I was truly awake.

The sun was more or less behind him so that at first I couldn't make out who it was – but that was only for a split second. As soon as I blinked and looked again I recognised the pink healthy glow of Robin Carstone's face. The sun made a halo of light behind his fair clean cut head and the freshness of his complexion heightened the blue of his eyes which had their usual hungry anxiousness about them. My heart, which until that moment had ceased to exist, sank at the sight of him. If I had only thought to check from behind the front room curtains first I would never have opened the door. As it was I had been well and truly caught. I blinked again, hoping it was a mistake, but when I re-opened my eyes he was still entirely there.

'Oh, good' he said, moving towards the door as if to enter, one hairy muscular thigh upbent, one white trainer shoe already on the hall carpet 'I thought you must be in when I saw the car. I kept on ringing because I couldn't tell if the bell was working or not ...'

You liar, I thought, if it could wake me out on the patio you could certainly hear it from where you were standing.

I said nothing and moved no facial muscle, just stood there helpless, one hand holding the door open, the other propped against the wall of the hallway. The body language should have been very clear – would have been to anyone else not so bent on gaining entry. I was barring the way as effectually as I possibly could.

'I've brought you that book on D. H. Lawrence we were talking about. I know you were too busy this morning but I thought you wouldn't mind now – the weekend ...'

He was peering over my shoulder, devouring the hallway as if its schema would tell him something about me.

'What a nice hall' he said and we executed a nice little pavane of heads, me moving mine as he moved his to look beyond. 'Not interrupting anything am I? No-one here?'

He smiled showing broad white teeth.

'Thank you for bringing the book' I said holding out my hand. 'I'll have a look at it over the weekend and we can talk about it on Monday.'

He clutched it to his tee-shirted chest and moved closer to me, like a rugby player bent on going for a try or whatever the correct term is. For half a second I thought he was actually going to shoulder me out of the way and make a run down the passage, throwing himself on top of D. H. Lawrence when he successfully reached the kitchen. He was dressed for it.

'I was just going out' I said politely.

He looked down at my bare feet and back at my face, blinking his pale lashes, owl-like. Then he broke into a smile and reached out one hand (the other still held the book tightly to his chest) and rubbed it very gently on my cheek.

'No you weren't.' He smiled in triumph. 'You've been asleep. You've got creases here and here ...'

'Look' I said, very nicely, 'I don't invite people in. I just don't – that's all. It's got nothing to do with you. I just like to be on my own.'

It was the wrong way to go about it. I could hear my own voice sounding soft and unconvinced – unconvincing – and having just woken up my wits were blunt; if I had been him I wouldn't have been convinced either.

He blinked again when I concluded my speech and there was a sly light in his eyes. 'Oh come on' he said cheerfully. 'I've cycled three and a half miles in this heat. Ten minutes and I'll be on my way.'

And then he did make the rugby tackle, sliding his shoulders sideways past mine and firmly planting himself inside the hall so that I had to turn and look at him. A far off emotion, once called anger, welled up inside, but it died before reaching any kind of peak. Oh no. I wasn't going to get back into the world of human emotions and frailty just because of him. I smiled politely and said 'I really am going out I'm afraid. Sorry but I'm late already.'

He didn't budge.

We were breast to breast in the narrow passageway. Suddenly his hand came up to my neck and I could see, like the pink frills of a clam shell, his lips descending towards mine. I ducked – with that sixth sense borne by woman, coming out of nowhere – so that my eyes were level with his chest and with the title of the book which he kept clutched there like a talisman. It was called *D. H. Lawrence: Prophet of Sexuality*.

So this was to provide the background to our afternoon's literary little *tête à tête* was it? I nosed back towards the front door imbibing an acrid pungency as I negotiated the curve of his armpit. A half forgotten human smell that caught me by surprise

30

with its lure. I pulled the front door as wide as it would go and said 'Goodbye' very firmly, looking down the path and into the street, willing him to leave.

'You've got a lovely evening to cycle home in' I added, with peculiar consideration.

What, you may ask, stopped me from leaning towards him and jabbing my finger into his powerful pectoral and saying 'Piss Off – Go Immediately – Do not come back – I don't want you here – See?' Jab, jab ...

I suppose what stopped me was that I had been taught from birth, like so many young women, not to be rude. I had been well brought up.

It is all very well knowing that someone is violating your space (let alone assuming that you want to exchange saliva with them) – but it is considered pretty hysterical to point it out to them in harsh unequivocal terms. Oh yes. What stopped me from doing the jab jab then was exactly the same thing that stopped me from wearing a G-string when I went to see Jack and had me sitting in Irish's low level seat without once saying anything cross or bitter – feminine breeding. Quite unseemly to make a scene. May we all, in future, spare our daughters this fate. When I was six years old and coming back home from the park a man stepped out from an alleyway, revealing his all to me and coaxing me with sweets and soft words. He barred my way. I knew something was wrong. I also knew that one should be polite at all times and – above all – never make a scene. So I said 'Excuse me' in an effort to make him move so that I could get past. 'Excuse me' again. He advanced towards me. In the end it was only the deeper primeval instinct for survival that had me racing past his outstretched hands, home to my mother. But I hadn't been rude to him.

What could be more ridiculous now than to be trapped in my own house by a man whom I did not want to be there, and yet be unable to tell him so? All I was doing was holding the door open so that he would go quietly. And, of course, he had no intention of doing that.

There was a sort of rustle and flapping of pages and a thump. He had dropped *D. H. Lawrence: Prophet of Sexuality* while righting himself after his misjudged try. I watched him bending to rescue it from the floor and although the circumstances leading up to that posture were ridiculous there was a certain strength in his well developed lines and curves – Charles Atlas rather than Michelangelo but potently muscular all the same. And that, combined with the half memory of his freshly sweating cyclist's armpit, was – oddly – disturbing. I looked away from him quickly – back down the garden path whence he had entered and whence I most fervently wished he would leave. I didn't want him here, yet – well – being desired is often half the battle towards desiring. What I wanted back was my absolute calm detachment; I wanted him to plonk his straining buttocks on my staffroom chair and continue to leave me cold. Most certainly I did not want this.

'Look' I said in a humouring way, 'I really do have to get ready. I'm sorry to hurry you out ...'

'Joan ...' his voice had an edge of tragedy to it 'I'm sorry about trying to kiss you just now ...' His face pinkened further and the sandy lashes blinked at a wicked rate.

'That's all right' I said inventing joviality. 'I was flattered.'

A mistake that.

Up came the hand which was not holding *D. H. Lawrence: Prophet of Sexuality;* the fingers and thumb encircled my face and drew it towards his. It is quite impossible not to pucker up when your jaw is being squeezed. This time the clam shell found its mark, very briefly, very lightly, and I had that tickling sensation in the lower intestine that often occurs when an erogenous zone is engaged.

It was all like a pastiche of a 'fifties Hollywood close up. He, still holding me tightly about the jaw, drew away and said 'I wasn't going to leave here without doing that once ...'

Cue for violins.

And me, who God knows had the right to bring my knee up or bite his nose or something – just gave a little nervous cough as prissy as any nineteenth-century maiden and backed off fractionally – there being a limit to how far you can back off when your jaw is clamped in another's hand. Just go! Go! I pleaded inwardly – but he still held on, fixing those earnest blue eyes so close to mine that it was a constant effort not to go cross eyed.

'Can I come again? When you've got more time?' He was not at all embarrassed now, much more assertive. And all because of a kiss, the stolen kind that a kiss-chase boy might exact from his prey in the playground. I suppose it means so much because of the taboo surrounding faces – touching a face is a very intimate thing – but that by engaging his lips on my unwilling ones he felt a barrier had been removed was both ridiculous and wrong. I've always thought kissing was an odd pursuit. Why not tickle somebody's back or massage their neck if you want to establish intimacy – and give them some pleasant physical sensations at the same time?

My whole being panicked at his question. I was beyond feeling angry. All I wanted in the world was to be left alone and now he had come here and destroyed that. And still I wasn't able to say piss off, jab jab.

Which accounted for the tears. My first since Jack left me. There they were, suddenly, but their fount was not sorrow – it was sheer frustration, sheer crossness, like a hedgehog being pulled from its warm winter leaves and shaken awake in the frosty air. They were misinterpreted of course.

'You poor girl' he was murmuring, pulling me (by the jaw) towards his tee-shirted chest. I did not want to be anywhere near its disturbing propensities. 'You've had a rotten time, haven't you?' I nodded into the white cotton. He was obviously talking generally while I referred to the last five minutes. 'Your divorce and everything ...'

'How did you know about that?' I pulled away in amazement. I hadn't told anyone about that side of things.

'I found out. I asked Pimmy about you.'

It all had a peculiarly medieval ring to it. Sort of enquiring about my pedigree first. I stared up at him for a moment and then, wits recovered, I took my opportunity and slipped out of his arms and down the garden path, mopping at the tears with the back of my hand.

I felt braver out in the sun, in full view of anyone passing, but he didn't follow me out. As if facing the cave of a beastie I called into the dimness of the hall 'You can put the book on the hall stand if you like. I'll look at it later.'

Just for a second or two I could feel him weigh up the situation. He didn't move out of the house and I remained on the path. Stalemate. I opened the garden gate. There was his bicycle chained to my fence. I went and stood by it so there could be no more rugby tackles and no more intimacy. It occurred to me that I was not acting like a character in the round; a character in the round would surely have been feeling immense anger by now, immense *something*, but all my inner

33

emotions seemed to have a great concrete ceiling fastened just below my solar plexus. On a scale of nought to ten they only achieved one – and that one was not anger but panic, simple panic that he be gone and quickly. I wanted him away from here and out of sight so that I could once more withdraw into my house, my territory, my life. I hadn't invited anyone, least of all him, to violate it.

He hesitated on the garden path and then came out of the gate slowly, joining me with reluctance by the bicycle. He began fiddling with the gears, eyes cast down like any street corner adolescent.

'I apologise' he said, addressing the gears.

'Accepted' I said looking away down the street in the direction I hoped he would soon by cycling.

'The thing is I really would like to see you again. I find you – well – very attractive – that's all. A bit different somehow. Mysterious.'

'No' I said 'I'm not at all mysterious – '

'You only think you're not mysterious because inside you know who you are. But I don't know you at all. So you are mysterious to me.'

This was irrefutable logic.

'I must go.' I moved towards the gate. Up came one of his great beefy hands gentle as a leaf on my shoulder. Eye contact at last.

'You're not angry?'

'No.' Leaf turning to paperweight as my body language said I was about to move on.

'And – um – can I see you again?'

'At school.'

'I didn't mean that. I mean – can I take you out some time? Or come and visit you again? Please?'

Pressure of paperweight increased to hot spot on shoulder. Little tug of – what? Anger? Sadness? – beneath the concrete plateau.

'I never go out' I said as kindly as possible. 'And I never have visitors.'

I could see this only compounded his view of things. Mystery Woman. I went on hurriedly, recognising the look in his eyes. 'That is not a challenge, Robin. I don't go out because – quite simply – I don't want to go out. And I don't see people because I am happy with my own company.'

34

'You're not happy at all' he said. 'You cried in there. You need to cry. It's the divorce. You're bound to feel like this.'

I should have used the opportunity there and then to tell him exactly why I had cried. But kindness combined with aforementioned good breeding forbade it.

'Robin. I am happy. I assure you – I am perfectly happy.'

I should have added, until you came along and spoiled it.

'Let me come and see you again. I promise not to ... um ... you know – ' he nodded in the direction of the open front door '... that. I could bring a bottle of wine and we could talk – about books – anything you like. Or we could go and see a play ... I haven't done that since I left university.'

I am a play, I wanted to say, one act, one character. I broke away from the weight of his hand, looked away from his searching sincerity. 'No. No thank you. I really am happy this way. I don't want any kind of relationship with anyone, male or female. I'm much better off like this.'

'Not really you're not' he said. 'I know sort of what you mean. I don't find it that easy to have close relationships.'

It was my turn to score. 'What about Barbara?' I asked.

'How do you know about her?'

'I asked Pimmy' I lied. And *touché*.

'She's keener on me than I am on her. That's all.'

I thought that was reasonably honest of him.

'But you're engaged to her.'

'I'm not' he said stoutly. 'We sleep together sometimes. Not very satisfactorily – ' He blushed.

Spare me, I thought, from this turning into garden path co-counselling. I slipped back on the other side of the gate, and closed it.

Safe.

'Sorry' he said. 'I don't know why I told you that. I just find you so – ' He leaned against the little white palings of the fence so that it creaked ominously. 'You can't go on living like this forever. It's a terrible way to behave. You should go out – meet people – have new friendships – ' He raised his hands in a gesture remarkable for its eloquence. 'It's like – Oh God – I don't know – like someone who has a bad crash. The first thing when you're well again is to get back in the car or bike or whatever and ride again. Before you lose your nerve. Not this –

35

this' more gestural eloquence 'complete cut off.' He seemed genuinely aghast.

'I'm happiest like this.' My voice sounded far away – a cold bored voice that had nothing to do with happiness.

'Rubbish!' he said.

I began to move away. I was tired of this dialogue. It was as if I was in a little white fenced cage being goaded to perform by a sporty trainer. His hands clenched and unclenched over the peaks of the palings. Another minute and he would be leaping them to stand, yet again, at my side. Crunching into my lavender bushes and crushing the daisies with his sparkling white trainers.

'I must go, Robin. I'll look at the book and give it back to you on Monday . . .'

He shrugged. 'Keep it for longer if you like. I've marked one or two passages that interested me. We'll talk about it sometime.'

'We will.' I nodded. And then without further demur or turning around, I rushed indoors, into the cool darkness of the hallway, feeling the relief of its emptiness like a physical sensation.

Like any pedestrian actress might, I closed the front door and leaned my back against it, just waiting and breathing and feeling afraid. I was afraid that he wouldn't go and that if he came back I had no reserves with which to make him leave a second time. Curious that no matter how uncontentiously solitary I attempted to be, it was not to be allowed. A sort of dog in the manger attitude on his part, and on other people's too I had no doubt, if they'd been given half the chance. Just about the only people I could trust not to impose their panacea of gregariousness on me were Fred and Geraldine; they had left me alone. Suddenly, standing there in the hall, I felt an immense rush of affection for that – and made a vague kind of vow to myself to be a little warmer towards them – perhaps chat to them over the hedge this weekend – something, anything, to let them know that I still cared about them even if I couldn't go back to the kind of relationship we once had. If I had known where this tiny fissure of my otherwise perfect citadel would lead I might not have felt quite so disposed towards them.

Later, calmer, with Robin Carstone firmly folded away somewhere dark and inaccessible, I wandered out into the garden.

Sure enough the Durrells were out in theirs. I was glad

because all I had to do was call them over the hedge rather than knock on their door or make a formalising telephone call. I pushed my way through the tall crisp dried up stalks of last year's – what? chrysanthemums probably. Noticed the fresh green luxuriance of some kind of spreading weed that bound itself around whatever it met in its path. Ignored and suppressed the urge to bend down and begin pulling at it, and leaned on the unkempt privet hedge that almost came up to my nose. I watched the two of them for a moment. In his old straw hat and pouchy beige linen jacket Fred looked more like a country cleric than ever, and Geraldine with her small neat legs encased in black ski pants and her diminuitive body swamped by a man's white shirt (Fred's probably) looked as girlish and fluttery and doll-like as ever. They were completely absorbed in whatever it was they were doing and I wondered whether any other nation on earth potters in its garden like the British? And in London, capital city, too. I could scarcely imagine a New Yorker, or Parisian or Roman doing it. Nice, kind, happy people; I felt like a creature from another planet.

I called them a Coo-ee so that they both looked up, smiled and came over.

'Joan dear. How nice. How are you?' Geraldine spoke as if the intervening months of silence had never happened. Her actress training perhaps.

'I'm fine. And you?'

'Hot!' They both laughed.

'Thank God you've stopped her' Fred said. 'She's had me at it all afternoon.'

'I know' I said. 'I heard you out here earlier. I fell asleep. All this sun ...'

'All right for some' he said and removing his hat he wiped an earthy hand over his sweating dome.

'What are you doing?'

He made a grimace. 'Turning the unfriable into the friable.' He pointed at Geraldine. 'She's decided that we can't live without pelargoniums. Just when the garden seemed finished Capability Durrell here decides it needs something else ...' He turned to her and gave a mock salute. 'Permission to down tools? I need a cup of tea – or something stronger.'

Geraldine laughed. 'You're showing your age' she said. And

37

then to me 'Squeeze through the gap and come in and have a drink.'

'I'd love to – but I can't' I lied. The closeness, the bond, the affection between the two of them was too sharp.

'Oh go on – just one. Fred's got involved with his cocktails again. He makes a whole shaker full which we have to drink and it's always too much for the two of us. We always end up pie-eyed and incapable ...'

'I'd love to but I've got some work to do.'

'Too much work' began Fred 'makes Jack a ...' His voice trailed off and he looked horribly embarrassed. I felt for him. Geraldine pushed her fingers through her popping curls and looked equally uncomfortable. Our eyes met. I smiled at her. She raised one eyebrow to say, most eloquently, forgive the blunder. Of course I did. It meant nothing to me, only to them.

'Don't tempt me' I said.

'Tell you what' Fred rushed into speech now, 'why don't you come over on Sunday and we can get out the barbecue?' He looked up at the cloudless sky. 'It's perfect weather for it.'

'And if anything is guaranteed to turn the hot spell it's us planning a barbecue' said Geraldine, wryly amused. 'Still – we can but try. Would you like to come, Joan? It'll only be us so it won't matter if it gets rained off ...'

I suppose it is the same for everybody. Even when I was with Jack and everything was happiness and future plans, Sundays were always difficult unless we were doing something specific like going to the boat or meeting friends for lunch. Sundays had that slough of despond time, that suspension of reality, when you had to galvanise yourself in order to overcome lethargy. Sundays since I had lived alone had been the weak point, a long unbroken day stretching into the evening, bearable and in a sense to be celebrated on dark cold dismal days when you could congratulate yourself for being indoors and free to slob, but now that the bright sun of May had arrived it would not, perhaps, be so easy. I felt the rough scratch of untended vegetation around my ankles, looked into their lovely cared for garden, and was tempted. Why not, I thought, for I had only to slip back through the gap in the hedge to be insular again. So I nodded, and agreed, and was rewarded most painfully by their obvious delight that I would come.

'Cocktails at twelve then?' said Fred.

'Cocktails at twelve' I agreed solemnly.

'Take a hearty breakfast, my girl' offered Joan, 'because the drinks will be lethal and you know how long the food takes when Fred's being chef.'

Back indoors I felt as if I had climbed the Eiger, immediately regretting that I had agreed to go and astonished at how much it meant to me to have ceded some of my inviolability. I shivered for the sun was going down now, and decided to fetch a cardigan. Then I would settle and write to my parents – I hadn't done so for weeks. Since I hadn't actually told them about Jack and me no longer being together it was, not surprisingly, a task I tended to put off.

Two things irritated the customary calm unsullied routine of my indoor existence. On the hall mat lay a brochure. On the hall stand lay the cheerily alien volume that Robin Carstone had left. *D. H. Lawrence: Prophet of Sexuality* gleamed in its bright dust cover. I picked up the brochure first. It was from some Commonwealth organisation. 'Have you got room' it urged 'for a short course student? Nigeria, Kenya, Malaysia [it gave a list] – all independent but still they need our help ...' It went on about the kind of courses and their duration and the kind of accommodation required. I screwed it up. There was no room here. *D. H. Lawrence: Prophet of Sexuality* was annoying but at least I could give it back after the weekend. Robin Carstone's literary ruse had been unsuccessful. Good. I have never much cared for Lawrence; too many purple patches with the earth like a sensual woman for my liking. And his poetry – too redolent of vague mysticism and the rural myth for my taste. His best works were his essays of which there are too few.

I picked the book up. Sexuality was no longer my style but I ought to skim it so that when I returned it on Monday I could at least make some suitable comment. Well bred as ever. Really, if I were to be true to myself, I should have hurled it in its owner's face and said Sod Off.

The book was very new. It was not a library book at all. When I opened it it had that new smell and the spine creaked. Predictably it seemed preoccupied with *Women in Love, Sons and Lovers* and the latter day case for *Lady Chatterley* – but there was a smattering of his poetry dotted amongst the pages. And – even more predictably – some lines had been marked out with thick

39

black ink. It was the last stanza from a poem called 'Fidelity' – not a word I chose to bandy about.

And when, throughout all the wild orgasms of love,
slowly a gem forms, in the ancient, once-more-molten rocks
of two human hearts, two ancient rocks, a man's heart and a
woman's
that is the crystal of peace, the slow hard jewel of trust,
the sapphire of fidelity,
The gem of mutual peace emerging from the wild chaos of love.

I closed the book up sharply. I had had a lucky escape. We could by now have been sitting somewhere in this house together, heads close and reading those very lines aloud. Which would have been intolerable.

I went upstairs to fetch the cardigan and the writing paper, light of heart to have had such a lucky escape. This place was my domain. Not a student's from the Commonwealth, not Robin Carstone's, not D. H. Lawrence's – and certainly, Oh certainly, not Fidelity's.

Jab. Jab!

Chapter Four

The weather did not change that weekend, except perhaps to grow hotter. For the whole of Saturday I lay around in the sun turning a nice shade of golden brown for no-one's satisfaction but my own. Tristram eventually got born which might have been the highlight of my weekend had there not been the Sunday invitation and its aftermath on the horizon. But it was not surprising, in all that heat, to find myself thawing, and by late morning on the Sabbath I was ready to go next door, and even looking forward to it.

Clothes have memories. I went upstairs to put on something cool and Sundayish before going next door. It wasn't until I had got the dress on that the reality of this hit me. Hanging there it was just a white cotton dress; as I slipped it on it was like slipping into a film of the past. I had worn it and worn it last summer. Jack had loved it – the transparency, the looseness, the skimpiness of the style which made wearing a bra an

40

impossibility. Whenever we were going somewhere and I asked him what I should wear this was always the dress he chose. It was too late to put it back in the cupboard and pretend it held no past. Like a great wave of images the memories swamped me. Screw up your eyes, close your ears, it doesn't matter – things go on working away in your head – inner images, private thoughts – strong as you say you are you are never a match for them. If I were a dog I would have howled; being human I swore violently, again and again – but they were still there when the sounds had finished reverberating – fading and dying one remained, sharp and clear and worse, much worse, still keenly erotic. Let it then, I thought with anger, Let it –

His Old School cricket match. How peculiarly British. What an apt setting for erotic memory. But no amount of acid commentary would deny that it was. There we were, sitting in our deckchairs watching that most English of activities – backbone of Empire; how much it says for love that I was there and happy to be there, me in the summer's heat with my husband beside me. Hah! Jack leans towards me and whispers that he wants to show me something – a schoolboy something though the tone of his voice and the look in his eyes has little to do with earning house points. He leads me to a small thicket some way off from the pitch. It is cool and dark after the sunlight and I have to pick my way in my Italian sandals, he pulls on my hand, I giggle half knowing – and we stop in a circle of trees, struggling grasses tickle the backs of my legs and the peaty leaf-mould crackles underfoot. He says that this was their den, this was where he and his cronies used to come and hide and do naughty things. Like what? I say, playing the game. His face twitches, he gives me a look that makes me shudder. Oh, he says, like smoking and looking through nudie magazines and dreaming of – he slips the first strap off my shoulder and kisses it, there is hot moist breath on my neck and my arm – Girls, he says, and what we would do with them one day. I ask him, What was that? He slips the other strap. Oh, this – and this – the dress falls of its own accord and gets held somewhere around my hips – he eases it down and I step out of it. It is one of those perfectly choreographed moments when everything works – buttons don't resist, zips don't catch, like an edited version in which each piece of action works perfectly. He is inside me in seconds and I lean against the tree loving him and the sexiness and the weird

41

juxtaposition of the cricket match with its cries of Howzat and the sound of cracking leather as it hits willow. When you give up your body so profoundly you are begging for trust. It doesn't mean that you get it.

Washed and worn and washed and worn this dress might have been, but it still had the grass stains on the hem, the marks where his heels ground it into the soil as he ground himself into me. And, believing, I had opened myself and sucked him in. Faint, but there, the stains remained. I should have used something biological on them.

My first thought, after plunging that sick memory back down below the ice-line, was to wear something else. But that would only compound the untenable notion that he still had a hold on me. The second thought was, to Hell with it; I kept it on. Never, never, never again, I told my reflection, brushing my hair with every word – not ever, ever, ever. And then I saw in the mirror something that was so cruel, so bloody cruel, that I just stood staring. Beneath the white cotton there were new stains, my own flesh, my unremarkable breasts once only hints of movement were now defined by the clear outlines of my nipples. Positive shadows. I had not noticed how the dress defined them before. And then the truth of it dawned. Cruel, wasn't it? For of course, I had been pregnant since last summer. No biological soap powder would wash those stains away, the darkening of fecundity glowing like a pair of vicious beacons. Pretence had protected but only up to a point.

I ran from the room and its reflection, scudding down the stairs as if I could leave the whole sordid scene behind; in the hall I hurled the hair brush at the front door where it made a satisfying cracking noise and broke in two. That felt better. By the time I reached the garden and the sunlight I was almost calm again. I stood facing my wilderness seeing it as if for the first time – overgrown – a tangle – a mess – the analogy was too bitter to contemplate. Quickly I pushed my way through the gap in the hedge to the Durrells' planned and cared for world. I thought I might scream and tear the dress from my body and fall naked and twitching to the ground, but no – I could act too. I gave Geraldine my cheek to be kissed and was led, demure as a lamb, to the little patio chairs and the little patio table and the signs of civilisation as manifested in a pile of Sunday papers. Fred was sitting there wearing his battered straw hat and loose linen jacket and Geraldine wore a long peach-coloured Indian skirt with a flounced blouse topped off with a grand disc of honey-coloured straw that threw her remarkable eyes into shadow. The scene looked so like something out of Chekhov that I almost felt some entrance line was called for but I couldn't think of one. Still, the idea was amusing and helped rid me of that bubble of hysteria that had been lurking around. Geraldine put her head on one side in her usual birdlike way and looked at me.

'Well' she said, 'you've certainly caught the sun – and it suits you. You look very pretty, my dear – really lovely. No need to ask how you are.' She turned to her husband. 'Fred. Joan's here. What about those drinks?'

'It's all ready.' He stood up and leaned over to kiss my cheek. 'You two sit down here and I'll get the tray.' He went off into the house.

Geraldine flopped down beside me and leaning slightly in my direction she whispered 'Just say thank you to whatever he brings and sip it and if it's too awful tip a bit on the garden when he isn't looking. That's what I do.' She winked at me. 'Some of them are lovely but some of them would blow your brains out if you had more than a glass.'

'Right now' I said 'I can't think of anything better.'

She gave me a look, considering this, and then squeezed my arm. 'Well, you've certainly come to the right place for that.'

'Thank you' I said, and meant it.

'Harvey Wallbanger' Fred announced proudly, carrying the tray aloft and setting it down with a flourish. He rattled the shaker and poured generous measures into the glasses, topping them up with a great deal too much Galliano. Geraldine looked critically from the glasses to him and said 'I think you'd better check the charcoal is getting under way before you begin on yours.'

'Everything is perfectly under control, I can assure you.' He waved his hand in the direction of the barbecue which was smoking dully. 'It will take about half an hour.' He set his watch on the table. 'Twelve fifteen' he said, 'we shall dine at one' and he raised his glass. 'What shall we drink to?'

I raised mine to his. 'Anything but absent friends' I said and smiled at them both. 'To us, how about that?'

'To us' they repeated.

We all drank and then I realised that I had to say something so

I put down my glass, studied my hands and said 'Jack and I are now officially divorced. You've both been very good not to pry and to let me go my own way – so thank you for that. I don't really want to talk about it because it's all in the past but I want you to know that I am fine, quite on top now, but it has changed me. Made me more insular. But I still feel a lot of affection for you both, even if it doesn't look like it – and I'm more grateful than I can say to have such good neighbours as you two – '

'You don't have to say another word on the subject' said Geraldine. 'The matter is closed. Just so long as you are all right and you know we're here if you need us – '

Fred nodded. 'So let's just get this one under our belts and enjoy ourselves.' He patted the pile of newspapers at his side. 'Because I'm going to read you a few bits and pieces out of these – some of the juicier things – unless anyone objects?' He picked up one of the shock, horror tabloids and flicked through it. 'Ah – here we are – you'll like this one – all about a vicar in Bury St Edmunds and his lady church warden – ready?'

Gradually, gradually, I settled down. Fred selected some of the more outrageous bits of righteous journalism and read them with great humour and gusto. 'Should this man be allowed to manage a Co-op' he would declaim, and go on to read the complete details of the manager in question's predilection for his lady customers. Or the story concerning the bankrupt starlet and how she paid her tradesman – the Dynarod man had spilled the beans. By the time the barbecue was ashy hot we were all in excellent humour, slightly drunk and had overcome any restraint that my previous six months' withdrawal might have imposed.

But of course such joys could not be allowed to continue, could they? Not, at any rate, for someone so blessed as me.

We had eaten. The sultry day with its heavy air was not atmospherically conducive to the barbecue. It had smouldered and slumbered and never really got going so that we ate smoke blackened chicken (Geraldine had whispered to me that it was quite all right because she had cooked everything first, Fred being a medical man she did not trust him an inch so far as salmonella was concerned – I always think of the maxim that the cobbler's children go unshod so far as Fred's medical considerations are concerned – was how she put it – the family had, apparently, to be near death before he ever noticed

44

anything wrong) – there had been leathery bits of blackness, possibly steak, and shrunken, shrivelled sausages that seemed to owe no allegiance to anything that had once been alive and walking. But none of this mattered. Fred was praised in much the same way as we had praised his Harvey Wallbangers, the debris of bones and sausage skins was deposited in the compost bin, and the three of us, looking more Chekhovian than ever, sat back in our cocktail haze to enjoy the late afternoon as it cooled towards evening. I had borrowed one of my hostess's hats because the sun was still fierce and I had nothing to worry about in the world except the little beads of sweat that broke out from time to time on my upper lip. Bees hummed, there was a strong scent of lavender mingling with the scorching smell of the dying barbecue, and I stretched myself like a cat in the sun feeling that my penance was over, that I could thaw now, that after all the cutting off need no longer apply. I was back in the world again, thawing in the sun, a divorced woman like countless others and no more special.

Naturally enough, the talk moved on to holidays.

Fred had his hat pushed well down over his eyes so that he seemed to be asleep – I had my eyes slitted against the sun and almost was. Only Geraldine moved – up from her chair suddenly, darting and flitting about the garden, talking to the flowers – or possibly us – I couldn't be certain. Suddenly Fred sat up and pushed his hat back and looked at me.

'What are you doing this summer, Joan?'

I had to shake myself, come out of the stupor a little.

'Nothing particular' I said. 'I'll probably go and stay with my parents for a week or two – ' Oh God, I thought, how can I do that without Jack? Still they did not know. I had begun my letter this weekend determined to spell out the truth but had got nowhere near it. 'Or maybe I shall just stay here. I don't know. Why?'

'Well – we wondered if you would like to come to Italy with us. Portia and the children can't come and so there's plenty of room. We've got a farmhouse near Sienna for the first two weeks and then we're going to stay with Vera Ferrante, in Venice – did you meet her last year? I can't remember. Nice woman, very fine singer. I'm sure you'd like her. The apartment is huge and always full of interesting bods – actors, writers – that sort of kidney – ' Geraldine's flitting form stopped its pottering.

Above the top of a flowering currant her eyes stared, round as polo mints, as if awaiting my answer. I looked from her blue ones into Fred's hazel ones, and read the same message – that they really wanted me to go, that the invitation was sincere. In all that heat, I was beginning to thaw. I thought about Italy and was tempted. Perhaps all this ice-maiden stuff was a thing of the past. I smiled from blue to hazel and said 'I'm very tempted. When are you going?' Geraldine gave a little look of triumph, like a midwife who has just pulled a new life into the world. She began picking at the decayed frond ends of the currant blooms. 'We shall be in the farmhouse from the middle of July and then travel up to Venice at the beginning of August. You could pick up with us wherever you like – '

'It would have to be Venice' I said half to myself 'because of the school holidays ...'

'We'll be there at least until the first week of September' she said. 'You could come any time.'

Fred pushed his hat back over his eyes and slid down in his chair again. He spoke with such studied nonchalance that I realised the two of them had discussed all this in detail before, almost to the point of rehearsing who said what. 'Of course it's not the best time to go – in fact, apart from February August is probably the worst time – but beggars can't be choosers. We usually go in September when we stay with Vera but she's got one or two specials there and they have to get back to London for rehearsals or somesuch – so August it is. But the villa is on the Dogana so it's fairly quiet and it's got a nice garden leading down to the water which picks up some breeze.'

'And you can always come home again if you find it unpleasant – '

'Or go to Padua for the day – '

'Or Verona – '

'We shouldn't organise you in any way at all – '

'You'd be quite free – '

And then Geraldine delivered her pivotal heart-wringer. 'It would be so nice for us to have you there – especially now that Portia can't come ...'

I was quite seduced. The heat of the day, the friendship, the booze and the flattery of being wanted all worked their charm. Yes, I thought to myself, it would be good to spend some time abroad; I had never been to Italy and the names they reeled off

46

so matter-of-factly filled my head with romantic notions. Had I really sought permanent solitude? Suddenly it seemed completely undesirable. I could not even remember what I had felt that had made me think it was the best way to exist. Instead I wanted to know more about the villa in Venice and the people who would be staying there; I hadn't quite committed myself to saying yes, but in my heart I knew that I was going to. I could feel all the ice melting away, the concrete breaking up, and myself emerging into the warmth of this Italian fantasy.

'Do you know who else will be staying there?' I asked.

Geraldine laughed, moving away from the misty pink bush and setting her trug down on the table. 'I don't suppose even Vera knows that yet.' She flopped into her chair. 'Get us some tea, darling' she said, pushing his hat brim off his eyes, 'before you fall asleep and start snoring.' Fred went off into the house. 'I hope he doesn't decide to lace it with anything. Honestly, Joan – he can't leave that weird array of bottles alone – ' she scanned the plant tubs and clematis that surrounded us and then, with the superb timing and expression of a fine comedienne added 'I think all these have only survived because I've pickled them.'

I laughed.

'It's nice to see you happy again' she said. 'Where were we? Oh yes. Vera's place – Well, there's usually a writer or two – and someone who can play the piano – ' she smiled 'Molto importa for those romantic canal-side pre-prandials.'

'Sounds lovely.'

'Oh it is. She always manages to surround herself with interesting people ...'

'You must be very flattered ...'

'Why?'

'Going there so often ...'

She smiled at me and patted my hand. 'It's very sweet of you to say so, dear – but really Fred and I are just like pieces of furniture in that villa now. Comfortable, useful and quite undemanding.'

'You don't give yourselves much credit.'

'Come and see for yourself then' she retaliated, amused.

'Who else is going?'

'A couple of actors – you may have heard of Finbar Flynn?'

I shook my head, the name meant nothing. 'Not son of Errol?'

She smiled delicately. 'Er – well – not *quite* ... No – he's just finished Broadway – *Oedipus Rex* – very well received. He'll be there – and another actor, a friend of his I think, Richard Dean.

47

He's more a telly chap. You'll know the face.' She winked at me. 'That's if you come.'

'It all sounds like something out of Scott Fitzgerald.'

'It is. Exactly like that. Lots of romance and secret undercurrents jealousies, tensions, the paper thin glitter of jazz-age living – ' She was teasing me with her theatrical posturing.

'And who is Vera?'

'Oh – Vera. She's an old friend. She was a very fine singer – born in Birmingham but she overcame that. In Italy she met and married the sculptor Paolo Ferrante. They were only married for three years before he died ...'

'How sad' I said, and meant it.

Geraldine threw back her be-hatted head and laughed. 'Not really' she said. 'Vera was twenty-five when they married, and he was eighty-one. In the circumstances three years was a good innings.'

I must have looked shocked because she went on. 'You needn't feel there was anything wicked in it. He died extremely happy – basking in the flattery of having a young and beautiful wife to wear the black veil for him. That was over twenty years ago now. She never married again.'

'Poor thing' I said.

'Nonsense! She very sensibly wanted to keep all she inherited to herself. She has a wonderful life. You'll see for yourself when you come. You are going to?'

I was about to say that nothing would keep me away when Fred called from the steps of their back door. 'I think you've got a visitor, Joan. I think that's your doorbell I can hear.'

We waited. Sure enough, faint on the sultry air, I heard my own doorbell. I said 'Excuse me, I'd better answer it. I can't think who it might be.'

'Well, if you want to bring them back here for some tea ...'

'No. It won't be anyone like that. I'll get rid of them and then come back.'

It occurred to me that it was either some kind of door to door rep – or, just possibly, it was Robin Carstone. Either way I intended to make short shrift.

I squeezed through the gap in the hedge and called over my shoulder that I'd be back in a minute. Fred had set down the tray of tea things and the giant silver teapot, gift from some of his patients, looked like an ornate samovar. I thought again how

48

Chekhovian the scene looked in the sunlight, with the plants and shrubs beyond, and that summery interesting looking couple waiting for me at the table. I was still thinking about Italy and Venice and the seductive idea of the whole thing when I passed from the bright hot sunshine into the gloom and coolness of my house.

Chapter Five

The shadow on the glass of the front door was masculine. I saw it lift its hand to ring the bell again. Whoever he was he was insistent. I bent down to pick up the two pieces of hair brush and felt only the merest twinge of self pity for the memories that had put them there; I laid them on top of *D. H. Lawrence: Prophet of Sexuality* and found myself smiling for Robin's naïveté; the chasm between myself and ordinary mortals was still there all right but it was less one of pain than a sort of older-than-time arrogance now. The Durrells, the sun, the prospect of Venice – and perhaps Fred's concoctions – had contrived a turning point. I felt on the brink of being better and that maybe, maybe, the protection of isolation wasn't necessary any more.

That was until I opened the door.

He was leaning up against the side of the porch – easy, relaxed, hands in pockets, head on one side with the sun shining behind him – perfectly lit. I stood there holding the open door, beyond speech. He moved towards me and reaching out a hand touched my hair. 'You've had it cut' he said. 'Can I come in?'

Immobilised I let him come past me and closed the door. Shock passed into anger and anger into control. By the time I had closed the door and turned to face him a pillar of salt had nothing on me. I gave him the kind of bright smile you reserve for the milkman. 'Hullo Jack' I said. 'What do you want?'

It was very dim in the hall. I looked him full and unblinking in the face, he looked back at me sheepishly, our eyes met and I was not going to be the one that looked away. Eventually he did. Leaning up against the hall stand he began playing with the two pieces of hairbrush, fiddling with them mindlessly, those familiar hands of his moving about as if he were playing with my nerve endings. I waited, silent. I could not trust myself to speak.

49

He could not know how those two pieces of plastic damned him. Then he reached out again and put both hands on my bare shoulders and looked me up and down slowly, as if to memorise what he saw, as if I were a piece of meat at auction; I was as stiff as any carcase. His hands dropped down to my breasts, touching them lightly, but when he looked back at my face and into my eyes there was nothing for him to read but that same blank brightness. I did not move towards him or away but waited. His eyes were pink rimmed and moist and full of questions. He took his hands away one by one and riffled his fingers through my fringe. 'Oh Joanie' he said, in a voice rich with misery.

'Jack' I said evenly. 'What a surprise.'

He gave a series of sobs and stroked my hair.

'Have you been drinking?' I asked sternly.

'A little' he mumbled. I could smell the sharpness of spirit on his breath 'I was afraid ...'

'Afraid?' I laughed 'Whatever of?'

'You've cut your hair' he repeated.

'I like it short.'

He bent and put his forehead on the top of mine. 'I used to love it tumbling down your back ...'

'You *are* drunk' I said, moving at last. 'You'd better sit down.'

He followed me into the front room saying 'Yes – I'm sorry. I needed a bit of courage.'

'Don't worry.' I plonked myself down. 'I've been drinking Wallbangers so we're quits.'

'Wall-what?' He sat in the chair opposite.

'Forget it.'

He sat forward in the chair, hands between his knees, staring at me. His hair looked a little greyer, or perhaps I imagined it. It was cut close to his head, the curls forming a tight cap so that he looked like some Roman patrician. He was tanned and healthy looking, if a little red about the eyes – and he exuded attraction. Even in the hour of his sorrow he could still manage to turn himself out well – pink tee-shirt that hadn't come off the rack of a chain store, caramel coloured slacks, certainly Italian, that fitted his long legs beautifully – white belt, white shoes – gorgeous to behold. How I hated him.

By contrast to his forward tension, I leaned back in my chair and looked at him through half closed eyes.

'How's Lizzie?' I asked and was surprised to find myself

50

giving a natural yawn as I said her name – though with all that afternoon's sun and alcohol and food it was hardly surprising. His eyes widened at such a soporific gesture. He knew enough about acting to recognise it and he knew the yawn to be genuine. Jack, I thought, I can read you like a book.

'Mmm?' he said

'How's Lizzie?'

'She's in Morocco' he said.

'Really?' I finished the yawn with a small stretch. 'Is that a state of mind or of body?'

Wisely he ignored this. 'I've just come back – '

'I thought you looked brown.'

He gave his bare arms a self-conscious appraisal.

'Did you have good weather?'

'Not bad – ' he began and then stopped with a look that clearly said, What the hell is going on here – and rearranged his expression into suitable misery. 'We've split' he said dully.

There was nothing to say to that so I waited.

He waited too. And then, when nothing was forthcoming, he raised his eyes, made bluer by the pinkness of their rims, and said 'God – I made such a dreadful mistake, Joanie.'

Joanie? Joanie? Who was that? Someone who no longer existed.

'What was that, Jack?' I asked politely.

'Leaving you for her.'

Somewhere inside good manners had me on the brink of saying 'Oh well, never mind' or 'Surely not.'

But I remained quite silent. From very far away blood began to pump and hiss in my head.

He wrung his hands within the silence. It was very theatrical.

'Joanie?'

'Hullo?'

'I want you back.' He sobbed once. 'I want you back so badly.'

'Nothing doing.' The slang must have doubled the power to hurt for he flinched visibly.

'I don't blame you' he said.

'Oh good.' I was about to go on with acid sarcasm as the blood made waves of crescendo in my brain but I controlled it. I wanted to release as little emotion as possible, to deny him the expected storm of anger and recrimination. He would not afterwards be able to report that I had acted like a wronged neurotic.

51

'You've been badly hurt' he said.

'That is true.'

Stone and ice fought with the deluge of heat.

'But I'm over it now.'

'Oh?'

'Quite over it.'

He struck the perfect posture for suffering hell on earth; head dropped down on hunched shoulders, hands clasped, arms resting on knees. 'I must have been mad to leave you for her.'

I was not sure how I felt about hearing that. I was so intent on staying frozen. But I think that somewhere inside there was a satisfied sense of I Told You So. And I felt that I had earned it. He went on. 'I've thought about you so much these past weeks. In Morocco we did nothing but lie around the pool until I went mad with the boredom. And all I could think was, if Joan were here we'd be off exploring this place instead of just lying around wasting time. Lizzie was so young, you see – she only thought of pleasure.' He rubbed his hands over his face, looked across at me, and suddenly threw himself down on his knees, burying his head in my lap. His breath was very hot and moist and my dress was very thin and the feeling of inner satisfaction began – fractionally – to become softened. I didn't touch him as he ground his face deeper and deeper into my thighs. He began speaking again, his voice plangent in my body. 'She was sexy, she was beautiful – but she just wasn't you – '

Down came the portcullis. Retrospectively it has its humorous side but at the time it wasn't at all funny. Jack's idea of replighting his troth was to offer me a series of insults. First I was some crashing blue stocking hacking off into the Moroccan mountains; then some ageing puritan to whom pleasure was childishly irresponsible; and finally – finally – I was neither sexy nor beautiful. And although I could forgive the latter – the former I most certainly had been. This self-pitying creature before me had no idea how profoundly he had wrecked his prospects; I shall never know whether I was likely to love him again – but at that particular little moment I despised him. All resolve faltered. The citadel, the pillar of salt, the woman of ice – whichever analogy you choose – failed. All my pain rose to the surface and spilled over.

'Is there anybody else?' He mumbled. 'Say there isn't, Joan. Say there isn't another man ...'

52

'There isn't another man – '

He exhaled a long, slow, hot breath –

'Has there been?'

I was about to say yes. I was about to say that I had had a series of lovers each with bigger and better organs of delight. His voice betrayed how much it would wound him. But the wound wouldn't be deep enough. And so some Bona Dea breathed its own words into my mouth and I heard myself say 'No. Not another man.'

He relaxed. 'No-one then?'

'Oh yes – there has been someone.'

He looked up at me puzzled, that beautiful handsome face of his ravaged with his drunken tears; wallowing in his own sorrows at my expense.

'Not a man though, Jack. I couldn't risk that again.' I cupped his face in my hands. 'You see – I have come to love my own sex as much as you do ...'

I leaned back in the chair and closed my eyes savouring every second of his distress. The jaw muscles beneath my hands clamped and he jerked his head away from me as if I were Salome and about to twist it off his neck.

I heard the rustle of his clothes as he stood up, the crack of his knuckles as he clenched and unclenched his hands. He made to say something but it only came out as a strangled noise. He swallowed and tried again. This time he managed to speak but it was in a hoarse whisper, very stage-like.

He said 'You can't be serious ...'

'My my' I said. 'Hark at the ego talking.'

'But you're a lovely, sexy woman. You can't have changed like that – not into a lesbian?'

'You presuppose the two attributes deny such a relationship then? Thank you – by the way – for that kind description – '

'Have I brought you to this – ?'

I opened my eyes. He was standing in front of me looking horrified.

I stood up. 'Don't be so bloody arrogant. It's nothing to do with you – '

'Of course it is. You wouldn't have done – that – if I hadn't behaved so badly – '

'Rubbish.'

'Where is she?'

53

'Who?'

'This female.'

'It's none of your business.'

'My God, Joan!'

I was angry now. Really angry. And I believed the part. 'It's so much nicer than anything I ever had with you. So much softer, so much more caring. It's wonderful. And it's so much less complicated and *healthy*.'

'Healthy? Joan – are you mad or am I? It's the very opposite of healthy – '

'Oh no – it's both uncomplicated and healthy. No fear, you see. No fear of getting pregnant, is there? No need to risk thrombosis with the pill – no unwanted babies to worry about – '
Nothing was going to switch me off now. I was shouting. I hadn't shouted since he left me, not even at the most wayward of my pupils. I both enjoyed the release and hated him for standing there creating the need. I pushed him out of the way and went back into the hall. 'You'd better go now.'

He followed me and put his arms around me and I began to shake all over in a fury of pain. He looked down at me as if I was a tantrumming child needing to be humoured.

'It's no way for you. Be calm now, be calm. It's early days for me to get you back. You've been badly hurt. I'll look after you – I won't leave you again – '

'Oh yes you will – ' I pushed him away so that he bounced against the hall stand knocking both hairbrush and book to the floor. He bent to pick them up and I screamed at him not to touch them. He grabbed my shoulders pulling me into a stifling bear hug – there was too much of him, too much familiarity, too much half forgotten smell, too much temptation. I could hear the tearing of pages as his heel ground into *D. H. Lawrence* – I thought of the explanations I would have to give Robin Carstone, I thought of the broken hairbrush – a tumbling jumble of thoughts while he held on, murmuring endearments and kissing the top of my head – the boozy breath swirling all around me. 'You don't need that kind of love' he whispered. 'You need my kind.'

Something in the pride of his tone controlled me. I ceased to struggle and rail. I did what the tantrumming child would have done. I held my breath and went rigid.

'There' he said. 'That's better. Now look at me.'

I did so. He was smiling. He thought he had won. I stepped away from him.

'Now get out' I said.

Still he smiled and said cajolingly 'What was all that about the pill? And being healthy? You've just got a bee in your bonnet, my love – that's all – '

I moved even further away, reached for and began to open the door. 'Better that' I said 'than a bun in the oven. Don't you think?'

He laughed in a kind of confused amusement.

Arrogant swine.

'Now what are you talking about?'

It was getting too dangerous. 'Just go, Jack. Will you? Just get out. Please?'

I released the latch on the door but he pushed it closed again.

'What on earth have buns in the oven got to do with all this?' He was leaning against the door, arms folded against his chest, still smiling that humouring smile.

I gave him a humouring smile back. 'Didn't you know?'

Flash of impeccable white teeth. 'Know what?'

'When I visited you and your little Notting Hill Carnival – I was pregnant ...'

I suppose there lurks beneath the civilised surface of all of us the desire for power. For a few moments I had it and it was, as the poets say, sweet.

He wasn't acting any more. The disbelief in his eyes was very real. The luminous horror of their blueness was quite without artifice. He looked down at my stomach and back to my face.

I patted my flatness and said 'Gone.'

All the male energy went from his body. His arms hung loose at his side – he stared and then said 'My poor baby ...'

'Which one?' I asked. 'Me or the little clot of protein I got rid of?'

'You Did What?' He spoke in capital letters.

'You heard.'

'I don't believe you.'

'I've got a doctor's letter somewhere. Would you like to see it? Hang on a tick and I'll find it for you ...'

The cruelty was nectar. How long I had suppressed that need to hurt back, that need to bathe the wounds of losing my baby in his tears of outrage. I had saved the best part of my gall for this one moment of brutality. I could share it with him pitilessly.

'You're lying, you must be.' Dame Kindness would have had me nod my head. I shook it. You must suffer as I have done, I vowed.

'Why didn't you tell me?'

'What – and have you and Irish offer to adopt it or something?'

'I'd never have left you if I'd known.'

'You already had.'

He began to cry. First with little whimpering noises and then in true hiccoughing sobs.

Inventiveness intruded the sweetness of the moment.

'It was a boy' I said. 'A fat little baby boy. They took it from me and lay it in a basin until its heart stopped pumping and they could shove it in an incinerator.'

He put his hands to his mouth.

I pushed him to one side. He moved as easily and lightly as an aspen twig. I opened the front door.

A little zephyr of wind sent a cooling draught into the hall; the honeysuckle that I had planted to grow wild and free bounced and swayed in the breeze, the first florets opening in the sun. I touched one and smelled it, the perfume was very faint but there. I knew I should never again smell it or touch it without remembering this glorious and bitter moment. I moved so that he could pass me on the step. He had his hands over his face.

'Complications' I said. 'You see what I mean?'

I closed the door.

If I was to have suffered remorse I was given no time. Right on cue, as the door clicked shut, the telephone rang. Exit stage left, I muttered, wiping the sweat from my face. I took a deep breath and answered it. Of course, it was my mother. And so I moved from tragedy to comedy without the grace of even an Interval in between.

'Hallo darling.'

'Hallo mother.'

'What's the weather like down there?'

Thank Christ for banalities.

'Very warm.'

'Same here. It's so unlike Edinburgh. Your father's positively wilting in the heat. The bank's not air-conditioned, you know.'

56

'Poor Dad' I said politely. 'No – I didn't know that ...'

'Well – you know how mean the Scots are supposed to be; too close to pay for such extravagances. Why did we ever come? I ask myself ...'

She'd been asking that for ten years.

I didn't say anything. I was suddenly shaking and couldn't trust myself to speak.

'Well – how are you?'

Her tone implied aggrievance. Justifiable since I hadn't seen them since before Jack left me – and never rang them but waited for them to ring me.

'Hot' I said. 'But otherwise all right.'

'How's Jack?'

I thought for a moment.

'A bit under the weather.'

'Working too hard, I expect. We just caught his film on the Vienna boys' choir last month – so good, and so sad about all those little boys – you can't hide it, you know ...'

'Can't hide what?' I asked sharply. I'd only been half listening and the statement seemed disturbingly astute.

'When their voices break. They can't hide it once they go – and then that's it – it's all over. They just have to pack their bags – all that travelling and excitement suddenly gone – very sad.'

'Yes' I said. 'It must be.'

'Anyway, tell him that we did enjoy it. We watched it at the Briggs' – you remember them ...'

Memories of a fat lady with a blue rinse and an angular old man came to mind.

'Vaguely' I said.

'Well – we were playing bridge and they suddenly said they'd seen Jack's name in the *Radio Times* – so we looked it up and it was on that night. We abandoned the game for it!'

'Good heavens' I said. 'He would be impressed.'

'Yes – well – it was very good indeed.'

I waited.

'So – you're well.'

'Yes.'

'Good.'

I knew she was building up to something.

'It'd be so nice to see you both again.'

Tell her, whispered a voice, tell her now ...

57

But I couldn't. 'It would be nice.'

'We've been thinking – your father and me – that if we can't get you up here on a visit – we could come down to you.'

Panic galvanised me.

'Really – when?'

'In time for the tennis. About three weeks. Your father – ' She always invoked my father if there was anything tricky in the offing '... thought we could come and stay with you – '

'How long for?'

'Ten days or so – '

'Just a minute' I lied. 'There's someone at the door.'

I stood holding the telephone and looking at it. Desperation brought no enlightenment. I couldn't face telling them about Jack and me, not yet. I could picture my mother sobbing into her little lace handkerchief and my father sipping an embarrassed whisky while I confessed the failure. I looked all around the hall as if it would yield up an answer. It did. There on the floor alongside the pieces of hairbrush and the crumpled book, lay the leaflet about Commonwealth students. I picked it up.

'Sorry about that. Now, what were you saying?'

'Your father and I want to come to London. We thought we could stay with you since we haven't seen you for ages.'

'Ah – well' I said.

'Well what?'

'There's a bit of a problem at the moment.'

'Is there?' she said understandably frosty. 'Well, of course, if you don't want us to come you must say – '

'Oh it's not that – it really isn't. It's just – ' I looked down at the scrunched up Commonwealth leaflet 'a matter of not having room.'

'What are you talking about, Joan? You've got plenty of room.'

'No we haven't. Not at the moment. We've got a student staying with us – an overseas student – '

'Really? Where from?'

I scanned the details. 'Nigeria' I said.

'Really?' Her voice sounded less positive. 'How nice. Boy or girl.'

'Girl.'

'And what is she a student of?'

'Health' I said vaguely.

'And is she – er – a – um – native of Nigeria?'

58

'She's a black African – yes.'

'How very very nice' she said, meaning the opposite.

'She'll be with us until Christmas.'

'That's not very long, is it?' I could hear the underlying relief in her voice. 'What sort of a qualification is it?'

'I don't know' I said feeling I was getting out of my depth. 'We don't have much contact – '

'No – well – I don't suppose you would really ...' meaning, my daughter has nothing in common with an African. 'Well, if she's in the big spare room perhaps your father and I could squeeze into the box room.'

'Why not?' I said – thinking Oh what the hell 'She cooks some wonderful things – and her family's coming over soon – I expect they'll be in and out while they're here. It could be great fun. A sort of mingling of the two cultures. Yes – by all means, Mum – I think you'd both enjoy it, don't you?'

I suppose I was bordering on hysteria but for the short moment in which I made the suggestion I actually believed she existed.

'Well – what about it?'

'No dear' said my mother faintly. 'I don't think your father would like it – '

'Oh he wouldn't mind – I'm sure of it.'

'No – no – we'll come another time. Or maybe we could persuade you both to come up here. Autumn perhaps?'

'I really don't know what Jack's movements will be.'

'Then you must come on your own. He could join you for some of the time. Honestly, Joan, it's been a ridiculously long time since we saw you. And you never ring us nowadays. I do think you might do that at least ...' She displayed understandable irritation.

'Christmas' I said, feeling that was far enough away to risk suggesting 'I'll come up for Christmas for sure. Can I speak to Dad now?'

'He's bell ringing.'

I looked at my watch; nearly six o'clock. 'Of course. Silly of me. Give him my love. I was going to write to you both this weekend anyway.'

My last word to my mother was sorry.

*

59

There were a few other sorries to perform after that weekend. Sorry to Fred and Geraldine on two counts; one for not returning to their peaceful Chekhovian scene that afternoon; two for changing my mind about going to Venice with them; and three, a tacit sorry for withdrawal of tangible friendship. It was back into the ice-age for me.

Sorry also to Robin Carstone when I returned his mauled book, rather appositely, I thought, ground beneath the heel of my prodigal husband. I gave it to him in the staffroom.

'I really am very sorry it's damaged' I said. I was too weary to do the polite thing and offer to replace it.

'What did you think?' his eyes all eager.

'What I always think about Lawrence.'

'Which is?' He moved closer despite the smoke hazed teachers thronging all around us.

'That his attitude to sex is boringly moralising.'

'Can I visit you again?'

'No.'

'I might be going to Canada for the autumn term. Someone from the school over there is coming here on an exchange. I could go out there early. If there's nothing here to keep me – ' he added this last wistfully 'Spend some of the summer vac there.' If he had been a puppy his tongue would have hung out.

'That's nice.'

'I'll come and see you before I go.'

'I'd rather you didn't.'

'You're too cold, Joan. It'd just be a friendly visit. Please?'

'No.'

He did call but this time I was cautious and checked the window first. He looked rather beautiful standing there on my step, one muscular arm leaning against the wall, the other raised, finger pointing to the nipple of the bell. I scarcely heard the noise it made; it didn't matter how long it went on for because I was quite inviolable now – he was outside, I was inside – I enjoyed looking at him surrounded in his honeysuckle frame. He was remarkably persistent, the rhythmic pumping of the bell seemed to go on for ages. Then, suddenly and rather disappointingly, Maud Montgomery came up her garden path, paused and gave him a penetrating look. I heard her ask if she could help – in that tone of voice that really means what are you doing – and I heard

60

him say he was waiting for me to open the door. She stood her ground, pretending to pick at a lavender bush so that he, feeling understandably self-conscious, gave one more ring before admitting defeat and walking out of my gate. He gave the house one fierce look that said very clearly he knew I was in, before getting on his bicycle and riding away. It was the middle of August.

He wrote to me a couple of times on thin airmail paper with his address underlined in heavy black ink. He had crossed by boat and had thought of me as he leaned over the ship's rail looking out to sea. Very romantic. He later wrote that the school was wonderful, that this was how education could be if the resources were there to fuel it and that he wished I would write back to him. You haunt me, he wrote, and I don't know why. I thought I detected a flavour of Lawrence about the style. If I had written back to him I might have congratulated him on that.

Sorry to Robin, then, for not getting in touch.

Not sorry to Jack. I quietly replaced the telephone receiver whenever he rang. Shook my head at him when he came a-calling with flowers, champagne, angry scenes on the doorstep. Maud Montgomery had something of a field day over all this but even she, towards the end, got more embarrassed than curious because he was there so often and so noisily. It was odd how angry Jack was – yet I felt calm and cool and only slightly irritated at the attempted intrusions. After one particularly loud exchange between him and Maud, in which she, understandably, asked him to go away and not make so much noise, he did depart. Only to begin a postal campaign – letters recommending psychiatric help (this I found especially amusing since I was the cool relaxed one, and he was the poor soul driven half demented); books sent through the post on – broadly – the psychology of women under stress; books left on the doorstep on – broadly – the psychology of men under ditto. He even left me a note one day saying he was working on a film for BBC2 about abortion – the video of which I duly received later that summer – it was on – broadly – the psychology of women under stress from abortion. There was silence after this and I assumed he had met someone during its making with whom a romance had blossomed across her ravaged uterus. Anyway, it was very peaceful again. With Robin in Canada, Jack dealt with, my parents in abeyance, Fred and Geraldine in Italy, I could at last settle

61

back down to a quiet withdrawal. Even – I decided – to feel a little sorry for myself. And what, I argued to myself, is wrong with that? Whoever began the stupid platitude about it not being good for you? One of those phoney Victorian aphorisms now regurgitated by the current trend towards red-necked righteousness. Of course feeling sorry for yourself is good for you – who could be better at it and more understanding than you? What possible virtue is there in the moral majority who swing down from the trees now and then and tell us to 'Buck up ... put a brave face on it ...'? Oh no. Give me Oscar any day – where there is sorrow there is Holy Ground.

I did indeed feel a kind of holiness, a kind of purity in my cold, white state. Nobody could touch me and I didn't want to touch them. It was beautiful arrogance. I floated above the world again, that ice goddess, that shaft of pure cold light – ephemeral, alone, emotionally impenetrable.

Or so I thought.

PART TWO

Ice maiden
Nice maiden
Frosted free from germs
Pure as any saint should be
From earth's corrupting worms.

Chapter One

Contrary to one's beliefs, one's parents tend not to be entirely witless. By late autumn my mother was distinctly suspicious. I agreed to come home for Christmas.

It was a nice snowy one, just right for my temperament, and when the day of departure for the frozen north arrived I have to admit that I was pleased to be going. This was nothing to do with my needing familial comforts and Christmas trees but more to do with the seasonal upswing in social pressures. You can go on avoiding and being avoided up to a point on the calendar but when the season of goodwill arrives it is not so easy. The kind hearted Margery had bounced back at the end of the Christmas term and insisted that I join the rest of the staff for their turkey lunch.

'And we won't take no for an answer' she quipped. 'It's in the room above The Three Bells – three courses and all the trimmings – five pounds a head – ' She raised a plump hand. 'No – don't even begin to make excuses.'

So I didn't.

I sat between Arthur Blackstone and the sumptuously colourful Rhoda Grant. Arthur taught chemistry and his doleful, ageing features reflected little of the expected Christmas cheer. Rhoda looked very splendid, all flashing eyes and fiery hair and features that snapped on and off like fairy lights. The wine heightened her colour and intensified her snappy manner.

'Come on, Arthur' she admonished across my plate of pudding. 'It's about time you cheered up. What have you got to be so miserable about?'

He leaned back and gave her a pitying look. 'You'd look miserable if you taught science to teenage girls' he said. 'It's rather like selling contraceptives in a nunnery; they think they'll never need it.' He sipped his wine. 'And of course – providing they never leave the nunnery – they never do ...'

I thought that was quite witty and laughed. 'Well, well' said Rhoda. 'Our mysterious lady of literature has a sense of humour after all.'

'Not much of one' I said.

'*Are* you married?'
'No – divorced.'
'Perhaps that explains it?'
'Not at all.'
'You live alone, don't you?'
'Entirely ...'
'I envy that.'
'Yes' I said 'I prefer it that way.'
'One husband, two kids and three salamanders.'
'Pardon?'
'That's who I live with.'

She was holding up her glass and looking through it at the people on the opposite side of the table.

'I like salamanders' said Arthur.

I saw her curl her lip and snap her eyes.

'So does my husband, so do my sons. Perhaps it's a masculine trait.' She took a drink. 'The salamanders are males too.'

'Not breeding them then?' Arthur said.

'Oh no.' She shook her head. 'Nothing so lustful as that. Not in our house anyway.' She took another sip from her glass; the eyes that stared above it were hard, angry suddenly. The very faintest of tintinnabulations rang in my head as she swivelled herself to face me.

'Perhaps I'll come and visit you during the holidays. Cheer you up a bit.'

The tintinnabulations increased. Beneath the brittle flippancy was an unmistakeable note of pleading.

'By the way' someone on the other side of the table said. 'Has anyone heard from young Carstone? He must be due back any day now. He won't be staying on for Christmas surely?'

In my ear Arthur said 'My wife and I would be pleased to have you over some time if you're on your own. I'll get Molly to give you a ring.'

Margery leaned across and said 'Joan dear – I shall be around this Christmas. We must get together. Let's get our diaries out afterwards ...'

Quasimodo's had nothing on these bells. Loud and clear, triumphant in their pealing call to a gregarious Noel, they rang out.

'I shall be going away' I said. 'To stay with my parents in Scotland. But thank you all the same.'

66

I had toyed with the idea of faking 'flu at the last minute and just not turning up in Edinburgh – for, naturally enough, I would have preferred to stay in London, quite alone, eating chocolates and reading into the night, but I knew it wouldn't happen that way. Even Fred and Geraldine had made their overtures, though restrained, about meeting up at Christmas. They were too kind hearted to be able to imagine me next door in my isolation without doing something about it. My Christmas card, dropped through the door, had a little note attached.

Joan – if you are going to be in London we would love to see something of you. We shall have one or two of the people we met in Italy staying for a few days. Be in touch – Love F&G

After the lunch I bought a card and wrote on it

Thank you both for the invitation but I am going to stay with my parents. Have a lovely time. Joan

Late that night, shivering in the frosty air, I sneaked up their path and pushed the envelope through their letterbox. But I was not quick enough. Geraldine appeared just as I was going back down my own path.

'It's my card for you' I said. 'I'm going away so I won't be able to meet your friends.'

'What a pity' she said. 'You'd like them. One of them is opening at the National in March. Exciting young man. Brilliant actor – he was staying at Vera's – it is a pity that you couldn't come – Italy was lovely.'

'Well, never mind' I said. 'I shall be getting my holiday now instead.'

She nodded and pulled her cardigan around her shoulders. 'All that sun seems a lifetime away' she said.

'Yes. Doesn't it.'

'When are you getting back?' she asked.

'I'm not sure.'

She took the hint and went in, wishing me a merry Christmas and telling me to wrap up warm.

Funny that no warning bells rang in my head that night. Perhaps they had been overworked that day. But there is no doubt that they should have done. Instead, in the bliss of unawareness, I went indoors and telephoned my parents.

The next day I made a sortie into the baubled tinsel world of seasonal shopping to buy them a present each: a compendium of Dorothy L.Sayers for my father, a small vase for my mother and the two biggest boxes of chocolates that I could find – one to take for all of us to scoff, one to leave for my own private greed when I returned. The shopping trip suddenly became unpleasant when I passed by the stall in the market that displayed the Christmas trees. Just for a moment I saw another young woman standing there, choosing one – smiling up brightly at the man, her face full of expectancy and hope – laughing at his winks and quips about the early bird getting the worm. How very true that had been.

The weather was cold and getting colder. The snow that had fallen was set now, a deep, crisp crunching whiteness that sparkled with the frost. When I looked out at the back garden it looked beautiful – what had seemed just a tangle of weeds and a jungle of unkempt unpleasantness in the summer was now a series of pristine sculptures, the outlines smoothed and the contours heavy. Like me it was at its best in the blanket of impenetrable whiteness, all messes hidden under the unifying rigor. It would be good if it could stay like that.

And the journey up was intensely beautiful beginning with the morning sharpness of frosty sunshine and changing gradually as we pulled north into that low afternoon light making the white landscape a pinkening peach and the sky more orange than blue.

My thoughts on the train were the same old ones really. That I wished everyone would continue to leave me alone and that so long as they did I was perfectly happy. It wasn't until we had crossed the border that it suddenly occurred to me what I had discovered. I had discovered that there was a fifth dimension after all – and that as they say – it was Good. We were just clattering out of Dunbar when the thought crystallised – and it was such a pleasant moment that I found I was smiling and waving at the guards on the station. And that they, curiously, were standing and waving back. I put this unusual behaviour down to its being Christmas but then it occurred to me that I had never behaved that way to station staff before. Perhaps all over the country they are only waiting for smiles and waves to respond like that. After all, there is something manifestly moving about seeing a train pulling out of a station – journeys of any kind tend to touch the subconscious innards of those left behind. I would try to remember that in future.

The thought that had struck me so pleasingly during the last bits of Dunbar Station was this. That up until now, in the civilised West, four categories of human relationships exist inviolable; that is to say once you live in one of them, no-one feels they must set about changing them much. Each of them in their own way is considered autonomous. I can, of course, speak only for my own sex.

The first and most popular is two people of the opposite sex living together in a sexual relationship – commonly called marriage but not always blessed as such. (Out of this comes widowhood – a sorry state despite Rhoda's sour cynicism.)

The second is two people of the same sex living ditto.

The third is living with a companion or companions of either sex but not carnally.

The fourth – for a woman anyway – is living as a spinster or divorcée; alone, it is considered, not out of choice but out of rejection.

My fifth dimension was living alone, choosing to live alone and – more to the point – enjoying living alone and being as cut off from my fellow human beings as possible. But short of having a banner embroidered with this message strung across my front door, no-one seemed to take the choice seriously. But I did. I was in my fifth dimension, happily in my fifth dimension. I felt a good deal better after that thought crystallised itself, and as the evening darkness gradually began to intensify the snowy buildings of Edinburgh I alighted from the train with a cheerful heart. Everything was just right for me to make my visit and my peace up here and return home with an unassailable right to my privacy. Good.

Both parents were waiting for me on the station. My father banging his hands together against the cold, their black leather gloves making a satisfying slapping noise, saw me first and gave me a big red-nosed smile from beneath his astrakhan hat; my mother had her fur coat on, big boots and a headscarf. She may have been smiling as well but I couldn't see beneath the knot of the scarf. They both looked like a scene from a Russian drama; steel yourself, Joan, I told myself. It was all very well having my fifth dimension epiphany on the train, it was all very well being thirty-one years old – but these, after all, were my parents. So far as they knew they had handed me over forever on my wedding day to one Jack Battram; and now I had been handed back. Parents have a somewhat blinkered approach to such things.

I decided to tell them at once, there on the station, with the train still standing being made ready for its return to London. If necessary I could always jump back on it and go home again. I gave my mother due warning of this as we all sat together in the station bar.

'Jack and I are divorced' I said. 'And if you make too much of an issue of it I shall get straight back on the train and go home.' She obliged me by wetting only one handkerchief. Her main pronouncement was Poor Jack, Poor Jack – rather, I thought, like a refrain in a pantomime. My father, who on hearing the news immediately got up and replenished our glasses with triples, rubbed my knee under the table and said Poor Joan, Poor Joan. Which about sums them up. I didn't feel at all vicious – why should I – so I said to my mother 'Don't feel you have to tell anybody unless you want to. I'm quite prepared to pretend nothing has happened.' This drew a few more tears and a little sigh – probably of relief – and then I admired my mother's new, discreet shade of gold in her hair and said I liked the perm. She patted it and thanked me – albeit a little waterily – and told me her new hairdresser had been trained in a London salon. To my mother Edinburgh was and always would be the provinces – anything that arrived there vaguely connected with the capital was greeted much as pre-war Raj wives greeted their Debenhams catalogue – with heartfelt relief that civilisation still existed somewhere on the map. Then she admired my hair, took out her compact and dabbed her little pink nose with the scented powder that was always essence of mother, re-tied the Jacquard on and not under the chin, and was ready for life again.

My father did not like my hair. I knew by his silence. I suppose we women do, after all, marry our fathers. He, like Jack, preferred it long and curling – romantic to look at and difficult to maintain. He was altogether less easy to pacify since he showed scarcely any emotion at all. I knew he was going through a bad time inwardly because, having removed his hat, he now ran his fingers through his thick grey hair from ear to ear, a sure sign of being upset, a kind of physical attempt at remission of sin or absolvement. There was only one thing to do and that was mention Communism to him – rather like smacking someone round the face when they've hurt their foot – to take their mind off the former pain.

I said 'I like your Russian hat, Dad. You look just like a Commissar.'

He stood up, straight and tall, and said 'Rubbish!' and retrieved my suitcase from beneath the table. I winked at him but he did not wink back – only blinked. The hat he crushed beneath his arm – I knew he would never wear it again and felt a small pang of conscience in case he caught cold. But at least he was galvanised. He took my mother's arm and walked very stiff and proud towards the car. I shuffled along behind them and then when we reached it, leaned over and whispered in his ear 'Pre-Revolutionary Commissar. Keep wearing it – it suits you.'

'You still say the silliest things, Joan.' He was mollified.

The inference was that despite being a divorced woman I was still his little girl.

Thank God, I thought, that they both live hundreds of miles away.

Neither of them asked me why. Why we were divorced, nor why I had not told them we were divorced. My mother assumed it was my fault since, to her, Jack was the most perfect son-in-law; talented, reasonably famous, handsome, witty – everything sophisticated. He was also a great flatterer of women when he chose and my mother had fallen prey to this countless times. My father assumed it was Jack's fault but not for the real reason – his assumption was based on Jack having a career that took him away from home often, leaving the little golden-haired woman-at-home pining.

On the morning of Christmas Eve we went for a walk leaving my mother at home to prod the slowly defrosting comestibles. We walked up the hill to the monument and looked out over the white meringue landscape.

'It's still beautiful' I said.

'Very' he replied, viewing it as a captain might look out to sea. He was wearing the check cap. The astrakhan was, as I had suspected, permanently tainted. 'Is there another man?'

'No' I said – and had the fleeting tickle of mischief to say what I had said so effectively to Jack, that there was another woman. But since we were quite high up, and since I really loved my

71

father despite everything, I desisted. He was quite capable, in his proud Englishman mould, of hurling himself off the walls at the idea of such foul corruption.

'You should come back here' he said, pushing his hazel stick hard into the ground and leaning on it, still viewing the hills like a Nelson. 'We could look after you then.'

'I don't need it' I said. 'I'm very well organised at home.'

His eyes were very watery, though whether it was the cold or sorrow I couldn't tell.

'I have found the fifth dimension' I told him. 'And I like being alone.'

'We'll come and visit you in the spring.'

He took his cap off and ran his gloved fingers ear to ear across his head.

'No' I said. 'Don't do that. I'll come up here instead.'

As before with Christmas – in all this ice and snow the spring seemed a long way off.

Apart from a few sobs into the turkey bones, my mother did very well. Once or twice – usually after a gin and tonic – she would tap a bauble on the tree and sigh as she watched it dance and catch the light, but on the whole the visit went off without any real recriminations.

I managed some long walks alone in the pristine snow feeling in perfect accord with the white unyielding landscape. I even went to church and was happy to find that the fund still hadn't reached the required target for a proper heating system. I put two foreign coins in the collection plate. After all, I wasn't the person to help them warm up those ancient stones.

By way of compensation to God I put real money in the Missionary box. Not that God existed where I lived – but he might – possibly — still be alive and well and living in Africa.

On the whole, after being up there for three days, I was beginning to feel like going home. Not tearing my hair out or anything – just nice and relaxed and at peace with having made my peace. I was also so grateful for my parents' reasonable attitude about the divorce that I didn't want to test the harmony more that I could help. At any moment I expected my father to suggest acting as intermediary and attempting to retie the sundered knot, or my mother to start perching on the edge of my bed in the mornings for woman to woman chats. So far I had escaped this but I was on borrowed time. For while Christmas

Day and Boxing Day can reasonably be regarded as private family times, the following days are social free-for-alls – at least, so they are in my parents' house. And naturally, everyone who came asked where Jack was.

'Working.'

Which brought sage nods from the men and smiles of sympathy from the women.

The prospect of further social sessions in this mould was not at all pleasing – so when the last guest had left I told my parents that I would be going home the following day.

'And you'll be back in the spring, you said.' My father's voice was mildly accusing.

'Which bit of the spring, Joan?' My mother was right to ask – I had thought to stretch it to – possibly – late May; now I couldn't.

'Easter-ish I expect.' It still seemed far enough away.

So really I could scarcely believe my luck – a reasonably undramatic arrival and visit – and an equally undramatic departure. And, of course, I was right not to believe it – but the threat came not from within as I had expected – it came, completely unexpected, via the telephone and from without.

Chapter Two

I was packed and ready to go and we were just about to sit down to an early lunch, when the telephone rang. Since I was passing I answered it.

The male voice said 'Is that you, Joan?'

'Yes' I said.

'Happy Christmas. It's Jack here.'

'Yes. I know.'

I could neither move nor think, beyond making sure my parents would not find out who I was talking to.

'You don't sound very surprised.'

'Oh but I am' I said evenly. My father called from the dining room asking who it was.

'It's a friend of mine' I called back. 'Start eating without me.'

'Sorry' said Jack. 'To interrupt your meal.'

I waited in silence.

'Hallo? Joan?'

'I'm here.'

'I came round to the house last night to see you but you weren't in.'

'Obviously.'

'I hope you don't mind but I let myself in and stayed the night. I still had a key, you see.'

My mother, passing by with a tureen of soup, stopped and said in a stage whisper 'Is everything all right? You look a bit shocked.' I beamed at her and nodded. To Jack I said, in as controlled a voice as I could muster.

'Why?'

'Because I forgot to return it to you. Perhaps that was Freudian ... '

'I don't mean why the key – I mean why stay?' Why call, come to that.

'It's Christmas. And I missed you. I wanted to see you.'

'You should have telephoned.'

'You would have said no.'

'That's true.'

'When are you coming back down?'

'Not for ages.'

'How long?'

'Not sure.'

'I could come up there.'

'Don't you dare.'

'No – that was a silly thing to suggest. I'm sorry. We must talk sometime soon, Joan.'

The close proximity of my parents was a powerful restraint. 'I don't think so.'

'When you're back.'

'I doubt it.'

There was a pause and his voice changed its slightly sorrowing tone to bright pleasantry. 'How are your parents?'

'Fine.'

'Give them my regards.'

Regards indeed!

'A funny thing happened here last night. That's how I knew where you were.'

'What?'

'The Durrells thought I was a burglar. Fred and one of their friends who's staying – that actor – Finbar Flynn – crept round to sort me out. It was quite funny really. In the end I went next door and had a drink with them all. They don't change.'

74

'No, they don't.'

'And you seem to be running a rave of a social life.'

'What do you mean by that?'

'Your telephone this morning. Hasn't stopped ringing. I've written down the messages.'

'Thank you.'

Rage was bringing me dangerously close to tears.

'Don't you want to know who they were from?'

'Leave them. I'll see them when I get back.'

'One was a chap called Carstone. I told him I was your husband.'

'But you're not.'

'We'll talk about that sometime. Hold on – I'll just get the list – '

Perhaps some small good had come out of all this if he had got Robin's potential overtures off my back. He returned.

'There were three others – all women.' He added this rather darkly. 'Someone called Molly asking you to lunch tomorrow; someone called Margery who left no message; and someone called Rhoda who asked who I was and rang off when I told her.' His voice changed again, this time towards pomposity. 'I presume that she's the one you – er – told me about.'

'Jack' I said. 'Get out of my house. Get out of my life.'

I rang off.

Fortunately, if they had been listening my parents had become bored with what they heard, for they were having an animated conversation about bridge when I took my place at the table. With luck they had not heard me use his name.

'Who was that?' asked my mother, ladling out some soup.

'Just a friend' I said. 'Someone I don't really want to see. Would you mind very much if I stayed on for a few more days? They'll have gone by then. Otherwise I won't be able to avoid them.'

'From the expression on your face' said my father 'they are an unwelcome aquaintance indeed.'

'You're damned right they are' I said, tearing my bread into three savage pieces 'and I want to make quite sure that I don't bump into them again. Ever. By the way, Dad – does it cost a great deal to change a front door lock?'

Pure selfishness is like a drug. By the time the next few days of enforced sociability were over I was suffering acutely from my own kind of cold turkey and I just wanted to get home and be on my own. I found I was analysing each social event I was part of, each convivial exchange, and asking myself, What, at the end of the day, had its value been? I had not brought a little sunshine into their lives, nor they mine; I had not changed the way they thought about anything, nor they me; none of us had eaten because we needed to, nor drunk because we were thirsty, nor talked because we had anything to say; they made no impact on me, nor I on them. There were no Mother Theresas nor Albert Einsteins in my parents' Edinburgh sitting room, just ordinary people like me. I did once try to tackle the vicar on points of religion – just for something exercising to do – but he was such a liberalised pastor that it was no contest. To any suggestion of debate he just smiled and would have patted me had his hands not been full with sherry glass and cake plate and said 'Just keep Jesus in your heart and you cannot go wrong ...' He only really got going when I became inexpiable.

'What about the Ku Klux Klan?'

'I'm sorry?'

'They kept Jesus in their hearts as they strung blacks up in trees.'

'They were misguided – '

(Misguided?)

'They only thought they worked in the name of the Lord.'

'So how do we know we're not misguided?'

'My dear Joan – no-one is hanging anyone in this country in the name of religion.'

'We sanctify marriage in the name of God and urge the recipients to go forth and multiply.'

'Yes.' He nodded with a saga smile obviously waiting for the punchline and completely at sea.

'Well – in the light of overpopulation this is creating death, isn't it?'

'Oh no – I don't think so. Even in the worst parts of Glasgow people are not quite dying yet from lack of food.' He smiled pityingly at me and popped the last of his cake into his mouth.

'Not here. But in Asia, Africa – people are starving to death – there aren't enough resources to go around. And still you're telling people to go out and have a lot more unnecessary human beings to sap the world's resources ...'

'Our missions to these parts of the world are very keen on population reduction – it is part of our education programme ...'

'But the trouble is, vicar, that sex is a pleasurable business – and after a tiring day in the paddy fields there's nothing like cuddling up with a willing body – '

He blushed a little but carried on gamely 'We are not like our Popish counterparts; we do not deny birth control.'

'But it doesn't seem to have got the world very far in population reduction – I mean – it sounds a bit like Pilate to me. The church washing its hands of the whole question. Consider how much famine and disease there is affecting the Third World and consider that despite this natural reduction we are still overpopulated – and then I think, if you have any real belief in saving lives as well as souls – you will look for a way to cut down on progeny.' I was really into my stride now and began to think I was getting somewhere – of course, this may have been due to my father replenishing my sherry.

'Educational programmes and medical programmes take time' he said, a little crossly I thought. 'You cannot expect primitive man to have vasectomies without a deal of education getting through to him first ...'

'In the meantime the world comes closer to the abyss. What we need to do in the West is something radical.'

'The West – if you are thinking about population – is in decline.'

'But it supports a system of marriage and normality that has a far-reaching effect throughout the rest of the world.'

'Yes?'

'Marriage between partners of the opposite sex.'

Unfortunately my father had happened along for the third time with the sherry decanter and if there is one drink that affects me like no other it is amontillado.

'Indeed it does. Nothing wrong with that, is there?' He said this with a slightly roguish twinkle – since he too had been replenished by my father. 'I am sure you are finding your own marriage a delight?'

'Never mind that' I said. 'What about offering an alternative kind of sex? What about suggesting that two people of the same sex can have a loving and sexual relationship – without adding to their burdens with a whole lot of unwanted children ...'

'Pardon' he said.

'I am saying Why doesn't the church sanctify homosexuality?' He opened his mouth like a fish gasping for air. 'The Greeks did it perfectly responsibly – had their children to keep the race going – but also had their homosexual pleasures which the state and the church thought perfectly honourable.'

Even as I said this I knew what his answer should be – he should have completely destroyed my sherryfied argument by saying that while this worked for the men it did not work for the slaves and women so I couldn't really seriously countenance *that*, now could I?

And then I would have trotted out the hoary old chestnut about Sappho seeming to do all right and we could have diversified nicely on the gentle art of poetry or something and forgotten my sacrilegious pratings. But of course, being a man and the champion of a male God, it didn't occur to him to use this sensible piece of artillery.

Instead he said, very red in the face now and still opening and closing his jaws like a beached and blushing haddock 'Joan – I am horrified – horrified – at the very suggestion. Can you seriously expect the Christian church to advocate, or even countenance, carnal knowledge between two people of the same sex?'

For a moment I thought about saying Why stop at two? (For the sitting room was closing in on me.) Why not three, or four, or five at the same time? But I only said 'Give me one good reason why not?'

He released one of his fingers from their stout hold around the sherry glass and wagged it at me; the spirit of evangelism lit his pale blue eyes. 'Thy wife shall be as the fruitful vine upon the walls of thine house. The children like the olive branches round about thy table.'

He regarded me with triumph.

'Beautiful poetry' I said, quite sincerely. On the whole I have never thought that poetry had much to do with real life.

'Not just poetry, Joan – the official text of spiritual guidance: the Solemnisation of matrimony, laid down for us in our prayer books ...'

I decided to hold my fire since he looked so intoxicated with his own proselytising ... the words What about the barren vine? died on my lips. What was the point? All this talking that we do in sitting rooms and at dining tables, the way we call certain recognisable noises between ourselves Communicating and glory to the human race for being the only ones to do it ... what piffing self-congratulatory poppycock. *I'd* been living without it for the last year and I couldn't say that *I'd* missed it much at all. If anything I'd found it something of an improvement this not having to take anything I said seriously, and I recommend it. So, eyeball to eyeball we stood – me silent – he taking his pastoral role seriously and arguing (albeit in oblique embarrassment) for the joys of heterosexual union as sanctified by the church, and against (even more embarrassment, it was a good job he had a stout heart) my proposals of world harmony through homosexuality.

And then my mother joined in.

'Well' she said in her floral frocked innocence 'you two are deep in conversation. I'm quite envious. What have you found so interesting?' She looked from the vicar to me and then back again.

'World problems' I said quickly.

'Marriage' he said simultaneously.

'Make up your minds.' My mother beamed at us.

'Well' I said 'they could be construed as the same thing.'

'Another drink, Father Robert?' my mother said quickly, but he covered his glass with his hand and shook his head. She meanwhile caught my eye and frowned, so I said 'Yes please.'

She frowned even deeper. 'Your father is over by the window ...' Women are so good at oblique commands. I ignored this one. 'We were really talking about the population explosion – that's all. And I said I thought the church actively encouraged it by propounding marriage as the only allowable way to have sex ... and sex only as the gateway to begetting children. I said it was too nice just for that ...'

She kept her eyes absolutely at the same size and stared absolutely without flicker as I spoke. I almost put my arm around her and congratulated her at the self restraint.

'Interesting' she said, in the tone of one who has been served up a disgusting looking dish at a dinner party.

'Joan has some very wild ideas' Father Robert added smiling.

'Wild?' I said. 'I think they are potentially very sensible. Especially with AIDS around ...'

This was in the early days of its provenance. I think my mother thought it was some kind of church associated charity.

Certainly she thought it a safer point of discussion than my wild ideas.

'AIDS?' she said, blinking at last. 'And what is that?'

The vicar stared into the empty depth of his glass and rocked very slightly on his heels.

'It's a disease, Mum. Mostly transmitted sexually. It's been decimating the – ' I was about to say Gay but then realised she'd only think I meant jolly 'the homosexual community in California.'

Father Robert stopped rocking and looked up. His evangelism overcame his propriety: he was about to bear witness.

'So there you are, Joan' he said firmly. 'You cannot expect the church to countenance such relationships if that kind of thing is the outcome ...'

'But it doesn't apply to women, Father. Perhaps we should be advocating sex between women as the solution to everything and only consort with men when there's a population shortage. Or just keep a few in a pen somewhere in case the freezer in the sperm bank breaks down ...'

My mother had been twisting her pearls round and round her fingers – now, almost strangled by them and certainly sounding it, she said 'Joan! Go and get the decanter at once. Father Robert's glass is empty.'

'Well?' I said, not moving away. 'What would be wrong with that? It would certainly put the brakes on famine and disease. After all, men have eulogised about the female body for years as being the height of desirable beauty: why shouldn't women enjoy women for a change? I think it's worth considering, don't you – tell me, vicar – what does the church say about this? It seems a reasonable alternative to me. Rather a good one actually ...'

But before the vicar could answer my father arrived. Presumably my wild-eyed mother had signalled to him. He waved both decanters around at us with the social abandon of one who assumes the group he has entered is discussing the weather. 'Sorry to neglect you all' he said, filling the glasses. He gave me the most fleeting of winks, as if to say that he was sorry I had got caught up with the vicar for so long, and added 'By the way, Joan – I meant to ask you – how's that nice Nigerian girl you've got living with you nowadays? You've been quite mysterious about her – ' He gave a roguish chuckle and added 'Nothing we shouldn't know about, is there? Ho Ho ...'

Both the vicar and my mother choked.
Very definitely it was time for me to go home.

The external frost seemed to have penetrated the house. My father was still warm but there was a definite chilliness about my mother. If I looked up suddenly I would find her regarding me with a sort of odd despair and if I returned the look with a smile she returned that with the slight rictus usually reserved for lunatics. I decided to travel home on New Year's Eve.

'I expect there will be a lot of parties, darling' she said at the station 'with lots of nice people?'

'There's always a lot going on in London.'

'What about this African girl?' asked my mother.

'Oh, she won't be there.'

'And will you be seeing Jack?'

Come on, train, I thought, rescue me. 'No.'

'But you'll be meeting plenty of new people? Parties and all that. Some new romance ...?'

'I don't know until I get back. I might just want to spend the evening on my own.'

'You can't do that. Not on New Year's Eve. Not in London ...'

My father said 'Give us a ring. When you get home. What time does it get in?'

'Six-ish.'

'Plenty of time to have a rest before you go out.' My mother sounded almost hysterical. 'You must, Joan.'

I heard the rumble of wheels in the distance.

'Actually' I said 'I've grown rather fond of my own company.'

'Don't be silly' said my mother, unaware of the unintentional insult. 'You can't have ...'

'Give us a ring when you get to London' my father helped me aboard.

'Of course I will.'

I kissed my mother's cheek – still that powdery essence of mother – and then it was my father's turn. He brushed my forehead with his cold lips and whispered at the same time 'Don't get too drunk ...' I laughed but his eyes were serious. He still knew me better than anyone else. Or perhaps he had seen the bottle of vodka packed into my suitcase.

'Be good' called my mother as they waved me out of the station.

'Don't do anything we wouldn't do' added my father.

Both sets of parental eyes were watery which was not solely occasioned by the cold. They each had their own reasons for their tears.

'See you in the spring' I shouted, thinking Not before, please, Not before.

Did a teardrop descend from my cold-blasted eyes? I don't recall. But if one squeezed its way out it was swiftly transformed into an icicle. It was very cold outside that train. I watched the countryside flash by for a while, the rime on the hedgerows seeming set for eternity, before closing the window and sitting back on my seat. I had the whole carriage to myself since this train was heading in the wrong direction for Hogmanay. All the way to London I read *Wuthering Heights*, laughing out loud at the absurdity of the two central characters whose unbelievably contrived passion got them into such a melodramatic pickle.

Chapter Three

I had completely forgotten my conversation with Jack until the taxi was turning into Milton Road; he might still be there. I got out a few houses before my own just in case. But when I reached my gate everything was dark and silent. I did entertain one fleshcreep moment when I imagined he was in there, hiding, waiting, but of course – he wasn't. By contrast next door at the Durrells' there was a great deal of light and noise – waves of stomping jazz beat out into the night, laughter that I did not recognise thundered and pealed from their curtained windows and shadows showed the idiotic posturing of party guests doing free dance. I was glad all this was going on because it meant I could return without being noticed; providing I was discreet no-one need know that I was back for days. There was a strange kind of comfort in hearing the noise. In my silent, empty house it echoed through the walls and emphasised my solitude – which was pleasing. A kind of confirmation that I was all to myself again. Besides, I didn't need theirs – I had my own party planned. It became a bit of a game – creeping around in the dark, renewing old aquaintance with position of doors, furniture, windows. Like an enchanted house that had lain dormant, Sleeping Beauty's palace or Miss Havisham's dead room: at least, it was like that until I pulled the blind and turned on the dimmer in the kitchen and saw how the whole pleasing enchantment had been broken. For plonked right in the middle of the table was a great vase of flowers – well past their prime – chrysanthemums drooping and shedding a few brownish yellow petals, orange lilies like dried up tongues. Very symbolic, I thought crisply, as I picked up the note that Jack had left with them. It said (if you please)

> Darling
> Not sure when you are getting back but welcome. If you are back in time for New Year's Eve give me a ring. I'd like to take you out to dinner. If not, hope you had a good Hogmanay and I'll ring you later in the week.
> On with the New Year and on with the old love.
> Jack.
> PS I've left the messages by the telephone.

I turned the note over and wrote a reminder on the back – to get the lock changed. Steady, Joan, I told myself, as I felt the anger rising – remember the concrete solar plexus. I pushed back at it and reduced it to a cold hard lump just below my diaphragm. I think if I had not done so then the rage would have engulfed me entirely and I might have gone shrieking out into the street screaming for vengeance. For everywhere I went in my house I found the unmistakeable signs that he had been there.

By the telephone were all the neatly taken messages – one from the Blackstones, one from Margery, one from Rhoda and not one but two from Robin Carstone – both asking me to call him. Good for you, I thought, for not being put off by Jack the first time you rang. All the same it reminded me that he had stayed here for more than one day. This was confirmed when I went up to my bedroom for even though the bed was made and everything orderly – there was a definite change in the pattern of things, a definite feeling that Jack had slept in this room, in this bed. I looked at myself in the mirror in the moonlight and took myself completely by surprise by laughing at she who looked back. Still in her coat and scarf the angel-faced demon, breaker of hearts and desirable property, was inviolate. I wouldn't even change the pillow cases, let alone burn the bedding his tres-passer's bum had sweated into. If he could only know the gift he had given me he would weep. For I knew with a profound certainty that I had come through the hoop of fire he had set a year ago and that he could never touch me again. I felt tough, ten foot tall, strong as rock and certain of myself. High as a kite on my own positivism. Impenetrable as an ice nugget calmly adrift in its own private waters. Until that moment I had never really been certain that my obliviousness was genuine; now I was certain. In a great sweeping shaft of understanding I knew I had exorcised Jack. Two epiphanies within a fortnight is not bad going for any woman. My singular life was going to be just great. Great.

I unpacked my case upstairs in the moonlight, still chuckling at the delight of it all. Out came the vodka bottle which I put reverentially to one side while the rest of the things were neatly disposed of. I doubted if I should feel like doing it tomorrow. My parents' gift to me had been a cashmere sweater – bottle green, plain as a pikestaff, irresistibly soft and perfect for a divorced schoolmistress. In the classroom it would look correct and severe while at the same time its silky warmth would pander to the skin-touch sensuality. Rather like wearing real silk knickers under a pleated skirt and twin set. If my father understood my inner self, my mother, who had chosen it, could always be relied on to understand my dress. She had even wrapped me separately a box of Mothaks – possibly the strangest gift-wrapped item ever to adorn a Christmas tree. Now that they were both far away and out of my hair I could love them both again. I felt quite sentimental as I replaced the tissue paper around the jumper and slid out the drawer of the wardrobe to stow it away. Which, quite possibly, had a bearing on what I did next.

You have to remember that all this was going on in a moonlit bedroom at about seven thirty at night, and shortly after our heroine had experienced an epiphany. It is no good looking for another word. Epiphany is exact.

I was smoothing the jumper into place in the drawer which was very full; one of those storage places into which you put all the things you will probably never want but have not got around to throwing out. Not that I was castigating the jumper to such a fate – it just seemed the appropriate place. Or maybe there were

84

deeper, darker powers at work that night to make me think so. Anyway. When I tried to push the drawer back shut it did not respond easily; the jumper was, as it were, the straw that broke the proverbial. I removed it and removed the layer beneath it. Sheets. Unwanted wedding presents. Funny how things occur to you: I put them to one side thinking how ideal they would be for the school props cupboard. Underneath them (this was all becoming like an Aladdin's Cave of my past) were some views-of-London table mats and a red leather-bound visitors' book (still in its cellophane); and beneath them? Why, what else nestling there in tissue paper? My wedding dress. Still, no doubt, with its champagne stains for I had not touched it since the day. Well, well.

Well, well, well.

Before imaginations run riot let me harness them. I did not walk down the aisle in froths of white tulle and organdie, nor wear ancient lace cascading down my back. I did not walk down the aisle at all. We were married in a very pleasant Register Office and the dress I wore (remember it was Easter) was only slightly soppy. It was long sleeved, long skirted, scoop necked and made from ivory seersucker – just to give the right perspective; retrospectively I must have looked like an up-market café table-cloth. Of course on the day I wore pink roses with it, in my hair and pinned in a small cascade at my shoulder, and I also had a very neat pink velvet neck band with a gold drop locket; decorated like that it had looked fittingly festive. But now, as I shook it out and smoothed it on the floor, it was bathed in the bluish moonlight and looked – well – rather like a shroud. I couldn't resist it. Perhaps *Wuthering Heights* had had more of an effect than I realised. Because I put it on.

It was cold. I was cold. The room was cold. Picking up the vodka bottle I slid downstairs, gliding like a phantom. Now here is melodrama, I told myself, and you can only do this sort of thing when you are quite, and absolutely, alone. The pumping beat from next door only enhanced the peculiarity. I whirled, triumphant, at the bottom of the stairs, and went into the kitchen. The Victorian mood was lost a little when I turned on the central heating and the boiler gave its rumbustious leap into life but – well – you can go too far with fancies. I riffled my hand among the half dead blooms so that they shed more petals, a nice piece of symbolism, and got myself a glass from the cupboard. Then the whole lovely mood was shattered by the telephone. Shrieking and sounding three times as loud in that dark hallway it pealed and pealed and pealed. Ring away, I told it, but you can't catch me. I am in a different century now and you haven't even been invented.

Of course, when it stopped, I realised that it could have been my parents – though something made me sure it was Jack. So I rang them. Dad answered.

'Safe journey?'

'Fine. Thanks for a lovely Christmas.'

'And what are you doing tonight?'

'There's a party next door.'

'That's the ticket.'

'Did you ring just now?'

'No.'

'Happy New Year. Love to Mum.'

'She's here. She'd like a word.'

'No – Dad – don't ...'

Too late. On she came.

'Joan?'

'Happy New Year, Mum. Thanks for Christmas.'

'You're not on your own, are you, darling?'

I looked through the door of the sitting room, also bathed in moonlight. There was the vodka bottle and the glass, winking at me from the little table by the chair where I had set them.

'No' I said truthfully. 'I'm all dressed up and ready to kill.'

'Oh. Well – that's good. Happy New Year then.'

'And to you.'

Duty done I set about organising my props.

I pulled the front room curtains and turned on the low lamp in the corner. A nice, cool, soothing light. Next to the bottle and glass I put the Brontë book – there were a few chapters left of Cathy and Heathcliffe. And then – *pièce de resistance* – I opened the kitchen cupboard and took out the enormous box of chocolates. Rain on me, spots, I commanded them – bring forth your pestilential pimples and sluggish countenance – I shall eat you all and damnation take the consequences. The telephone rang again. I poked my tongue out at it and glided into the sitting room, clutching the picture book box to my cold, hardened breast. Curling into the chair I poured out a gallant measure of

86

the thin, cold spirit, and ripped the cellophane from the box. Eeeny, meeny, miny, mo, I intoned – and then peeped to make sure the first chocolate I selected had a hard centre.

Chapter Four

Vodka and chocolates do not, actually, go together. The spirit encounters the cloying sweetness and destroys it. But I was not going to admit this to myself and went on resolutely drinking and eating and reading. The noise from next door remained at roughly the same decibels which made me certain they had no idea I was back. Despite my disappointment with the planned gastronomy I was beginning to feel that wild, inner sense of freedom. The hope that such wickedness as alcohol and chocolates would promote my sense of singular emancipation was right – even if it tasted slightly disgusting. Later I noticed that the party seemed to have stopped – no music, no revelry floated into my room. I listened hard and then thought I could hear something – but from a very far off – as if they had all moved into the upstairs bedrooms or something. Despite Fred and Geraldine's open heartedness I doubted this. Not an orgy, not even in their house. But the silence disturbed my own private party. The spirits of Heathcliffe and Cathy had wuthered their last across the pages, I was tipsy enough to feel pleasantly at one with my eccentric outfit and situation, and had eaten enough chocolates to feel a good rush of satisfactory self-indulgence – and one of my feet had gone to sleep. Time for a wander, if only to get the circulation going again. I limped into the kitchen and for no reason save the two or three tots of neat vodka, pulled a more or less whole chrysanthemum from out of the mess in the vase, snapped off its stem and stuck it in my hair. Perhaps I was squiffier than I had thought. It was at this point that I realised I could hear voices – laughter – coming from next door, not in the house but outside it. And not imagination either. For when I (somewhat wobbly) stood on a stool and peered through the skylight of my back door, I could see into the Durrells' back garden, and there they all were wrapped up in coats and furs, holding up candles in the frosty air and looking like a scene out of a Scandinavian Christmas. No, Joan, I told myself, blink and they will be gone. But I blinked, and they were not gone. Still there, beautiful in the flickering yellow lights – like a fantasy – the group of revellers stood facing down towards the massive shadow of the sycamore tree. And as if such surrealism were not enough, the object of their interest was standing on the white wrought iron patio table, about halfway down the garden, and lit on each side by a couple of Fred's barbecue flares. Was it any wonder that for a couple of seconds I was sure I was hallucinating? Delirium tremens perhaps? But then it occurred to me that if this candlelit crowd were to turn their heads for a moment and stare into my kitchen, they would see something even more weird, Myself, chrysanthemum, wedding gown and all, spying on them. Which, as Johnson would say, concentrated the mind beautifully. What I was looking at was real enough.

The figure on the table was male and stood in the pose of Donatello's David, though he was taller and more substantially built. Instead of the sculpture's delicately rustic hat the man wore a gangster's wide-brimmed slouch, with a dark band, which was pulled at a rakish angle over the brow. Unlike the sculpture (and not surprising in this frost) he was not naked but swathed in a brilliant white coat which reflected the light and hung about him in the perfection of tailoring. Instead of David's sword he held, with just the right slack elegance, the party-goer's equivalent – a wine bottle. And with the light of the flares, the flickering of the candles, and the figure's dramatic presence I realised that I was holding my breath, just waiting. Watching and waiting like the audience next door.

And then the figure began to move – a slow, controlled movement, removing his hand from his hip, reaching upward to the blue velvet of the diamante sky – fingers spreading like a magician about to create a new Universe. Beneath the shadow of the hat the mouth moved. He was speaking but only the timbre of his voice reached me, the words being lost across the distance. I wobbled on my perch, righted myself and stood mesmerised, wishing that I too could be out there standing with the rest, candle in hand, soaking it up. Whatever it was.

Reason nudged me in the ribs and told me I was overreacting: she said that this was only a performance, that once it was over the charisma would die. She counselled me to stay where I was

88

and not do what I was contemplating. Do not, she said, give yourself up to this passing moment of passion. This is the beginning of a New Year when all things seem possible and never are. Stay where you are, enjoy it for the moment, and be safe.

Unreason told me to fling open my door and rush out, vaulting the hedge to land superwoman-style at the beautiful orator's feet and participate in the collective adulation.

Unreason used fewer words and would have been the victor had not the group beyond the window become too affected themselves. For as I watched, torn between staying and joining them, they began to press forwards. I think he had lowered his voice for I could hear nothing now, only see, and as they pressed forwards he suddenly stopped, mid-gesture and leapt down from the table. There was a shriek, and then another. I thought perhaps the emotional pull of his performance had been too much for them but it wasn't that. It was that one of the candle-holders, moving closer, had shoved their flame too near to the person in front and ignited their hair.

The shrieking may have come from the shock, or from the pain of the heat, but most probably it came from the affront of having everybody suddenly pounce on its source and start beating hell out of its neck and shoulders with their fists. And striding into all this, a good half a head taller (as befits, after all, a romantic hero) than the rest, strode he of the swirling coat. Lifting up the wine bottle he poured it over the suffering creature whose shrieks then turned to howls. And in the middle of all this came more light, piercing and artificial, raking across the space of my garden into the Durrells' like ack-ack beams. Two powerful torches which brought with them the perfectly recognisable, furious voices of Maud and Reginald Montgomery.

'Have you no consideration for others?' barked Reginald. 'We're entertaining in here.'

The white hat, pushed back on the head now, appeared over the hedge. In the shadowy light the face beneath was sardonic. 'We're pretty entertaining in here, too, as a matter of fact ...' it said.

'I appeal to you' said Reginald.

The white hat shook with laughter. 'I'm afraid you don't, old chap ...' This was said in such good imitation of Reginald's regimental tones that I began wobbling on my stool with

89

laughter. The affronted Reginald retired wounded and Maud's acid voice took over. 'We'll call the police if you don't stop. This is supposed to be a nice neighbourhood ...'

'And so it is, Madam, and so it is' said the hat. He then put a finger to his lips and slid down out of sight. From Fred and Geraldine's patio came a swell of raucous laughter as, one by one, the remaining candles were extinguished. I heard the Montgomerys' back door slam and very quickly I slid down off my stool. I did not want that hat to reappear and accuse me of being one of the neighbourhood watch, nor make fun of me which, given the dying chrysanthemum and wedding dress, would have been all too easy.

Suddenly (and not surprisingly) I felt very silly standing there dressed as I was with the opposing forces of vodka and chocolate swilling around inside me: the notion of 'Ah, is this not happiness?' seemed suddenly to be wearing rather thin. I faced the darkness in my house and wanted it to put its unlit velvety arms around me for comfort. I wanted it to hold me fast in its silence, to make my solitude within its walls desirable again. Instead, and despite my efforts to remain apart, I found that I was concentrating for all I was worth on the prodigal revelry still going on in the garden next door. Worse, I was concentrating on one particular aspect of it, one reveller's voice in particular, which, at this precise moment, seemed to be singing 'My Way'. And I was listening to it with all my heart and soul.

Reader, I trembled for him and a tongue of fire licked my womb. I shuddered. I shook myself. Absurd. Ridiculous. Drunk most likely. And went back to the front room.

Here the dim light and the almost silence put things into better perspective. I stood there shoving chocolates into my mouth, considering. I had just had a turn, that was all. My grandmother was always having turns. So – they ran in the family. And it was scarcely surprising considering the situation. My vodka had combined with the sheer theatricality of the scene and its protagonist; the candles delicately lighting the upturned faces of the group, the drama of the flares upon that white coat and the figure within – who wouldn't have been carried away with the overt spectacle of it all? (A little voice said Maud and Reggie wouldn't, but I ignored that ...)

I felt better after such reasoning. Cooler, calmer. Of course it had only been a passing turn. I had just been reading too much, that was all, and reading the wrong thing too – all that Brontë afflatus, all that rubbish about heroes with dark curls and fire in their eyes. I wasn't seriously going to swap all this, this lovely solitude, this fifth dimension, for Some Enchanted Evening Across A Crowded Garden, was I? Not me. Back you go, I told myself. Down, girl. And down I went, relieved to be safe again.

I cleared the goo from my teeth with a vodka mouthwash and felt much better. Soothed, you could say, by the almost total silence. The Durrells' party had obviously continued in the garden. Very faint echoes of it floated in my room but they didn't tempt me now. The turn was over. I leaned against the curtained window feeling pleased with myself and sipped my drink in the peace. Silent, solitary night. Lovely.

Then, suddenly, breaking into it, came the distinctive throbbing of a taxi engine pulling up and parking outside. The throbbing made peculiar little ripples through me and that little tongue of fire began licking away again, right where it shouldn't. Throb, throb it went as the engine ticked over. No wonder fairground johnnies have a reputation for being oversexed – it comes from leaning up against those pulsing machines all night. By the time it pulled away I was feeling extraordinarily nice inside – not post-orgasmic or anything but – well – nice – on account of the mechanically inspired frisson, I suppose. And I thought how lucky I was to be able to enjoy the simple pleasures in life alone and quite unaided. Hum, hum, I went under my breath. A sure sign of contentment.

And then the humming stopped for I heard my garden gate give its familiar creak and footsteps on my path which banished any thread of niceness flowing through my body.

Bloody Jack, I thought. Since I didn't answer the phone to him he had come to check.

The banished niceness was replaced by solid ice. And this in turn dispensed with any doubts I had about aloneness being A Good Thing. I didn't want to see anybody. And I certainly wasn't going to open the door to Him!

The bell rang.

Go away.

I waited. No footsteps retreated.

It rang again.

I thought, I can stay here as long as you can stay out there.

Save for the one small lamp there were no other lights on, no clue that I was in. The curtains were drawn. He could not know.

It rang for a third time and the footsteps shuffled.

And then I remembered. Sod, bugger and bums. He had a key. He had a key and he would use it in a minute.

I peeped round the door jamb. Moonlight threw his shadow onto the glass of the front door. Somehow I had to shore the citadel up again: make the entry fast against this wrecker of solitude.

If I walked to the door he would see my shadow. So I dropped to my knees and began crawling along the passageway, hampered not a little by the long skirt of my wedding dress. Good grief, I thought, as if seeing it for the first time, He mustn't see me in this, not this of all things!

I reached out for the bolt at the bottom of the door, which, of course, was stuck because I never use it. But I thought that if I could huddle up against the wooden panels of the lower half, and slide my hand up the latch, I could snag it without any noise or cast of shadow. I was just negotiating this delicate manoeuvre when the letterbox opened and a pair of eyes, glittering in the moonlight, rolled from left to right in their sockets – presumably trying to get their bearings with the silvery light in the hall. Those eyes, and my eyes, were about a foot apart. I didn't recognise them as Jack's – but then – I didn't recognise them as anything – not even human. What I did recognise was the moment when they focused on me. And, being female, with several thousand years of conditioning behind me – I screamed. Possibly primally. And the letterbox clattered shut.

'Cer-ist!' said a young male alien voice, and its owner ran back down my path, banging the gate shut after it.

'Finbar!' the voice then yelled. 'Finbar Flynn. Where the hell are you?' Followed by a stream of enviable obscenities. Vaguely I wondered what Lady Wilton would make of *that*. Weak from the scream I slumped against the wall only to leap to my feet with amazing alacrity as the first long opening chord of the Beatles' 'Hard Day's Night' came with pumping shudder through my walls.

The Durrells' party had apparently recommenced.

There is an advertisement somewhere that indicates that a certain brand of vodka will lift you from the realms of ordinariness into a world of wonderful fantasy. This is no idle boast. If I had had the sense to stop the reel there I could have avoided it. The citadel would have remained intact, the vision of Dunbar reality, but hurtling to our doom we go. It was curtain down on Act One, time merely for the taking of a deep breath, before Curtain Up, Act Two.

The shock and the scream left me feeling very weak. Which was hardly surprising. But also relieved and a little carefree that it had not, after all, been Jack at the door. I went back into the front room, now a-throb with music and the exuberance of party noise, and skulked in my chair. I insisted that I was now back in control, suppressed any bubblings beyond the solar plexus, and in a very wobbly fashion poured out some more of the fantasy fluid. Then, feeling much better, I hummed along with the Beatles, which was quite enjoyable until I remembered what had happened to John and then blubbed shamelessly to the slow joys of 'Imagine'. Some child of the sixties had obviously been mixing the tapes. I brought my knees up under my chin and clasped my arms around them, knowing that this was my pose of comfort, the way I had always sat as a child when life seemed to be too awful to take. Only now, at last, there was no-one to invade it and ask asininely what the matter was.

Peaceful self-indulgence. Who could ask for more?

And then – of course, since my solitude seemed about as solo as Piccadilly Circus – the doorbell rang.

And this time I didn't care if it was Jack, Ronald Reagan or Attila the Hun. This was *my* space – who dared to invade it? I jumped from the chair, upturning the residue of the chocolates and crushing them underfoot as I swore my way to the door. I opened it with a gesture worthy of Bernhardt on a good night.

'Yes?' I yelled imperiously into the darkness of the doorstep. And 'Yes?' again, more savagely.

'Well!' said a vaguely familiar voice. 'The spirit of the age! This I just do not believe ...'

And Oh My Goodness.

Neither did I.

For it was Donatello's David. Hat, coat, wrist on hip and still with a bottle for a sword.

I saw the mouth first, the rest of the face being shaded by the hat brim, quite apart from the only available light coming from the moon. The mouth was smiling in that same sardonic fashion of all hard won heroes ever born since romantic fiction hit the dewdrop hearts of desiring heroines.

'I'm come as emissary from next door ...' it said, and waved the bottle delicately before bowing the hat low. It righted itself and continued. 'My friend thought he had seen a ghost ...' The wrist removed itself from the hip and the hand attached reached out and pinched me lightly on the elbow. The mouth smiled. 'But I see he was wrong. You are, after all, made of flesh.'

All this made the taxi engine as relevant as a candle's heat in Alaska. The resonance of his voice carried right into a place that was well below the damped down solar plexus. Had this not been the mid-nineteen eighties I might comfortably have swooned. As it was I could only do what the modern woman is allowed and pretend to be quite unmoved by the catastrophic excitement his mere touch created. On balance and not wishing away an iota of my liberation, just at that moment I thought that my nineteenth-century counterpart had the better of the bargain. Swooning would have been infinitely better than standing at the doorstep pretending I couldn't give a fig for the possibilities. Gripping the edge of the door helped a little.

'And who the hell are you?' I asked in a tone that would have exonerated me at any feminist rally.

Inside I thought, you excite me beyond measure and please would you be so kind as to step in.

The hand that had pinched me took off the hat.

If only, if only, he had been bald.

But no, it had to be, here was a Heathcliffe if ever I saw one. And Lady Moon, Lady Moon up there, smiling down, decided to give her full beneficence to the crushed black curls and the dark glowing embers that were his eyes. If I looked up into the starry firmament I would probably see Barbara Cartland racing by in a tinsel bound chariot.

'Finbar' he said.

'Finbar who?' I demanded, stalling for time.

'Flynn.'

'You don't sound bloody Irish ...'

'I was born in Tunbridge Wells.'

'Bully for Tunbridge Wells.'

'Do I detect a note of deprecation?'

He took a step back.

Don't go, I thought. And fortunately, 'Don't go' I said.

He took a step forward.

I breathed again.

'You are obviously having a private party.' He looked me up and down. 'So I won't stay. I just wanted to check up on little Ricky's ghost.' He leaned his shoulders against the side of the porch and pulled the hat back down over his face. And sighed. Which sent another paroxysm through me. 'I seem to spend my time in Chiswick doing odd things with this house.' He pushed the brim up slightly with the hand that held the bottle and gave me the full view of his moonlit profile, a strong one (of course) and slid his eyes to look at me. He was a born performer.

'This is my house' I said. 'What have you had to do with it?'

'I made my first citizen's arrest here last week ... Pity it had to turn out to be your husband ...'

'My ex-husband ...'

'That's right. It made it very difficult.'

'He shouldn't have been here. I live alone. I like living alone.'

'Are you alone now?'

'Yes.'

'Can I ask you something?'

I wanted to giggle and say Your Place or Mine?

But all I said was 'Uh-Huh.'

'What are you doing on New Year's Eve, on your own, dressed in a long white dress with a flower in you hair and – if you'll pardon the expression – absolutely plastered?'

'I am not plastered!'

'You are. Very. I know because I'm halfway there but you – You, my dear girl, are swaying ...'

I looked down at my feet which were bare. They seemed quite still to me. Irrationality took over and I curtsied. So far as I was concerned this proved my sobriety. Righting myself very carefully I said 'You see? You couldn't do that.'

So – of course – he did.

Donatello's David curtsied to me on my doorstep on New Year's Eve and it seemed perfectly acceptable.

'Do come in for a moment' I said.

'If I don't get back I shall be missed.' And then he laughed in a sort of stagey kind of way and said as if addressing the upper circle 'But – what the hell – leave them while they still want you, don't you think?'

95

I laughed too, because as I stepped back into the hall, he followed.

'They say' he said, advancing 'that you are an odd little creature who never goes out and never asks in. And that this house is your enchanted castle ...'

'Who says?' I was still backing, leading him on.

'Fred and Gerry.'

'They said that?'

'Well' he had the grace to look uncomfortable 'not exactly. But it sounds better that way. More romantic.'

By now we were in the front room.

'I've got some vodka here.' I held up the bottle.

'But I've got champagne.' He held up his.

'Mix them' I said.

'Yuk' he replied. And I thought he was referring to the idea. But he raised one foot and looked at it. Attached to the heel was a chocolate. As I bent down to retrieve it I felt his hand on my hair. This is it, I thought, for the touch was like electricity. He's going to seduce me. Goody, goody, gumdrops. But no – all I felt was a sudden loss. He had taken something from me. The chrysanthemum.

'It's dead' he said wonderingly.

'Everything that touches me becomes like that' I said, inspired to pathos. 'Pretend it's a geranium.'

'Pretend it's a what?'

I sat back on my haunches with the chocolate held aloft.

'Don't you know your Eliot?'

He shook his head rather guardedly and the curls spilled about his neck. I was enraptured. He was here, in my room. I had him. But how to keep him? Well then, he was an actor. Actors love language. Ergo – I had language, the best of it, stored up in my brain. All the things I had not allowed to inspire me at school, memories of it locked away and now spilling over. I was fighting to keep him and I had to entertain and inspire him in turn if I was going to do that. He removed his hat in a gesture that meant he would stay.

'You're an actor. You must know Eliot. T. S.?'

'You mean *The Cocktail Party*?'

'Don't be such a Philistine. I mean poetry – wonderful, wonderful poetry ...'

He bridled. He looked so beautiful all scrunched up in the

edge of the settee with that white coat falling in its perfect folds all about him and that strange, half-handsome face above it.

'It's coming up to time' he said, looking at his watch.

'Have a chocolate' I said, as seductively as I could, offering him the crushed piece of ghastliness that I had removed from his foot.

He opened his mouth and I put my finger in. It was soft and warm and wet and I could feel the ridges in the hollow of his mouth as I pulled it out. I licked off the residual stickiness that was mixed with his saliva and thought that John Donne's Flea could not have been more metaphysical. I smacked my lips.

'What a very beautiful gesture' he said admiringly. 'Do you entertain men like this all the time?'

'I don't have much to do with men actually ...'

'You should.' He raised an eyebrow. '*Actually* – they're rather nice ...' He was still holding the chrysanthemum.

'Shake it' I said.

He laughed.

'No – go on – shake it.'

He did. Still laughing. The clock in the hall, found by Jack in a junk shop and once our pride, began to chime the hour of twelve. It was always five minutes fast rather like its owner.

'Is it dead?' I asked.

'Most certainly.' He looked at it solemnly.

'And is it a geranium?' I winked at him.

He held it up. 'This is a geranium' he said. 'A very dead one.'

I stood up ...

I smoothed down the front of my dress and faced him like a child about to do its party turn. 'Am I beautiful?' I felt it.

'You are unquestionably beautiful.' He had entered the game. It was either the realisation of this, or the vodka, that made my head go swimmy, but I carried on.

'Then I will perform for you.'

He sat back and settle further into the settee and waved the dead flower a couple of times.

'Ready?'

'Ready.'

So I began.

Twelve o'clock

The chimes had ceased but that didn't matter.

Whispering lunar incantations

I had forgotten some of it but that didn't matter either.

Dissolve the floors of memory
And all its clear relations
Its divisions and precisions

I looked down into those coal eyes of his hoping that the renewal of the flames licking at me would begin to fire him ... He was looking at me with pleasured concentration. That, at least, was something.

Every street lamp that I pass
Beats like a fatalistic drum,

I knelt at his knees, quite beside myself with the excitement of the moment –

And through the spaces of the dark

Perfect, perfect timing

Midnight shakes the memory
As a madman shakes a dead geranium.

He clapped.

The chrysanthemum shed a few more of its half decayed petals.

'That was simply wonderful' he said, and sighed.

I put my head on his knees (very bony they were) and I thought. Now he will take me in his arms and that will be that. I have given him the best I can do. If that doesn't work, nothing will. He put his hands on my shoulders, I could feel their heat. I stopped breathing and heard nothing but the ticking of his watch close to my ear. This is it, I thought, this really is it ...

And then

Of course

The doorbell rang.

He could very easily have knocked me out with those knees but I suppose, given the circumstances I was like rubber and just bounced off.

'Oh Christ' he said. 'That'll be for me. I'd better go.'

And while I was sitting there, dazed and befuddled and saddened by the sense of loss, he went out into the hall and opened the door.

98

'Finbar!' said a voice which I recognised as belonging to he of the glittering eyeballs. 'You're supposed to be at the party next door. You can't just piss off like that ...'

'I'm coming' I heard him say apologetically. And then he called me.

'Are you coming, Geranium? I'm sure there's room for you. Come on – join the fun – why don't you ... ?'

Fun? Fun? What were we supposed to be having here?

'No thanks' I called back, quite light heartedly. 'I'll stay here if you don't mind ...' I waited for him to come back into the room and take me by the arm and lead me, but he didn't. 'Happy New Year then' he called. And the front door closed.

I crushed two large chocolates into my mouth and washed them down with the remains in my glass. And then just made it up the stairs and into the lavatory before I was well and truly sick.

As a matter of fact, and *actually*, of everything.

Chapter Five

It was difficult in the fog of feeling ill the next day to even think about what had happened, let alone distil it for any real relevance. On the whole I decided that the experience had been an aberration without lasting meaning to my life. As I lay in bed for the whole day feeling too weak to move, life was not something I chose to contemplate. Death now – ah well – Death was another matter; there had been a point around seven in the morning when it seemed the perfect solution. But gradually as the day unfolded – first the darkness into dawn, then the sharp sunlight which crept into the bedroom despite the drawn curtains, then the sunlight into dusk again – and finally the blackness of the night – the urge to live overtook the urge to die. And at about eight o'clock I got up, weak and wobbly but alive to tell the tale. Going back to the womb seemed the obvious solution so I had a long warm bath before even attempting ground level. It was like washing away all the sins of the world, or at any rate, of last night. The whole piece of melodrama floating away down the plughole leaving me fresh and clean and pure again, in both mind and body. Thus absolved I went downstairs.

In the hall there was a note on the mat. Since my first hopeful thought was that it might have come from him, I realised that the purification process had not altogether been a success. Despite my wincing every time I recalled how I had invited him in and then performed in that creepy way there was no denying the little sinking feeling I experienced when I recognised Geraldine's writing and not a strangers's. The prospect of being a bookish spinster enclosed in a castle of ice seemed less inviting than it had done before last night's little episode and I felt too frail to do anything about that pro tem.

The note said

Joan Dear
We had no idea you were back until Finbar told us this morning. If we had known we wouldn't have made so much noise. I was going to call on you today but seeing the curtains closed I guessed you were resting. I hope we'll see you to apologise in person before the Year's much older.

I am sorry you were disturbed by F. He's a bit inclined to Bravura at the moment – or do I mean Braggadocio? It's while he's rehearsing *Coriolanus* – he does rather seem to be living the part and he is liable to rush in where angels fear to; I'm afraid he just didn't think that he wouldn't be welcome. Sorry. Sorry.

Love G.

I rang her and told her not to worry.

'I think you made quite an impression on our Superstar, Joan.'

I winced down the telephone.

'Yes – well – he made quite an impression on me ...'

'He had Fred chasing all over the house for any poetry anthologies. He said you'd been quoting T. S. Eliot at him.'

I winced again.

'Yes' I said 'I think I did do something like that. I might have had a little too much to drink – probably – '

(Might? Probably? tsk tsk)

'Didn't we all?' said Geraldine. 'Never mind. That's it for another year.' She paused and then added cautiously 'It would be nice to see you sometime. Socially I mean. I'll give you a ring.'

100

I remained non-committal. She took the hint and did not press. I opened my mouth to say Well, Goodbye Then – and instead out came 'When does the play open then?'

'What play, dear?'

'Sorry. *Coriolanus*, didn't you say?'

'Oh yes – that – Oh not for a couple of months I don't think. Tell you what – we'll get tickets for the first night and take you along if you like.'

'Maybe' I said, 'I don't know the text very well ...'

'Neither did we until last night. Then he gave us one or two of its meatier bits in the back garden. He was very good: breathtaking – not that I would tell him that – not that he needs to be told – But he's certainly got it – whatever IT is ...'

'Yes' I said. 'I don't doubt it.'

'You'll be back at school soon, will you?'

'Yes – next week. I don't relish the idea.'

'No – well – make the most of this free week then. We won't disturb you again. I really am sorry.'

I went off to coax the chocolate stains out of the carpet. Nothing like a bit of housework to remove flights of fancy. I left the ravaged vodka bottle on permanent view as a reminder of my folly. And life, singular, continued.

A couple of days later Jack rang me and this time I was well and truly ready for him.

'I really think you and I ought to have a talk, Joan.'

'What on earth for?'

'About our future.'

'My future is my own affair. Your future does not interest me.'

'I think you are still reacting to the loss of your child.'

(My child. Not his then? Nice shift of emphasis, that ...)

'What? You think what?'

'It's perfectly normal. And very natural that you turn to another woman for comfort in such a crisis.'

I had forgotten all that.

'You see' he continued, his tone as soothing as a male gynaecologist discussing the menopause, 'you turned to your own sex because it offered no threat to you; she could not make you pregnant and suffer that pain again.'

'Very true, Jack.' And so it was, biologically speaking.

'So when can we meet and have a talk?'

Demurely I said 'Jack – do you remember the flowers I brought to Irish's flat when I came to see you there about a year ago?'

He sounded surprised but considered the question carefully. After all it might hold a clue.

'Yes – vaguely – I think so. Red ones.'

'That's right. Did you keep any of them?'

'Keep any?'

'Yes – you know – press one between the pages of a book to keep as a memento?'

'Er – no – no, I don't think so ...'

'Neither did I with your chrysanthemums. Goodbye.'

He rang back.

A critic once wrote of him 'Like it or not, Jack Battram is one of today's most tenacious young film makers.'

'Jack' I said, weary with the whole business 'I'm sorry I was so vindictive when I told you about the pregnancy.' (I could speak of it like that now – just as a pregnancy and not a baby, my baby – well it was better all round that it hadn't been born.) 'It was a horrid way to behave and I am ashamed. But please believe me – I am not in any state of shock at all.' (I was almost going to admit that my lesbian lover had been a figment of imagination but resisted this. On the one hand it was too useful as a method of blocking his advances – and on the other my sexuality – whatever it was – had nothing to do with him.) 'I just don't love you anymore – not at all. That really is all there is to it. I don't love you and I don't want to see you anymore. For Christ's sake I don't even like you. So please leave me alone.'

'You really are upset, aren't you, Joan? I'm coming right over.'

Tenacious, you see.

'No' I yelled, despairingly.

'You can't suddenly stop all feelings for someone you once loved enough to marry. You can't feel nothing for me ...'

Egocentric and tenacious.

'*You* did.'

'Did what?'

'Suddenly stop caring for me.'

'When?'

'When you left me for ...'

'Oh that. That was just a hiccough. You know how sorry I am. I've said so. I want to make it up to you ...'

'A divorce is not a hiccough, Jack. We are divorced. All settled. We each have our separate lives now – which is fine by me.'

'I think you need help.'

It was becoming harder and harder to remain cool.

'When can I come and see you then?'

I thought hard and imagined a lump of white ice set in a glassy sea.

'Never' I said.

'You're cold, Joan. This is not like you.'

'Piss off' I said warmly and replaced the received which, mercifully, remained silent.

In the last few days before term began the temperature moved up a few degrees. The crackling frost, which had begun to look less and less appealing as a layer of London grime coated its virginity, started to drip from the trees. The back garden looked even more forlorn and uncared for. The shapes that had looked so sculptural and pure in the snow were now revealed as damp and rotting decay. There was slime on the patio where blown leaves had thawed into mouldering sponges. My grandmother, maternal, she who was given to having turns, was also given to making philosophical statements using the vernacular. She originated from the East End of London where her mother and three daughters ran a small laundry. Out of these humble beginnings grew my mother – who by a quirk of fate known as the war met my father. He came from a tier or two above her socially and had all the dash of a naval officer with none of the responsibilities (having poor eyesight and a good head for figures he had to stay at home). They met while fire-fighting and, the war being a great leveller of both buildings and class, she married above herself, and, I suspected, had felt insecure ever since. Hence the fear of what the neighbours might think, bridge parties and my cashmere sweater. Once when they came to London on a visit I suggested that we all go to Leather Lane market and was amazed to see my mother shudder and grow pale beneath her tasteful makeup. Outwardly she was Home Counties – inwardly she was still the Clerkenwell Road; it took more than a shift in the placement of the knot in her headscarf to alter that. London was ingrained in her even if areas of it could make her shudder at the same time. Anyway, this maternal grandmother, long dead, had sometimes stayed with us when we lived in Dorking and despite my mother's pleas that it wasn't the done thing for Surrey, she would sit in a straight backed chair by the front room window and look out for hours. And if the weather was bad she would peer at it and then shake her head and say in her strong growly voice 'If you didn't have the hump you'd soon get it ...'

Which picture fascinated me as a child for I longed for her to grow one.

Now, standing in my kitchen and peering out at the damp, depressing garden, I suddenly understood what she had meant. I had the hump. It was gloomy half-light within, and just as gloomy half-light without. A day when you keep the electric light on all the time and it only seems to exacerbate the dreariness. For a passing moment I understood why spinsters were renowned for keeping cats; at that precise moment I should have liked something soft and warm to touch and talk to. Perhaps I was misguided to think that my separate life could be sweet? I settled for second best and took some old crusts out into the garden.

Birds were already perching in the bare branches of the sycamore, eyeing the ground lasciviously as they saw the earth beginning to heave with worms and grubs and all the tasty things that had been kept hidden by the frost. I thought this was rather an apt metaphor for me; I imagined all the people who thought they had an interest in me, all sitting in the branches of their trees, waiting to pounce and peck at the bits any thaw revealed. The thought didn't exactly lift the humpishness but it gave me a sense of reaffirmation. I was not going to lose all the ground I had made over the last year just because the weather was dismal. Low spirits were to be expected when you lived alone. Low spirits were to be expected when you lived with your family (I thought of Rhoda Grant suddenly and her all male household including the salamanders), low spirits were a part of life, just like anything else. They would soon pass. What if, I wondered, as I made my way back to the house, I had a husband waiting inside or me, or a friend, or children – would their existence make me feel any more cheerful at this precise moment? Of course not. When you've got the hump, you've got the hump – and nothing will change it except you. At least I wasn't going to walk back indoors and be greeted by some fellow human exhorting me to 'cheer up'.

Which thought, did indeed, cheer me up.

A blackbird hopped across the flat, wet tussocks that had once been lawn; it cocked its head and eyed me suspiciously, but then gave in to temptation and jabbed its beak into the spot it had its mind on; up came the beginnings of a plump worm.

To think that it could have been me.

Chapter Six

The raw weather continued. A maundering prelude to going back to school. The air seemed raw rather than icy and I could never remember feeling the cold so acutely before. Perhaps it had something to do with being in my thirty-second year. Perhaps the blood had begun to run thin already; perhaps a willing spinstership brought with it a hastening of the ageing process; perhaps my bones were already a-brittling, my nose a sharpening and the whole life-giving pattern of hormones already in decline. Perhaps.

But all this was as nothing compared with the bother caused to me by the reappearance of Robin Carstone, whose healthy animalism seemed to have expanded in the Canadian Wilds and exacerbated his attractions. He looked even more well formed and picture book handsome and I sighed as I saw him sidling up to me in the staffroom. I had forgotten how peaceful (well – relatively) things had been during the previous term without him. As he shouldered his way through the queue for the coffee pot I could see a few maidens' hearts palpitating under their woollies at the sight of him. Oh why did he have to pick on me?

'Hullo' he said, perching in his usual close proximity. Did I imagine it or had his thighs got even broader?

'Hullo' I said. 'How was Canada?'

'Wonderful' he said. 'It has completely changed my life.'

His eyes looked into mine so soulfully that I cringed. No. No. Definitely not. I was not going to go back to all that.

Very quickly I said 'How's your girlfriend? Barbara, isn't it? I expect she's ever so glad to have you back ...' I tried to radiate that it was neither here nor there to me. Cruel to be kind now, cruel to be kind.

'I don't see her anymore.'

This was bad news.

'Ah Ha' I said, trying to sound like a fond aunt, 'Did you meet someone nice in Canada then?'

He blushed the deep pink that only the fair haired can manage.

'I – er – yes – I did. Oh Joan' he added feelingly 'I wish you'd written back to me.'

'I'm not one for writing letters' I said crisply. 'So you enjoyed yourself? And met some interesting people?'

'God yes' he said with feeling. 'In the school and out of it.'

'That's what those trips are for. Exchanging ideas on all levels … and in all ways …'

Fond auntie hinting coyly.

He blushed again.

'And have you given up D. H. Lawrence?' God knows why I said that.

'Oh no. I got much more into him when I was out there. The Literature Faculty at the University was really pushing the boat out for the Centenary. I went to a lot of lectures and things like that. I can't thank you enough for getting me interested – I've read everything I can get my hands on.' His eyes stopped looking soulful, which was a blessing, and went all dreamy.

'I hope you're not limiting yourself entirely to DHL?' The thought was appalling. 'He did have a rather blinkered view of things.'

'On the contrary' he said, hotly, roused from his dreamer's state 'he saw everything in the round, everything as pure – Nature, Religion, Men, Women.'

'He was a prating moraliser where most things were concerned.'

'He was not.'

'He was.'

'He was a visionary – '

I began to recognise the Trans-Atlantic academic style – Gimme a D for the deification of nature: D! Gimme an H for hagiology of religion: H! Gimme an L for Love of men and women: L!

D H L !! – LAWRENCE

'In what respect?'

'The way he had such advanced views.'

'On what?'

'On everything. Love for instance.'

'Prophet of Sexuality? You mean that kind of love?'

'Well yes. Even compared with our views today. He was years ahead of his time.'

'I don't think all the women in his books would have thought so.'

Somehow he had got me on a raw spot.

He mumbled something and turned pink again.

'What?' I snapped.

'I said he was very forthright on things that other people saw as – um – perversions. He saw them as aspects of nature.'

'What like? Coupling with goats?' Since Pimmy was not far off I did not go on.

'No' said Robin. 'Of course not. But he saw sex as an expression of love in every way possible: men could love men: women could love women ...'

'Goats could love goats ...'

'Joan! You know I'm not talking about that ...'

'Why stop there?'

Wisely he ignored this. 'He was years ahead of his time so far as his advanced views were concerned ...'

I thought about Oscar Wilde and Radclyffe Hall tearing their tomb-bound hair out.

'You've scarcely read any other writers. You said so yourself.'

'I've read him in context. You do that in Canada' he added pompously. 'They've based themselves on the American system. Much better than ours. Anyway – he was open to the validity of all kinds of love – '

'And Fidelity, Robin – don't forget Fidelity ...'

I could have pulled out my tongue as soon as I said it for his eyes returned to their soulful stare, so I rushed on 'I suppose Canada's as good a place as any for expounding the view of sexual freedom.'

'Why do you say that?'

'Remember Monty Python? All those lumberjacks wearing high heels and pressing wild flowers ...'

He looked perplexed, then stricken with embarrassment. 'No' he said, creaking away from me a little on the chair arm, 'I don't.'

107

Oh well, I thought, I suppose there really are people around who know nothing of the Flying Circus. 'I expect Lawrence would have had something to say about all that – don't you ...'

But he was not going to be drawn again. Instead he suddenly reverted to his eyeball to eyeball contact and said 'Look, Joan, I really must talk to you. I know you and your husband are back together again and I want you to know that I think that is terrific – just terrific [he really had been across the Atlantic – I shuddered inwardly at the emotional verbalisation] – but I should like – '

I stopped listening, realising what I had just heard, and roared at him.

'You know what?'

Pimmy's cup loup de louped in its saucer. 'Me and my husband ...?'

'Yes.' He looked puzzled. 'I rang you at Christmas. He answered.'

'Me and my husband are not back together again. And you can put that in your Lawrentian Fidelity box and store it!'

'Oh' he said 'But I thought – '

'I live alone' I said wearily. 'I still live alone. I like living alone ...'

'Well then' he said brightly 'that means I can come to see you and talk about what I want to talk about with you ...'

'You cannot, Robin.'

Too loud. Pimmy's spoon rattled to the floor.

'But I have something to say to you, Joan.'

'If it's anything to do with Fidelity, Robin – please keep it to yourself. Anyway. What about this Canadian romance?'

'Please – Joan – I have changed so much – and I want to share it with you. Please – Joan – I'd be so grateful if you'd let me.'

I remembered the rugby tackle in the hall and the frilly pink lips.

'No' I said. 'You're a dear boy [may I be forgiven] but – N O.'

And anything his crestfallen face was about to impart was conveniently drowned by the bell for resumption of duties.

'I thought' I said to my fourth years 'that we might look at some twentieth-century poets this term. Can anyone name me one?'

'Byron' said one of the brighter girls.

Mea culpa.

108

'Page thirty-one in your anthologies. T. S. Eliot.' I lingered over the titles and felt a small bubble of electricity as I flicked the pages and came upon, apparently by chance – Twelve o'clock – Along the reaches of the street – I turned the page quickly – neither they nor I was ready for that.

'We'll do some *Old Possum* first. Page thirty-eight.'

'Here, Miss?'

'Yes, Sharon?'

'Didn't he write that musical about cats?'

'Sort of.'

'Thought so. I went to see it at Christmas. Instead of the panto. We've got the record at home. Would you like me to bring it in? It's lovely music – really lovely ...'

Which popped the bubble as surely as a gunshot in a ceasefire.

They were on my doorstep with their cases and a flood of recriminations before I realised what was happening.

It was Friday night, the first weekend since school began.

My mother was in tears and my father was shuffling and looking grim.

'We had to come' she said through the sniffles and snuffles.

'Let us in then' said my father, picking up a worrying amount of luggage.

'What on earth are you doing here?'

'Let us in for goodness sake, Joan. We can't talk here on the doorstep.' He put the cases down in the hall, removed his cap, and ran his fingers through his hair, ear to ear.

Here was real trouble.

'What is it? What's the matter. Why didn't you let me know?'

They moved in further.

'Are you on your own?' my mother said, peering wetly over the top of her handkerchief.

'Of course I am.'

'She's not here?'

'Who?'

'That black woman.'

Memory distilled itself.

'No, no' I said cheerily. 'She's gone back now. She isn't here anymore.'

'Well' said my father following me into the kitchen. 'That's something, I suppose ...'

'Oh Joan' said my mother coming up behind him and speaking in the tones of profound tragedy. 'What have you been going through? Why, why didn't you tell us at Christmas how bad everything was?'

I filled the kettle and tried to gather all the shreds of thought that their arrival had so successfully shattered. I mean – here I was – just home from school – feeling quite happy, quite normal, with a new selection of library books for the weekend, looking forward to a nice, peaceful couple of days. And now this.

Perhaps I'm dreaming, I thought. Turn round slowly and they will be gone. I turned round slowly, but they weren't. They were still standing in a queue of two; father steely-eyed, mother damply querulous.

'What is all this?'

My father held out a chair for my mother and then sat himself down at the kitchen table.

'At least take off your coats.'

'Sit down' said my father.

I did.

'Joan. We've had a long talk with Jack.'

'What about?'

I had managed to catch the anger at chest level and my voice came out sounding so even and easy that I congratulated myself.

'You know perfectly well what about.'

'He's very worried about you, Joan. Very worried indeed ...' My mother dissolved into tears. 'And so are we-e-e ...'

'But there's nothing to be worried about.' The anger chanced its arm and raised itself to throat level. 'And anyway – you shouldn't be talking to Jack about me. He has nothing to do with my life at all. He knows nothing.'

'On the contrary' said my father with unusual pomposity. 'He seems to know a great deal. Much more than we do ...'

'And then we talked to Father Robert about it and he told us what you'd been saying to him at Christmas and – well – we just had to come. We caught the morning train.' She cried into her hankie again.

'You've been very silly, Joan.'

'Dad. Please don't speak to me like that. I am not a little girl anymore.'

110

'Well – you're acting like one.'

'How?'

'All this – ' He waved his gloved hand about. 'This – female nonsense ...'

Pennies fell, bells rang, lights flashed on and off and the jackpot of understanding poured out its wealth. I put back my head and roared with laughter.

Given the circumstances this only compounded their terrors.

'None of it is true' I said, regaining some control with great difficulty. 'I just made it up so that Jack would leave me alone. I'm not a lesbian.'

My father froze in a rictus of disgust. My mother closed her eyes and rocked slightly.

I got up to make the tea.

'What about the girl who's been living here?'

I just shook my head and counted teabags.

'And what about the baby?'

'That' I said, fitting the lid neatly into the pot 'was true. The rest' I set out the mugs thinking act normally, whatever you do act normally, 'was pure fantasy.'

'Jack thinks you've become a little unhinged after the experience.'

Where would we be without our euphemisms?

'Look. I didn't like having an abortion, Dad. But it hasn't sent me cuckoo. A decision like that is a terrible thing to make – but of its many legacies, madness is not one – '

'What was all that about a Fifth Dimension then? I didn't know what you were talking about.'

The anger, confident in its righteousness, rolled over my tonsils and gathered momentum across my tongue.

'Then you should bloody well have asked me what I meant – instead of nodding away as if you knew ...'

'All right, all right ...' He was by my side, stroking my hair, just as he used to do when things went wrong. But he was no longer infallible Dad.

'Calm down, Joanie, it's going to be all right. We're here. We can help. That's what parents are for. Just tell us what we can do.'

'What you can do' I said, an adult again, 'is to drink your tea and listen.'

And so – like some bizarre finale in a comedy of errors I told

111

them everything. Very honestly. They didn't like it but they seemed to accept it. I knew they had when my mother began to powder her nose. There was only the merest shadow of doubt on their faces when I had finished, and the teapot was stone cold.

Because of the shadow and because, perhaps, I was weary with using so much truth to defend myself, I added a little lie at the end, just to be sure.

'Anyway' I said 'you need have no further worries about whether I'm normal ...' (What is normal?) '... or not. Because I have a boyfriend.'

'Oh how lovely' said my mother. 'When can we meet him?'

Which is why I ended up sneaking round the corner at some unearthly hour of the night to ring up Robin Carstone. While my parents settled themselves into the spare room (they had set a week aside for my absolution, so a week with me they would spend) I asked Robin if he would mind helping me out and making up a fourth at the theatre. I told him no more than that.

And retrospectively all this has taught me that honesty is by far the best policy. For if I had been honest none of what followed would have taken place.

Unless, of course, those Calvinists are right, and destiny is indeed a foregone thing. I should like to think, for my own self esteem, that this is the case: it is not a pretty thought to have to accept full responsibility for what later transpired.

The four of us set off for the Aldwych in good humour. My parents had their normal little girl back again, and my mother had all the thrills and spills of a week in London before her. I was now exonerated and had the prospective delight of finding some wonderful vengeance for my ex-husband when all the current difficulties were over. And Robin, only marginally cognisant of the reasons for his presence, seemed perfectly delighted to fill in the gap as my accredited heterosexual companion.

The play was good. At least the first half. Certainly I recall that we were just saying so over the interval drinks when a hand touched my shoulder and a voice, strangely reminiscent in its effect as the purr of a taxi engine, said into my ear

'Hullo, Geranium. And how are you?'

Chapter Seven

There really is nothing to acting. It was at this precise point that I realised this. Actors are born, not created. LAMDA and RADA are quite unnecessary. You've either got it or you haven't. Someone once said that there are two schools of acting: the British school where if you don't feel it you fake it, and the American school where if you don't feel it you go out and invent the situation whereby you will. He cited as example an American actor playing a wounded soldier – a head injury case. The actor felt he wasn't quite getting the suffering across strongly enough, so for the entire filming schedule he kept his bandages on: day and night, night and day, the actor's entire head was swathed in properly applied dressings. At the end of the filming the rest of the cast had even started bringing grapes and fruit squash for him on set. He probably won an Oscar.

I discovered that I was of the American school. I had engendered the circumstances for my current piece of role playing perfectly. I was faking nothing. And I envied that head injury actor hugely. It would have given me more pleasure than I can say to have had my entire upper portions swathed in bandages at that precise moment.

To say that, on hearing that voice use its own private nomenclature, I froze, would be something of an understatement. Until that moment my ice-maidenhood had needed the occasional bit of help, reminders sent from my brain down to it, to keep it solid. But not now. Now only the brain went on working – but the body – Oh the body – it had frozen completely – not a flicker showed that it lived.

I could tell precisely where the voice spoke from by following the direction in which the three pairs of eyes of my party stared. Low and amused the voice spoke again, very close to my ear: a little flicker of flame attempted to lick at the adamantine ice.

'Still drinking, I see ...'

'Orange juice' I said automatically.

'Vodka in it?'

The warm breath on my ear made me shiver but the

newfound actress gave no sign. Winter had definitely come to the Aldwych.

'Joan' said my mother from that distant land of reality, 'aren't you going to introduce us?'

She and my father were still staring at the space beyond my shoulder with, understandably, mounting discomfort: my mother was giving little uncertain half-smiles and delicately patting the curls at her temple. My father just looked puzzled. Robin's jaw had dropped and his usual openness of countenance had been replaced by the two emotions of wonder and fathoming – I-know-the-face-but-what's-the-name …?

The hope that if I stood thus for long enough it would all go away, melted. I had to command myself to thaw, to move a little, even to speak – not easy with an icicle rammed up one's thorax. Two attempts at swallowing were useless but a third produced a kind of croak. Up came my hand in a gesture of introduction. Any doubts about my thespian talents were washed away, for this is where the real acting began.

'Of course' croak, croak, another swallow 'Mum. Dad. This is …'

'Finbar Flynn!' Robin said suddenly, in a voice that sounded loud as the ocean's roar, though it was probably quite an ordinary exclamation. 'The actor – ' He turned all pink and faced my parents. 'The famous actor. You must have seen him on the box. Just before Christmas …?'

'Finbar Flynn' I echoed weakly, having finally got my hand into the right position to say the words without turning my head.

My parents were still looking, showing no signs of recognition. Naturally enough.

Robin, by contrast, looked wonderfully animated. The passing thought, which was How Could He Possible Know, was dealt with nicely as he continued excitedly '*The Virgin and the Gipsy!* It was on the box just before Christmas. Didn't you see it?'

I groaned. *The Prophet of Sexuality* was certainly stretching out his tentacles. No wonder Robin was elated. My parents shook their heads. Robin glared at me. The groan, I suppose.

'And which one did you play?' said a voice. It was mine.

'Well, it certainly wasn't the virgin' said Finbar Flynn and laughed. Everybody except me relaxed.

'You really were very good' said Robin, looking up at him like a Nordic dog.

I was still staring straight ahead but had managed to get my arm back down to my side again. My father and mother were saying how sorry they were that they had missed it and Robin was enthusiastically suggesting that it didn't matter because it was so good they were bound to repeat it. I kept my smile and continued to look into the distance, nodding at nothing from time to time, thinking that this made me appear to be part of the proceedings, knowing only that in time a bell would be rung and we could all go back to our seats. Suddenly, appearing around the corner of my field of vision was Finbar Flynn's face – eyes, nose, mouth as close to mine as a mirror's reflection, eyeball to eyeball. His breath was minty, like a little blow torch.

'Do you ever behave normally?' he said.

Snap, crack, pop, click. Vision on, sound on, automatic transmission.

'Seeing an actor in the audience of a theatre is very odd' I found I was saying. 'Like seeing a priest sitting in a church congregation.'

'Lo – It speaks ...'

'Mr Flynn' said Robin

'Call me Finbar.'

'Finbar. Can I get you a drink?'

'Thank you – but I don't even know your name ...'

Up came my hand again. 'Finbar Flynn' I said, enjoying the sound. 'This is Robin Carstone.'

They shook hands deeply and sincerely. Robin glowed. Finbar managed to look imposing and unpretentious at the same time.

'And these are my parents ...'

'Mr and Mrs Geranium' he said. 'How do you do?'

Oddly enough no-one corrected him.

He gave them a smile, most perfect in its duration, and then said 'Thank you, Robin. I'll have a *crème de menthe*. So good for the throat.'

'Oh how lovely' said my mother. 'Do they serve that here? I think I'd like one too ...'

My father, very sensibly taking the easy route, said 'I'll give you a hand with the drinks' and departed in some relief. Leaving the mother and the actor and me.

I knew I ought to speak. I knew I ought to do several things like swing my head round gracefully on my neck and smile at this acquaintance of mine with easy charm. But for some reason which had only slightly to do with embarrassment – I was stuck facing infinity. So – knowing that I had to say something – I did – leaving the actual words to instinct.

And, as usual, it was wrong.

The kind of thing I hoped would come out was a reasonable comment on the First Act, or even a useful sentence or two about the baroque decor in the bar. But instead out came 'That's what tarts drink, isn't it?'

Which, obviously enough, did not best please my mother and hugely amused Finbar Flynn who poked me in the back and said 'By the way – we're over here ...'

I turned round with less of a graceful swing and more of a glacial creak. In a minute, I told myself, I will face him properly, but just for the moment I will settle on my mother, my ally. But she looked so vinegary – not surprising since the comment about tarts still hung on the air – that I had to give her a warm, rallying smile until appeasement honeyed her face. Eventually the minty blow torch, earwards again, said in a voice of penetrating softness 'Oh my Geranium – the teeth are smiling, but is the heart?'

This affected my knees so dramatically that I decided not to risk speech and stood dumb.

'Well' said my mother in a voice that I noted with horror held a flirtatious edge. 'And how did my daughter get to know such a famous actor?'

The 'my daughter' was delivered with a slight trill. In a film the man in question would have said 'Your daughter? Surely not? I thought you were sisters ...'

If he says that, I vowed to myself, I shall walk out.

He said it.

I did not go.

'Well' she repeated, having savoured the flattery for a moment, 'how did you two meet?'

He began 'On New Year's Eve ...'

'Oh – at that party Joan went to – '

'Funny kind of party, wasn't it? – ' He was looking at me. I knew that. And this was the time to look at him, if only to shut him up.

'We don't know anything about what Joan gets up to in London' said my mother as if all categories within the range dope peddling to light operatics were a matter of pride.

116

Sanity rapped me firmly on the knuckles and told me to stop this conversation fast.

'I bet you don't – ' he began confidingly, engaging her eyes with his. And then, quite suddenly, he shouted at the top of his lungs with only an actor's capacity for projection 'CHRIST, YOU BITCH!'

My mother reeled. Until that moment I thought this a figure of speech but – no – she actually reeled. And the whole of the bar seemed to suspend activity. My mother righted herself.

'Sorry' I said, for even I had been dragged from my muteness. 'I have trodden on your foot. So sorry, Finbar.

I smiled again at my mother but this time she remained vinegary, softening only as she looked sympathetically upon Finbar Flynn.

He was bending now, his head of black curls somewhere down by my knee.

'You are stark, staring mad' he muttered. 'Absolutely potty.'

I looked down and could see what he meant. My stiletto had completely pierced the front of his shoe. Undoubtedly there was blood underneath. I put my hand on the back of his head and gave it a little stroke, crooning a half-second's croon for forgiveness. It was undeniably better than stroking a cat.

Perhaps some of my thoughts penetrated his skull, or perhaps it was plain and unadorned and perfectly understandable anger that made him rise up from his squatting position in such an acute manner. Whatever it was it was unfortunate on two counts. One because I had been enjoying the feel if his hair and two because just at that moment Robin and my father returned with the drinks. And, unhappily, it was Robin who stood directly above the crouching Finbar; even more unhappily it was Robin who held the dual libations of *crème de menthe*.

Like the moor breaking free of his chains, the rising figure shot through Robin's outstretched arms and sent the two small glasses of lurid green in a dazzling skyward spiral. They landed somewhere near the bar, where the crowd was at its thickest. Finbar gazed about him in amazement – stunned by impact and stunned by result. All around him elegant theatregoers were dripping in a greenish ooze looking just like refugees from a panto kitchen scene. I peeked up at Finbar's face and saw the first genuinely uncontrived expression I had ever seen there:

117

such a shame it had to be horrified surprise. 'Why is it' he hissed 'that whenever I see you strange things happen?'

'Never mind' I said, as much for my own benefit as for his. 'In a minute a voice will announce Act Two and it will all be over ...'

But, of course, it was not. Semele was flying high that night and the ecstatic madwoman would not be leashed. Amid the terrible furore of people mopping themselves down and crying for vengeance (which diminished when they realised that the man who shouted so obscenely and then threw drinks about was the famous and therefore allowably tempestuous Finbar Flynn; presumably it was all right to be assaulted by him) a voice did come over the tannoy – but only to say that due to lighting difficulties there would be a delay in the resumption of the play.

Clearly Semele thought she was doing me a sisterly favour. I both blessed and cursed her for this.

'I shouldn't think anyone will mind' I said acidly, indicating the tannoy. 'What's going on out here makes a worthy alternative.' I glared, unfairly, at Robin.

'I think I prefer you when you're pissed' Finbar muttered. 'You're much nicer when you've had a few. It's not the poor boy's fault, is it, Robin?'

By now both Robin and I must have looked like a pair of twin sufferers from high blood pressure. He still bemused while I, with ever deepening blush, was almost able to smell the dry and dusty scent of a dead geranium. How could I have acted so creepily on New Year's Eve? It would have been bad enough with a ship that passed in the night but this one seemed bent on remaining in port. Worse – I wanted it to. And worse, worse, I didn't want to want it to ... if you follow.

'You could always leave ...' I said.

'You've gone brick red. Very fiery. It becomes you wonderfully and – alas – I am drawn to you like a moth to a candle flame ...' He looked around at us all. 'Besides – I'm bored with my party over there. Yours is much more fun. Never a dull moment with you, Geranium. You could hire yourself out for parties. You know – rent a happening – '

'Very amusing ...' I managed to curl my lip into what I hoped was a convincing sneer – something quite new to me. It must have been successful because he said

118

'You don't like me very much, do you, Geranium?'

I thought about this for a split second as it presented a poser so far as honesty was concerned.

And then I answered a straightforward 'No.' Which was true. Whatever all this was about it had nothing whatsoever to do with Like.

My father, either from diplomacy or despair, began remembering an incident when I was twelve and fell off my bicycle which was just the kind of thing I wanted to hear just then, but fortunately my mother, who was also in no mood for domestic remembrance, interrupted and said delightedly 'Nothing like this ever happens in Edinburgh ...'

Robin was still speechlessly looking at his empty hands wondering, perhaps, if this was some kind of acting business he had just experienced. And Finbar Flynn, who seemed impervious to my bluntness, just put back his head and laughed and laughed. Damn him.

I noticed he had a lot of fillings. Probably, I thought, because he drinks such sweet stuff.

'You've got a lot of fillings' I said. 'You should take more care of your teeth.'

'My only flaw' he said wickedly. 'And thank you for noticing. People will keep thrusting chocolates on me.' He shook his curls. 'And now I shall go and get some more drinks.' He blew me a steel-eyed kiss which was most offensive. 'Robin' he said 'I envy you ...' He patted Robin's cheek, the pink of which deepened amazingly. 'But more than that, my dear boy – I pity you ...'

And he limped off heroically.

'What on earth happened?' said Robin crossly.

'Joan trod on his foot.'

'You always were clumsy' said my father. 'Remember the bicycle?' And he sipped his whisky and sighed.

I was about to say that it was their fault for buying me one that was too big – like all those school raincoats that I was supposed to grow into and never did – but instead I just watched the limping figure making its way towards the bar.

'I wonder how much longer we've got to wait?' said my father.

Now that was a sentence to conjure with.

Either by dint of his famousness, or through fear, Finbar was served almost immediately. I watched his back view – the

119

breadth of his shoulders, the small peak of curls on the nape of his neck – and then he had turned round and was coming back – smiling and ducking past the crowd. He paused by a small group of people and shook his head, nodding in our direction and then, with a wonderful parting smile, headed on towards us, green glasses held aloft. He bowed on arrival and handed my mother her drink. Then, bowing again and winking at me, he extricated a glass from his pocket, chinked it against his own, and handed it to me with a smile. I did not have to be a candidate for Mensa to realise what was in it. Very loudly he said 'She does love her vodka – don't you, Geranium?'

'Can I ask ...?' said Robin.

'You can ask anything of me' said Finbar in a velvety cadence that had my knees wobbling again.

'Can I ask ...?' Robin's voice was a squeak now and his face had yet again turned to fire. He coughed to right it. 'Can I ask why you call Joan – Geranium?'

'Can I ask' said Finbar Flynn 'where you were on New Year's Eve?'

Robin blinked at him. The fire remained. He looked oddly appealing in his rosy embarrassment. 'Actually – I was phoning Canada.'

'When you should have been spending it with your sweetheart?'

'No. No. No!' I said. 'Not sweetheart!'

He looked from me to Robin and then back again. 'I'm sorry.' He put his hand on his hip in a delicious gesture. I could have eaten him. He was Donatello again only this time in a black blouson jacket and jet black jeans. It really was not fair. ' – So sorry. I just assumed that you two were ...' He shrugged, raising an eyebrow at me, then at Robin, smiling in that well-remembered sardonic way 'You know ...' He drank with his head thrown back which made his adam's apple bob.

'Joan is not – ' began Robin.

I began. 'We are not ...'

And then I looked at Robin and he looked at me and we both looked at my poor, dear, innocent parents on whom I had spent such careful and loving deceit just to convince them that indeed we were ...

'I expect you two had had a tiff' said my mother.

My father passed his hand over his head, ear to ear, and looked imploringly up at the tannoy.

120

'I lifted up mine eyes unto the hills' I said because it seemed so apposite. 'Whence cometh my strength.'

They all looked at me in various degrees of amazement.

'You' said Finbar Flynn, putting his face very close to mine 'have a gift for poetry.'

He looked at my parents. 'And you – have a very odd daughter.'

Then he turned to Robin. 'Never a dull moment, eh?'

'That's what I love about you, Geranium, you're a genuine eccentric. The kind that brings a bit of colour into our otherwise monotonous lives.'

It was at that moment that I realised all the ice had melted. Clean away. None of it was left. I took a great gulp out of my glass before I remembered it was no longer orange juice but the very liquid I had thought would never pass my lips again. It tasted like perfect fire. Colour I was. And he was colour. Two colours in an otherwise dreary world. Together we could lift the veil of greyness and set the world alight with brilliance. I gave myself up to the thought and said

'The purest and most thoughtful minds are those which love colour the most ...'

That went down even better than the hills. Nobody spoke.

'Was that Lawrence?' hazarded Robin after a while.

'No, it was not bloody Lawrence' I snapped.

'Another tiff?' asked Finbar.

'Oh I do hope not' said my mother. 'Are you in a play at the moment, Mr Flynn?'

'Finbar' we said in unison.

'Of course' I said 'you could change the whole meaning by changing one "s".'

Another silence. Followed by my father saying in exasperation 'Do speak plainly, Joan.'

'It could be "the purest and most thoughtful minds are those which love colours the most".'

'That's wonderful' said Finbar. 'You should be directing plays or something – not – not – what do you do by the way?'

'She's a teacher. We both are. In the same school.'

'Ah – love in the classroom, is it?' He gave Robin a long stare. Robin stared back, blinking his pale lashes 'Well – no – not exactly – um – er –'

121

'And do you also like poetry?' The dark eyes never wavered from the shining cornflowers.
'Um' said Robin.
'Oh tell him about Fidelity' I said, suddenly impatient.
Robin's face lit up with pleasure. He screwed up his forehead for a moment and then, like a child reciting, he began. He knew the words, more or less, only stumbling a little and getting one or two phrases mixed up – 'And when throughout the wild orgasms of love, slowly a gem forms ... etc. etc. ...'
I prompted him once or twice.
When it was over I said, thinking generally. 'Fidelity is a funny thing. It evaporates so quickly.'
I looked at Robin for no particular reason and was astonished when he suddenly clasped both my hands tightly and said fervently 'Oh Joan, Joan, I am sorry ... so sorry!'
'Isn't that nice?' said my mother.
'Very' said my father shortly. He was rocking on his heels now, hands behind back like the Duke of Edinburgh; waiting, waiting.
'You're in a play at the moment – Finbar?' my mother asked.
'Rehearsals. *Coriolanus.* You must come and see it.'
'How lovely' she said, fingering her empty glass.
'You must all come.' He gave a grand, expansive gesture. 'All of you. Come to the opening on March the third.' He gave Robin a little punch which had the benefit of making him release my hands.
And then, suddenly, succour did come from the hills and the voice over the tannoy announced that the play would shortly recommence.
'Thank God for that' said my father, almost hurling himself towards the exit. He pulled my mother after him and, with a queenly wave, she too disappeared, swallowed up in the swarm.
'Well – goodbye' said Robin, grabbing Finbar's hand. 'I look forward to seeing – um – You really were terrific on the box.'
'Even better in the flesh' said Finbar, returning the handclasp. Robin moved away and was lost, like the others, in the crowd. And we were alone.
'Sorry about the foot.' I said.
'So I should think. By the way, where did those lines come from?'
'Which lines?'

'The lines about colour – '

'Oh – from Ruskin. *Stones of Venice* I think.'

'Ah – Venice. I was there last summer.'

'I know you were – '

He looked down at me and raised that devil's eyebrow. 'You knew?'

'Fred and Geraldine invited me.'

'And yet you did not come?' He delivered this histrionically. 'You have been before?'

'Never.'

'Then you were very silly. It is perfection.'

'Yes' I said. 'I believe you. I wish I had – now – '

He gave his curls a little shake. 'Better perhaps that you didn't.'

'Why?'

He shrugged. 'No matter. Anyway – you will come to the opening of the play. I'll get tickets for you and – ' he pointed towards the exit 'him. Your boyfriend. I'll fix it up through Fred and Gerry. You can come to the party afterwards and do something dramatic. You won't find that too difficult now, will you?'

He put his hand on my hair very lightly, gingerly even, as if I might bite, and smiled down at me with a very sexy smile. At least, I thought it was sexy, at that precise moment he could have been grimacing in the early stages of appendicitis and I would have found it seductive.

'You can put a flower in your hair – a dead one – and wear that ethereal white dress – ' He smiled more broadly. 'That should liven up the proceedings. Ever been to a first night party, Geranium?'

I decided that my old comprehensive's version of *HMS Pinafore* did not count and shook my head.

'You'll enjoy it. Both of you.'

The bar was almost empty. The final announcement had been made. This was the time to speak, to deny Robin as a lover, to apologise for the peculiarity of New Year's Eve (You see, Finbar, there isn't a man in my life at the moment and – well – a girl gets kind of lonely on special nights so you caught me in an odd, not to say uncharacteristic, drunken state. But perhaps you would like to share a little of my lonely darkness sometime – [more poetic than saying bed] because I seem to have fallen

123

passionately, desperately, triumphantly in love with you … you attract me madly). Of course there was no time to say all this so I tried to make a snappy distillation of it which came out rather baldly as

'I live alone.'

'I know' he said. 'You're eccentric. That's what I like about you.'

Now that was an aspect of the available dimensions that I had left out at Dunbar. Women who live on their own may also be considered to do it out of a form of mild madness. If I had not found him so profoundly attractive I would have brought my heel down just as savagely on his other foot.

I opened my mouth to speak for time was running away, but closed it again. For some reason I was close to tears. The overflow from all that melted ice, I expect. I swallowed and tried again and managed to squeak 'Robin …'

'Robin?' he said sharply. 'What about Robin?'

But then a hand seemed to appear out of nowhere like a Saki spectre and it gripped Finbar's arm.

A very short fat man followed it saying in a pleasant, plummy voice 'We ought to take our seats now, Fin.' He peered up at me from Finbar Flynn's elbow and smiled. The beautifully modulated voice belied the dumpling face from which it issued. Despite the heartbreaking untimeliness of his interruption, I liked him and somehow managed to smile back.

Finbar patted his hand. 'Sorry, Jim' he said while continuing to look at me. 'Robin? Robin what?'

But the man at his sleeve pulled at the black blouson and said 'Shouldn't you introduce us?'

And Finbar gave himself a little shake that made those wretched little curls do their customary dance and said 'Jim. Sorry. This is a friend of Geraldine Durrell's – Geranium something.'

The fat man extended his hand which I took. 'How nice' he said warmly. 'And are you also an actress?'

'Oh no' I said. 'I'm a schoolteacher.'

'Stay that way' he said, with feeling.

'Jim is my agent' said Finbar.

'I pity you' I said.

He chuckled. 'I rather like you.'

'I rather like her too' said Finbar, with perfect mimicry.

'Good. Good' said the fat little man, and he bowed over my hand and kissed it.

As he did so a third voice said 'For Fuck's sake you two, are you coming or what?'

The voice and the slight glitter in the eyes was familiar.

'Ah Richard' said Jim with a sigh.

'Ricky!' said Finbar 'Meet – ' He turned but the young man had swept off in a wonderful motion of huff towards the exit.

'We had better go' said Jim sadly. 'I hope we shall meet again.'

'She's coming to the first night' said Finbar, already moving away 'I've asked her to. In a white dress. And to the party afterwards. Don't let the ordinary exterior fool you, Jimbo –'

(Thank you so much)

'– she's extremely odd. I'll send the tickets to Gerry. Don't forget now – I want to see you both there ...'

And fairly rapidly, though to my satisfaction still limping, he followed the young man through the exit. Every time he took his socks off he would remember me, at least for a while. Small consolation.

His agent gave a shrug of his stubby shoulders. 'He likes you' he said munificently. I could have picked him up on his fat little legs and kissed him.

Rather like Mrs Lincoln, I couldn't tell you what the play was about and I apologise to whoever wrote it. I had other things on my mind sitting in that darkened auditorium. I was just grateful not to have to enter into conversation for the next hour and a half. I sat there, all of a fluster, thinking 'steady, Joan, steady' but Joan refused to be steadied at all. However when the stage lights faded in the last bow and we all went back out into the real world everything resettled itself. The whole thing had been a silly piece of delight and it was now over. Nothing was going to come of it. Nothing at all. Normal service must be resumed as soon as possible.

PART THREE

Chapter One

But this positivism took no account of my parents who stayed with me for the full week. What the whole might of Chiswick and its environs had not managed, they almost did, turning my Fifth Dimension almost into rubble overnight. They were up and down the stairs, in and out of the bathroom, chatting at the breakfast table, until I thought yearningly of involuntary euthanasia. Why don't ageing parents need more sleep, not less? I tried sneaking up at dawn for a quiet toast and Weetabix but, no, down they would come with a whole battery of ideas for jaunts out on my free afternoons. I became immersed in that horrible clammer known as leading a full, rich life.

My mother, misinterpreting the pinkness of my cheeks as good health rather than suppressed fury, said that she could see how much good my having some company was doing for me and thought perhaps they should try to stay on longer. Dad raised my hopes by saying he had to get back to the bank and the bells but she, scraping out the last of my Greek honey, seemed prepared to consign him to the Edinburgh train alone. He was clearly prepared to put patriarchal duty above marital comfort if it came to it. Ergo – it must not.

I invited my father to come for a walk with me in Chiswick House grounds.

There was a pale winter sun lemoning the sky and the bare branched trees gracefully bowed us forward. The squirrel Olympics were taking place and the air was sharp though not bitter. It should have been a scene of tranquil harmony but all I could think of was my mother back in Milton Road preparing yet another well-balanced meal and considering herself indispensable. She had even mentioned Finbar Flynn's play in an if-only kind of voice that filled me with fear and sharpened my resolve dramatically. Mother must go well before the play opened. Even I wasn't thinking that far ahead. Besides it would probably not come to anything. And better if it didn't.

I put my hand in the crook of my father's arm and we walked in a nice, easy, confiding rhythm. I was scratching around in my head for a way to begin.

'Joan' he said, stopping suddenly. 'You feel very tense.'
'Just a bit cold' I said, and we walked on.

'So' I said, after a while and when I could be sure my voice was at normal pitch. 'When you get back you'll be getting in touch with Jack, will you? Just to tell him that everything is fine and he can forget all about me. I laughed. 'I mean – you can tell him that you've found me absolutely normal and that I just don't want to be bothered by him, or anyone, anymore . . . ?'

'Joan' he said 'you're squeezing my arm rather tightly.'

I took a deep breath and eased off, attempting nonchalance. 'I really do like living on my own, you know.'

He patted my hand. 'You're being a very brave girl.'

'No I'm not. I enjoy it.'

'I don't think it's very normal.'

'Oh come on' I said, exasperated beyond remembering to weigh my words. 'It's one thing to fly down here thinking I was locked in the arms of a lesbian . . .' His whole body stiffened, a piece of body language I stupidly ignored. 'But it's quite another to worry just because I choose to live alone. And anyway – what is normal?'

'Normal' he said 'is the opposite of abnormal. I don't think choosing to live alone is normal.'

'Yet if Jack had told you I was living with a man you would have stayed up in Edinburgh? Even if you didn't know anything about him? But because you thought it was a woman you abandoned bridge, bells and bank to come south and rescue me?'

'I can't say we would have been overjoyed but we would have accepted it. After all, it seems to be the modern way. But the thought of you living in the manner Jack suggested was – well – not on.'

'Why?' Interest completely overtook strategy. I had never discussed anything remotely like this before.

'Oh for Heaven's sake, Joan!' He stopped abruptly and struck the ground with his stick so hard that the squirrels' 300 metres was abandoned in chaos. 'It is not normal. It is against nature . . .' He pointed with his stick indiscriminately at nature. 'It's not the natural way.'

He resumed walking, looking straight ahead. I heard him take a deep breath. 'You mustn't underestimate me, Joan. I was not

130

always a respectable sixty. I happen to think that the – er – act between man and woman is rather a beautiful thing. Perhaps one of the greatest joys that God ever gave us. And what you never refer to – what those kind of people do – is not. In fact it is quite the reverse. It is abnormal – and – ugly.'

This was being well adjusted and very grown up. Talking about sex with my father. The kind of thing Dr Spock was on about, the kind of thing other people did, and usually in books. It made me feel very close to him and I abandoned making sure my mother accompanied him back to Edinburgh for this much greater matter. I squeezed his arm and watched a bird soar free from an empty tree, mistakenly taking it for an omen. His sexual bigotry was as nothing to this newfound honesty between us.

'It's lovely to talk to you like this, Dad ...' On we walked, arm in arm. 'But I'm not quite sure I agree with you about the beauty of the act. All that grunting and humping and sweaty red faces. And then there's penetration ... just think of that ...' I laughed up at the bird 'I mean – you couldn't call that beautiful, now could you?'

My father stood stock still.

'At least' I added, lemming like, 'lesbians don't have to do that, do they?'

The brief flowering of the well adjusted relationship was over. Totally decayed.

When my father eventually spoke again it was in the low reassuring tones of one soothing a wounded, cornered and therefore dangerous animal.

'Perhaps it would be best if your mother stayed on for a while.'

'Shall we go round the back and look at the staircase?' I said, admiring the charming way I said it. 'It's a real Palladian gem.'

He ignored the invitation.

'She can come on later. People up there will rally round.'

Good old Dunkirk spirit.

He patted my hand again. 'I think that would be best ...'

Cunning as a lunatic, I switched too.

'No need, really, Dad. Besides ...' My Bona Dea fought off Semele and won. 'I think Robin finds it a bit difficult when you two are there. You've probably noticed that he doesn't come round much ...'

131

'He doesn't come round at all, Joan. He's not been in touch since the theatre.'

'Well, yes – that's it, you see. I think he feels a bit inhibited with you two staying ...'

Inhibited?

Inhibited?

That was the wrong word to use. It smacked of outrageous things taking place as soon as they boarded their train – whips, leatherwear, Nivea and polythene bags –

'I mean – he's very tactful. He knows that I don't see you very often and he doesn't want to intrude ...'

My father relaxed visibly.

He could, after all, hand the baton on to somebody else.

'I expect I shall see a lot more of him when you've gone back.' I shivered. 'Shall we get in the car? I'm beginning to feel very cold.'

I watched him clunk click himself into the seat beside me. He looked depressed. That really was too much. What had he got to be depressed about? I could feel reproach all around me in the car so I began to hum a little song of reassurance in my head, to the tune of 'Yellow Submarine': Today is Tuesday, Tuesday, Tuesday – They're going home on Saturday, Saturday, Saturday. Pretty soon the tune was out loud and only the words were silent. My father liked the Beatles so he joined in the humming. If only he had known.

Yet despite all this easing of tension between us, I silently gave them both due and certain warning that if they were not on that Saturday train together I would instantly invent the most outrageous relationship, with a card holding member of the Communist Party, and travel up there to personally announce it to the Bridge Club.

They never knew what they had escaped by agreeing to travel home together and on the designated Saturday.

All I had to do was wait.

What with shoring up my defences and refrigerating my emotions both at home and at school, I might well have not given Finbar Flynn another thought. After all, it wasn't as if he was around for me to moon over and – well – he was an actor – so I couldn't rely on anything being real. Whereas the seductive prospect of my parents' imminent departure was never far from

132

my mind, and certainly took up most of my waking thoughts. And the situation might have stayed that way if it hadn't been for the media. And, presumably, little fat Jimbo.

Jack always spoke about agents with respect. He said that a good one was invaluable and that, given the option, he would always talk with the chef rather than with the raw ingredients; he also said that if you see the same face involved in some publicity twice in the same week, it means they have a first class agent.

Well, Finbar Flynn must have had a double first class agent because he seemed to pop up everywhere. And I know there is a theory about heightened consciousness but that had nothing to do with it. Jimbo certainly had. There was his client grinning from a colour supplement, giving the details of one of his rooms. To this picture I gave my microscopic attention as only the bewitched can do, studying every little item from the colour of the curtains to the invitations propped up on the mantelpiece. '... In fine disregard for ceremony' burbled the interviewer 'Mr Flynn appears to use his Oscar as a letter rack ...' Only someone in my state could possibly be interested in things like that. In the foreground of the photograph was a glass topped table awash with books. Finbar grinned from behind this as he stretched out on a creamy leather settee in blue jeans and cowboy boots. Presumably in fine disregard of ceremony he used his Italian furniture as a doormat. Uppermost of the foreground books and placed, I thought, with a good deal too much careless abandon, was the complete works of T. S. Eliot, face down and open. 'I have recently been re-reading Eliot's poetry for relaxation. It makes a good contrast to the text of *Coriolanus* ... Eliot has long been a favourite of mine ...' quoted the supplement. I read this in the normal way, and nodded over it until it suddenly occurred to me what he had said ...

Re-reading?

Long Been?

The tongues of men are full of deceits, are they not, Fair Katherine?

Oh well, I thought, I suppose we all do hypocritical things like that from time to time. In a way I was flattered – after all – it had been me who introduced him to its joys in the first place. I thought no more of the deceit than that, though I should have

133

done. For was I not also perpetrator? With first hand knowledge of how deceit can blossom until its perfume becomes the normal scent to the nostrils? And all the resultant muddles it can get you into. I had my parents staying with me right now as a result of all that.

But I did not stop to think about it. Finbar had just bent the truth a little – harmless enough. As I said, we all do things like that from time to time ...

For the moment, with my parents around, I could only concentrate on them. I was like a piece of matter suspended in formaldehyde; one movement from me in the jar and they would never let me alone again.

On the night before their departure we were supposed to be going next door to have dinner with Fred and Geraldine. I was not looking forward to it because the bizarre Aldwych scene was bound to be discussed; Finbar Flynn under my parents' microscope was a dreadful prospect. But the invitation was unavoidable. On one of her frequent sorties to the butcher my mother had recognised Geraldine and the resulting telephone call, later in the week, had been inevitable. The Durrells couldn't be blamed for stepping over the demarcation line that they had so tactfully respected throughout the year, though Geraldine's rather guarded telephone conversation had given me the opportunity to refuse. But with my mother at my elbow it was impossible. At least I had managed to put it off until the last night so that whatever further discussions transpired there would be no time the next day to go into them.

'Is Robin going to join us?' asked my mother. 'I'm sure they wouldn't mind if you asked him to come too. We should like to see him again before we go back. You don't seem to have a very regular relationship with him, darling. Everything is all right, isn't it?'

'Perfect' I said. 'And I do see him every morning at school.' I didn't add that this was from a distance, ducking and wheeling whenever he hove into view, and risking permanent eye damage from nose-in-book-itis at the morning breaks.

'Well – yes – I know' she said. 'But it doesn't seem very romantic, does it?'

'Well' I said, calling up inspiration. 'He's in training this week –'

'What for?'

'He cycles –'

Not bad. It was only equivocation after all.

'But not at night surely? Not every night. And not on Fridays. Why don't you ask him and see?'

'Because I don't want to tempt him.'

And that was the truth.

But in the end it did not matter. Because on Friday afternoon, while my parents were out having their final fling at the Boat Show, Fred rang to say that Geraldine had some kind of stomach bug and he thought it was hovering around in his entrails too: all in all, he said, he thought that they had better cancel the dinner. Great apologising from Fred was quickly curtailed as he himself had to make a sudden dash for the bathroom. His relief can have been only marginally greater than my own.

Instead I cooked the three of us a three course dinner that night, fingering recipe books that had not been touched for more than a year. It felt strange to be that old person again, the one whose *cassoulet* had made her husband sing, and whose *tagliatelle porcini* had stoked his lust so well that the blackcurrant sorbet had been unable to extinguish it. I exorcised that whole sorry history in the bathos of cooking like a demon for my parents – and I did not feel a thing. I cooked grilled red mullet with a sauce made from their livers (I sniffed the fish most indelicately at the fishmonger's since the last thing I wanted was parents too poisoned to travel), Beef Wellington, and a baked Alaska. I had to make the ultimate cook's sacrifice and let my mother help with some of it because she kept making noises about just popping next door to say tootle-oo, and I could not face the thought of the bug transferring to her bowels and scuppering everything. But, despite this, the meal went well.

I was happy and elated and they, not guessing the fount, responded similarly. Mum got slightly maudlin by the end of it – partly the claret and partly the idea of returning to the barbaric North, I suppose.

'You look so lovely' she said. 'I hope it won't be long before ...'

'Before what?'

'Before you get married again.'

I kept smiling and suggested that we leave the dishes and go

135

and watch some television – which is – after all – the greatest conversation stopper ever invented. So we did.

Fortunately it didn't matter to me what we watched; I had only to sit through it, go to bed, and – lo – tomorrow would be glorious freedom. This was just as well as whoever said that television was simply so much chewing gum for the eyes must have had Friday night winter season in mind. It wasn't until I heard the slightly-hysterical-with-hype voice of a presenter saying '... And here he is, ladies and gentlemen – Finbar Flynn –' followed by brassy music and riotous applause, that I realised we were watching that completely expendable institution, the Chat Show.

'Oh look' said my mother. 'It's your actor friend.' Even my father looked up from his brochures. 'Doesn't he look different on the screen?'

But I was quite beyond answering.

The colour supplement and now this. You see what I mean about Jim being a good agent?

Finbar looked wonderful. Sort of groomed and flamboyant at the same time. He was wearing clothes with a vaguely Brummel-ish style to them, his curls accentuating the sense of Regency. There was nothing ordinary about him, really there wasn't – nothing at all: even while striding across the set to be greeted by the interviewer he made an impression. Oh dear, Oh dear, I thought, here we go again.

I was sorry to see that he no longer limped; he must have forgotten all about me now. As he sat down on the low sofa he looked amused and self-conscious, like a small boy who has been dressed up for a party – a small boy who is rather enjoying it. It was clear that the chat show host was going to make some remark about his outfit from the way he eyed it up and down, making wry, admiring facial asides into camera.

'Well' said the actor after a while, extending his arms and swivelling his torso slightly, the better to display his clothes. 'What about the suit? It's the first one I've owned for twenty years. Do you like it?'

'Yes' said a voice which turned out to be mine.

'Pardon?' said my mother.

'Nothing' I said.

No wonder Georgette Heyer and her imitators did so well out

136

of their Regency romances. I thought about taking myself outside for a moment to compose myself but my mother said critically 'He's not handsome exactly – is he? But he's very striking. Don't you think so, Joan?'

My 'Yes' was about as apt as a pools winner saying a quarter of a million pounds would be very acceptable.

'And so' says the host 'you're all set for a glorious return to the British stage after your triumph in America?'

Finbar squirms at this and says 'Triumph sounds a bit strong – as if I had to fight a battle over there.' He smiles disarmingly, 'Which isn't true at all. I had a mild success and the Americans were very charming to me. They love successes ...'

Interviewer not too keen on this put down so there is a slight hardening of the muscles around his crinkling eyes. 'Well – anyway – you certainly made an impact –'

Finbar inclines his head in a movement of gracious acceptance. He looks enchantingly roguish.

They chat on for a while about theatre in general and his experience of it and I sit there like a piece of happy blotting paper until – suddenly – I find myself sitting bolt upright, hands clenched beneath chin, breath held – for the tone of the conversation changes. The interviewer says 'So much for the professional side of things, Finbar. Now – what about the personal side? Women for instance ... You seem to have a very enjoyable effect on them. At least my wife –' pause for studio audience to laugh '... seems to think so.'

Finbar drapes himself backwards in a gesture of perfect relaxation and stamps a delicate question mark on his features.

'But you have never married. Why is that, Finbar?' To compensate for the gap between them, the interviewer now leans forward and we get a good close up of his best profile. He winks into camera and closes the gap still further – like a smiling piranha – 'Can't make up your mind or –' leans back in chair now for pose of expansive relaxation 'are you going to disappoint all those ladies out there waiting on the edge of their chairs for your answer ...'

I sit back hurriedly.

'... and say you're not interested?'

Lovely warm smile from Finbar which implies that it was a good joke but enough is enough.

137

'I have a lot of wonderful friends' he says. 'And I love them all dearly.'

'Ah – Ha –' twinkles the host to the camera. He always seems to know where it is. 'But isn't there one special person in your life at the moment ...? Someone who is more important than everyone else right now?'

'Yes' says Finbar. 'You.'

Looking slightly discomfited but quickly regaining lost poise the questioner ploughs on. 'I mean – someone special in the romantic way?'

How very silent my room suddenly seemed. I could even hear the ticking of the clock in the hall. The brochures rustled slightly on my father's lap as he breathed, my mother scratched her arm and her bracelets rattled. I sat completely still and was fourteen again.

'... a girlfriend perhaps?' concludes the host, smiling for the benefit of his audience and then back to Finbar again. 'Of course I don't want to pry into your private life but you are – well – in the public eye rather a lot at the moment ...'

'Why don't you tell him to just piss off?' I said.

'Joan!' My father was shocked. All his brochures flapped onto the floor.

'Well – honestly – what a terrible intrusion. And anyway – who on earth wants to know about that sort of thing?'

Who indeed?

'... aren't you?' finished the host with a little deprecating shrug. Don't Say Anything, I urged silently, for I certainly didn't want to hear his answer. Just Refuse.

But he did not. He just went on smiling and mulling as if the question was deep enough to settle the Universe.

Eventually he said 'Of course there is ...' Interviewer cocks his head expectantly but Finbar then closes his lips, the small boy suddenly turned tongue tied, and twinkles at him silently out of those shadowy eyes.

If the interviewer and the Ladies Out There are on the edge of their seats, I have practically fallen off mine.

'What about a nice cup of coffee, Joan?' says my father.

'You won't sleep if you do –' replies Mum.

'Oh do be quiet you two – I want to listen ...'

'He is very attractive' says my mother wistfully as if she has finally made up her mind.

138

The interview continues 'Well – and is this special person in your life someone we all know?'

Finbar laughs. There are those dear little fillings again. 'I really would rather not talk about that side of things, you know.'

'Oh come, come' says his host with jovial dagger thrust. 'You've come on the show. You are in the public eye so you know that we are all interested.' He leans forward again. 'Or perhaps it is someone unknown. A struggling young actress perhaps. Come, come – we are all fascinated – aren't we?'

He turns to the audience who titter agreement.

Finbar seems to be struggling himself.

'Your audience awaits' says his tormentor.

Finbar's brow clears and he seems to have reconciled the struggle. He speaks. 'It is someone quite obscure and it is a relationship in its infancy.' He raises both hands. 'So – there you are. Next question.'

But his host presses him.

'In the theatre?'

'No' says Finbar a little wearily. 'Not in the theatre. A schoolteacher. And a poetry lover, like myself.'

'A schoolteacher?' Both host and audience register shock at this.

'Sounds like you, Joan,' says my mother. 'He said you were good at poetry. Does your Robin know about this?'

But I am speechless, stunned by the same realisation as my mother's. He could be talking about me. New Year's Eve, the Aldwych – each flashes back. I begin to bite my nails.

'Don't do that, dear' says my mother.

Back in the box the investigation continues.

'And what has a schoolteacher to teach the flamboyant Mr Flynn?'

The flamboyant Mr Flynn falls into the trap and says 'You'd be surprised ...'

'Ho ho' says the hunter. 'Perhaps ... helps you with your lines? That sort of thing. Or –' He leers quite openly now.

'No. I never take help with my lines. I always learn them alone and unaided when everyone else is fast asleep.' Finbar looks relieved because he has managed to swing the conversation away from his love life onto the safe ground of professional procedure.

Interviewer claws it back. 'I see. But they say – don't they – that behind every great man there is –' he shrugs and smiles with perfect timing – no need to finish the phrase '... So she is surely closely involved in your current preparations for –' he checks his notes '*Coriolanus?*'

'Not at all' says Finbar smoothly.

'But she will be there on the opening night?'

'Of course.'

Finbar is now showing marked signs of strain. The host, good at his job, understands this and eases off a little. Leaning back in his small success he can afford to be affable. 'I expect we shall see you both photographed together after the event and then all our curiosities will be sated. Eh?'

I think Finbar was supposed to nod with relief at this but he seems to get a second wind. 'I rather hope not' he says seriously. 'I think individuals and their private lives should remain private. There is no reason that I can see why my friends should become public property. Nor –' his voice holds an edge of bitterness now '... should they be subjected to the same kind of scrutiny that I am.'

The host recognises encroaching seriousness and this is, after all, a light chat show, so he laughs and eases the tension. 'You mean she would become as harassed as – say – Princess Diana did?'

Finbar takes the cue. 'I'm no Prince Charles, ho ho ...' he says, relaxed again.

'Some might say you were their Prince Charming though. Ho Ho.'

Interviewer gets the last word.

'Really' says my father. 'Can't they leave the Royal Family out of anything nowadays?'

'Hush' says my mother in an awed voice. 'He was talking about our Joan. No wonder we haven't seen Robin. He must be awfully jealous. I felt there was something when we were at the theatre ...'

I went on staring at the screen. There was my whole world, my whole citadel, my kingdom of ice, rendered to ruin. The little tongue of flame turned into an inferno. I was blazing merrily and the heat was hopeless.

'The media are not particularly scrupulous' Finbar was saying.

140

'This morning I came down to empty some rubbish and there was a reporter sorting through my dustbin.'

'And did he find anything?'

Pause for studio laughter.

'Mostly burnt toast ...'

More laughter.

'You should get yourself a toaster.'

'Perhaps I should.' Boyish grin, wry look.

'Or ask your schoolteacher to give you a lesson on making it ...'

Riot.

'And thank you, Finbar Flynn, for giving up your time to come along and talk to us tonight. We all look forward to your return to the British stage on –?'

'March the third' he says 'I'm looking forward to it. And thank you – all – very much – ' He extends a valedictory hand towards the camera. An actor to the last. I had a painful sense of betrayal – mine to myself or his to me – I couldn't say – and then my father said above the closing applause

'What about coffee, Joan?'

And I took the cue and ran.

Down the passage, through the cluttered kitchen, out, out into the clear, black air of the night. All I had ever asked was to be left alone and at peace. And now this.

Hot tears on cold cheeks in that blessed, velvet silence.

No surrender, I promised myself, and shook my fist at the night sky. It was full of imperial brilliants and quite unmoved by me. I looked down at the earth in the garden, the dark silhouette of it, reproachful stuff. 'You've never moved for anyone,' I sneered, and I could taste the spite on my tongue. 'Be warned – or I shall have you levelled with bulldozers.'

I had been so happy in that anchorless world.

I stamped on the soil and kicked at it, just to get the message across. A stone was sent flying into the undergrowth where it ricocheted satisfactorily against the Montgomerys' regimental fencing. I let out a long, loud yell of defiance and stood there trembling with rage for the control, the ice age, that I had lost. And then, like a ghostly puppet show, bathed in moonlight, two heads appeared above the palings, and the heads had mouths.

'Oh hullo' said the high well-bred tones of Maud. 'It's you. We wondered what the noise was ...'

Jesus Wept. Was there no place that I could be on my own in this teeming planet?

'It was only a stone' I said.

'We thought it might be something else' she replied. She gave the words 'something else' such a sinister edge that even in the depths of my pits I was curious.

'Like what?'

'I am afraid' said Reginald in a voice that was dark with shame 'that we think we've got rats ...'

My curiosity died.

'Rats don't throw stones, do they?'

Was I mad or were they mad? They certainly looked it. Maud had on one of those little red helmets with ear flaps and a small peak so favoured by county ladies in cold weather; the untied strings dangled from the side flaps and looked more like a baby's bonnet than the smart way to keep warm this winter. Reginald's tweed cap was pulled down almost to meet the tucks of his check scarf which hid most of his face except for a pair of dragonlike nostrils that issued forth staccato bursts of vapour perfectly in accord with his appearance.

Maud tinkled a laugh. 'We've been setting some bait for them.'

So that explained the costumes.

She flashed her torch across my depressing slum into the Durrells' garden. Seeing the beam raking across like that reminded me of that other time when they had done the same thing. It even picked out the now forlorn shape of the white patio table next door. I had been all right until then. Eventually she brought the light to rest on a spot beneath the base of Fred and Gerry's sycamore tree.

'That's the problem' she said. 'Those neighbours of yours and their disgusting compost heap.'

'No doubt about it' said Reginald between fiery snorts.

'Still' said Maud 'we shall get them in the end.'

I wasn't too sure if they meant the rats or the Durrells.

'Well, I haven't noticed anything. Nothing at all.'

'I expect you will. Let us know and Reggie can bait your garden too.'

'Goodnight' I said and turned to go.

'Goodnight' they said and then popped back above the fence.

'By the way, Joan' said Maud. 'We met your parents on the

142

path yesterday morning. So nice. I wondered if you would like to bring them in for a drink – perhaps tomorrow evening? It's such a long time since we invited you in.'

Fifth columnists cunningly disguised as my parents. Not only was the citadel lying in rubble but there were already plans afoot for an invasion. I had to begin rebuilding immediately.

'They're going home tomorrow' I said. 'And I'm going to be frightfully busy with a project of mine.'

'Shame' said Reggie, disappearing again.

Maud clung on. 'What a pity.' She smiled politely. 'What is this new project that's going to keep you so busy?'

'I'm sort of building something.'

I saw her knuckles go white as she gripped the top of the palings and Reginald's dragon head, positively drowned in vapour, reappeared instantly.

'Here?' they chorused together in panic.

'Yes indeed.'

'I hope you have obtained planning permission.' Maud's politeness was diamond hard.

'It isn't necessary.' I laughed. 'You won't see it. Nobody will.'

'Indoors then?' said Reginald calmly.

'All around me actually.' I kicked another stone.

'Joan. Joan!' they called, but I was already walking away.

There was no snow anywhere when I drove my parents to the station. And no frostiness from them either. They had enjoyed themselves. I was the perfect daughter. My father would ring Jack up as soon as he got home and suggest to him, as if he were an undesirable playfellow, that he should play elsewhere. I could face many things if I no longer had to face him.

I waved and blew kisses long after the train had clattered out of the station and was lighter than air now they had finally gone. I danced down the steps, pirouetted towards the car and drove with renewed delight towards that silent, empty house of mine where no tap would drip unless I left it dripping and where nothing would stir unless I allowed it to. As for Finbar Flynn? Well – who was he? Just a silly bit of fantasy. A moment of weakness on my part, engineered into my life because of other people. I had too many roots. I remembered the Christmas tree of over a year ago. That was how I should have stayed – a rootless stump happily growing nowhere, sending down

143

nothing, taking nothing back. Now I could return to that joyful state.

To celebrate I called into the library on the way home, like a child visiting a sweetie shop. I poked out my tongue at the volumes of D. H. Lawrence and wondered which book to select to have the old goat whizzing in his grave. Baroness Orczy seemed wonderfully appropriate. The mystical prophet of sexuality would have a quite different appreciation of the wayside scarlet pimpernel and would feel deeply affronted by her foppish Dan Dare. I took that, along with a few others, and whistled all the way home.

March the third was no more than the possibility of free theatre tickets – which, after all, are always nice. But if I didn't get them – well – so what? I could either buy my own – or not go at all. *Coriolanus* was not a play I was burning to see. And the chat show – ? Well – the chat show was just that. Finbar was an actor – British school – faking away for the benefit of his public. None of that mattered to me anymore. All I wanted back was the slumbering Fifth Dimension. Whoever invented that other emotional pinball machine out there needed their head smacking.

Chapter Two

There was a bit of Baptism by Fire at school during the following weeks largely because Robin insisted on telling every-one that I knew the famous actor Finbar Flynn. Even a couple of girls in my class asked me, shyly, if I could get them his autograph. Mass appeal. It was understandable given the man's genuine attractions and the skill of his agent. The media coverage that man got was outrageous.

Marjorie – hot with excitement – asked me what he was like and I said Like an Actor.

Rhoda suggested, with snappish envy, that I hadn't let the grass grow. And even Pimmy, grey haired and bespectacled and already knitting next summer's cardie, was moved to say how much she enjoyed (blush) watching him.

The more I tried to avoid Robin, the more soulful and inescapable he became, so that he no longer seemed to perch on my chair arm, but to slump there like a wounded but loyal dog.

I certainly did not want to discuss Finbar Flynn with him, though he kept trying – using it as some kind of middle ground, I suppose.

'I expect he'll forget all about getting tickets for us ...' he said mournfully.

'Probably' I said, still marking exercise books.

'Come out with me tonight, Joan?'

I studied Sharon's version of the Quality of Mercy.

'I can't talk to you here and there's something I want to talk to you about very badly.'

'How's the Canadian romance?' I gave Sharon's piece a large tick. She at least hadn't thought mercy dripped through something resembling a kitchen sieve.

'It's over' he said in a small voice.

So that was it.

'I am sorry, Robin.'

'Can we meet?'

I looked up and saw Rhoda nearby. She gave me a knowing smile.

'How are the salamanders?' I asked.

'Cold and wet' she said wryly, and winked. 'Just like the family. You lucky loner ... Have you got a cat yet?'

'A cat?'

'Marge has got one. For companionship.'

'Thank you, Rhoda, but I am quite happy without one.'

Dunbar was confirmed.

If I had shaken off Robin, it was not so easy so far as my conscience was concerned to shake off Fred and Geraldine; I was delighted when they told me they were off to America. With them gone, flying to their beloved and heavily pregnant Portia, I was free of all constraint. Pan Am would cut the silver thread that linked me with those golden apples. My Atalantahood would thrive now, unthreatened – in all conscience I could once more bow out of society.

'We'll stay until the baby is born' said Geraldine 'and be back for Easter. And we'll just have to let the garden go for the time being.'

Fred smiled 'There are, after all, benefits to being a grand-father three times over ...'

'But you can't do much anyway' I said, looking out of my back room window where we were standing with our coffee cups. 'It's dead as death itself out there.'

It certainly looked it. Damp sulphurous light on last year's decay.

'Don't you believe it, my girl' said Geraldine. 'It's all happening. Getting ready for the final thrust. In a week or so's time we should be starting work on it.'

'From Valentine's Day on, Joan, she never gives me a moment's peace. Most people get cards or chocolates as tokens of esteem. Gerry takes me to the garden centre and lets me choose anything I want. And then I have to come back and use it, or plant it. After that there's no let up until December. Two months off a year – that's all she allows me ...'

Geraldine poked his stomach with her finger. 'You have to work this off, you know – all that Christmas excess.'

Please, I begged silently, don't display your long-won affection all over my dining room.

I took back my library books. The Orczy had been a mistake; I had cut off my nose to spite my face by sniping at Lawrence, for I had forgotten how romantic the Baroness could be. There comes a point in her tale where the proud and haughty Sir Percy, having publicly rejected his beautiful wife Marguerite, watches her go, and then bends to kiss every place her little hand has touched on the balustrade. Some of the not quite frozen ice-pop had flowed from my eyes at that part. You have to be careful with literature. There seem to be star-crossed lovers everywhere.

Of course, a couple of days later Jack rang. Well, he would, wouldn't he? I was hardly to be allowed the euphoria of a free conscience for long. He had to pop up.

'It's Jack.'

'Jack?'

'Yes. Jack.'

Back to the panto refrain again.

'Did you speak to my parents?'

'What? Oh yes. That was ages ago.'

'Well then?'

'Look. Can I come and see you?'

146

'Absolutely not ...' I twined the cord around my finger, not so much cross as bored.

'Very well then, I shall have to talk to you about it over the telephone.'

'When?'

'Now of course ...'

'Only I've got so much to do ...'

(Hemingway, Woolf, Proust.)

'It's extremely important.'

'Fire away then' I said sweetly.

'The thing is – well – I've met someone else.'

I looked at the cord which was looped very loosely and painlessly around my finger.

'Oh but Jack' I said. 'You can't have. It's not Christmas.'

'Pardon?'

'Never mind. Oh – and jolly good –'

'What?'

'That's fine.'

'I really do think you're off your rocker you know.'

'Well – that's not really your problem – is it?'

'It certainly is not.'

'Fidelity' I said 'is a funny word.'

'Joan – are you taking this in?'

'I am. Is she Irish?'

'What? No, she isn't bloody Irish. Just listen, will you?'

'Yes' I said meekly, letting the cord fall free.

'Now – don't get all excited. But I'm going to get my share of the house back.'

I wiggled my finger and bent it a couple of times and thought of that old James Bond line, What's a nice joint like this doing in a girl like you?

It made me titter.

'Hallo. Hallo. Are you there?'

'You can't do that, Jack.'

'I'm going to do that, Joan.'

He sounded very cross indeed.

'Ah well. If you do I shall have to get my income from somewhere else.'

'You can damn well do what you like but I don't see any reason why I should lose out any more. We can sell the place, split it fifty fifty – I'm quite prepared to be fair. You can get a flat somewhere. Prices have gone sky high in that part of London – you should get something decent with your share. All right, Joan? Have you understood all that?' His tone implied that it was only a remote chance that I had.

'I'm more glad for you than I can possibly say ...' American school. 'And I mean that most sincerely. I hope you will be very happy.'

'Thank you.' He sounded somewhat mollified. 'And you understand about the money?'

'Oh I understand ...'

'Good, good ...'

'I just don't agree ...'

'Very well – it will have to go through solicitors.'

'Very well – I shall just have to sell my story.'

'What?'

I wriggled my finger again.

'To the Sunday newspapers.'

'What story?'

'Television director leaves pregnant wife. Lonely abortion in hospital ward full of prostitutes (with apologies to the phlegmatic Rosie) – He Made Me Do It. Television director leaves Irish tart and attempts to have ex-wife thrown out on the street. I've no doubt I could get in touch with Irish. We could draft it together. It could be sensational ...'

'You are mad ...'

'Sent mad, Jack' I corrected. 'Anyway – it's next to genius ...'

'Don't try it.'

'Don't make me ...'

'We shall see' he said darkly.

'Indeed we shall. Was that all you rang about?'

'Joan ...' Warningly.

'... and threatens violence ...'

Dialling tone.

Curtain on Jack.

Mean bugger.

Robin made another attempt to get me alone by suggesting that we had lunch together. His face had lost some of its well-scrubbed freshness nowadays; it looked slightly tormented, more mature, and lines appeared on the smooth map of it. The doggy look had been replaced by something less open, more to do with inner struggle. Since no amount of my counselling myself made me entirely free from guilt, I felt tempted to accept the date – but what was the point? Sooner or later he would make the inevitable pass and I should feel even worse then. I had to admit, though, as I saw him cycling off, that however badly his spirit might be suffering, his body was still in excellent shape. Despite the low temperatures he only wore the bare essentials for the ride to and from school and now, as I watched those glistening muscular limbs pedalling across the playground, I thought of Adonis and how odd it was that despite all his extraordinary physical attractions, I was no Aphrodite, no Aphrodite at all ...

I decided that this was a very healthy sign and refused the consideration that it might have less to do with a healthy mind and more to do with one distracted elsewhere ...

That, I decided, was largely Robin's fault for his persistent conjecturing about our theatre tickets. Without this I was certain I would have forgotten all about the slight possibility of seeing Finbar Flynn again.

Chapter Three

Normally February is the most despicable of months because it plays on the desire for spring. It will give you one warm, sunny day in which you feel the sap rising and a belief that there is soon to be lived a life devoid of the nightly hot water bottle and a nipped raw nose. But the following two days will be dark as Jupiter's shadow on Promethean light, casting you back down into the pit. Happily I was under no such delusions: each day came, each day went and I was content. Debates on the weather forecast meant nothing to me.

About a week after the Durrells' departure I received a postcard from them; a nasty scene of skyscrapers against a harsh blue sky. How anyone can possibly suggest that New York is beautiful is beyond me. There was a cheerful little message on the back about the delights of being there, how well Portia was, etc., and a final postcript saying wistfully ' ... and say hallo to the garden for us as it's probably feeling very neglected ... ' I stuck it on the hall stand and went off to school.

I thought it very odd, since I so seldom received any post, to be greeted by Rhoda and Marjorie in the corridor saying 'Well – did you get any post this morning?' Followed by a huge wink from Rhoda. 'Poor old Marge didn't, did you?' Poor old Marge giggled and agreed.

'Not putting herself about enough, is she, Joan? But I bet you did get something, didn't you?'

Puzzled I said that I had received a card. Possibly Rhoda was running a project about the postal service with her kids and while I never got embroiled in staff conversations as a general rule, there seemed no point in denying my postcard.

'Only one?' said Rhoda.

'Only one' I agreed.

'Oh dear' she said mockingly, 'Still – one is better than none. And we all know who that's from, don't we?'

'Do we?' I said, quite lost.

'Oh well.' She patted Marjorie on the arm. 'Better luck next year. We'll have you tripping down the aisle yet.'

'You are awful' said Marjorie, simpering plumply above her beautifully made jacket.

Rhoda laughed and then looked over her shoulder at the sound of the entrance door banging. 'Ho Ho' she said. 'And here he is. Come along, Marjorie – this is no place for us.'

It was Robin, fresh from his morning's pedal. I gave him a quick smile across the distance and hurried off. His trainers thudded behind me, catching me up.

'Any news?' he panted.

What was this? Some sort of inquisition?'

'About what?' I said crossly. 'And why is everyone suddenly interested in my mail?'

'The tickets. The theatre ... Finbar Flynn was on the arts programme a couple of nights ago' (this I knew) 'and it sounds like a really exciting production.'

A funny little tickle in an unscratchable place began and I am afraid that the irritation came out through my mouth.

'No, there is not – now just leave it, will you? I don't want to hear another word on the subject.'

'Perhaps I could write to him. Have you got his address?'

'No' I said 'I have not got his address. I have not got the remotest idea where he lives.'

'I suppose' he said thoughtfully 'I could write to the theatre –

150

you know – care of – it does sound like a really exciting production. Don't you want to see it?'

'Robin' I said. 'You can always go and buy tickets, you know. You don't need Finbar Flynn to arrange it.'

'I know' he said eagerly. 'But he did say he'd like us to go – both of us – do you think he'd be cross if I reminded him?'

The bell rang for assembly.

'Christ!' he said 'must go.' And he dived into the men's lavatory to effect his superman change.

Back home in the bliss of my quiet I dumped my bags in the hall. There was the amazingly interesting postcard with its ugly skyline. Remembering Geraldine's wistful postscript I thought that the least I could do was to oblige, so out into the back garden I went. I looked over their hedge at their sad orphan, which was still not half so neglected looking as mine, and said 'Hallo from your owners. They send you their love.' Duty done I tramped back across the soggy ground.

It was one of those in-between February days – as if Dame Nature could not quite make up her mind; warm and dull, not quite so bad as a hump-day but certainly not full of the joys of spring. As I passed one of the overgrown tubs on my patio I saw a fresh green finger poking up out of all that exhausted bindweed – and another, and another; these were the bulbs that Jack and I had put in the autumn before last, I had forgotten them. Narcissus, daffodils, tulips – all set before the final curtain fell on our jolly let's-do-it-together world. Somehow I had missed them last year. How far reaching are the tentacles of Nature.

Waiting for the pang I was happy it did not come. Jack was completely exorcised and no bruising remained. They were, after all, just pieces of growth and had no emotional hold at all.

I don't suppose the Durrells would have graced it with the term gardening, but all the same, I stayed out there for a while pulling weeds off the tubs and grabbing handfuls of wet greenery from the stone troughs that bordered the patio, finding evidence everywhere of the coming spring. I enjoyed the rhythm of it – grab, pull, chuck – grab, pull, chuck – and the satisfying piles of discarded matter that grew up all around me. Indiscriminate weeding is a real joy. I even found evidence of a rat – some half chewed lumps of bread – and our barbecue tongs,

151

now dignified into Roman artefacts by the weather. I decided it was the rat and me against Maud and Reggie: I would not betray it.

During this burst of horticulture I discovered the first real flowers of the year – some pink and yellow clumps of primulas – a little damp and unsure, their florets like newly hatched chicks, half unfurled. They were very pretty and I was pleased to have uncovered them. I cleared the soil around them and then, ready for my lunch, I went in.

Even such a short piece of physical activity gave me a sense of righteousness and I went to bed soon after, snuggling down under the duvet with a feeling of achievement rewarded. Life on your own is full of such perks. Virginia Woolf slumped onto my chest as I drifted into a deep and tranquil sleep. If the condemned man ate a hearty breakfast, the condemned woman went to her fate very well rested indeed. Considering the rigours of the night ahead, this was just as well.

Normally I listened to the Radio Three concert in the bath, renewing the water from time to time. But since the night when, lying there listening to the same arts programme Robin had quoted, I had reached out a dripping hand to switch it off smartly (in the name of protection from even more of Finbar Flynn), it had become useless for music. So I had to reassemble. Have the bath first, then go downstairs to listen. When you live alone such things become wonderfully important. I had a lovely long soak throughout the first part, Bartók, because I didn't mind that being loudly interrupted by raspberries. Indeed, it might even be considered an improvement. But when it was over and the soft voiced announcer (where do they get them? They are fabulous creatures) said that the first half was over and that there would now follow a short talk on medieval ivories before part two, which was Sibelius' First, I got out and dried straight away. Sibelius' First is not something to have interrupted by electronic farting. You could have an orgasm over that opening string crescendo. Indeed, I would opine, there is something seriously wrong with you if you can't.

So it was out of the bath while the ivory expert wittered silkily on, and into my Victorian nightie with lots of ruffles round neck and hem – very warm for the winter if a little recherché for the lone sleeper – and downstairs to the front room stereo. Perhaps

152

because of that afternoon's gardening I felt something stronger than cocoa was appropriate but looking through the cupboard there was nothing; I had finished off the brandy with my parents.

This was a blow. From the front room I could recognise from the slight rise in the speaker's voice that thirteenth-century carving was almost explained. Drone, drone, it went on its usual non-contemporary path – why don't they ever have some modern topic during the interval? Medieval ivories indeed!

So – no brandy or anything else – and Sibelius imminent. And then I remembered the vodka bottle which I had taken from its position of admonishment and hidden when my parents came to stay. Swish, swish went the ruffles and lace as I went off to get it. One minute to go. I poured just a little into my glass, banishing reminders, and swish swished my way into the front room to stretch myself out like some Millais heroine. Here, I told myself, is private joy, as those first bowel-liquifying strains of enchantment smote the air. I was glad the conductor had been kind to the score for he let it go slowly, slowly ... Supine in all the heat from my maximised central heating I lay there like some hot-house flower, a cream petalled orchid shut off from the world, only me and the music and the little splash of vodka in the glass.

Da dum de dee dum – plink plink – Da dum de dee dum –

When the doorbell rang I couldn't believe it. I really just could not believe it. And so much could I not believe it that I went to the door perfectly convinced that I was right. I even opened the door convinced of this. Swung it back on its hinges expecting only a blankness, still carried along by the soaring strains of Sibelius, drowing in the heat and the fullness of sound.

But doorbells need fingers and fingers are always connected to something, are they not?

Chapter Four

I hadn't turned the hall light on. Well – I wouldn't have, would I? Not expecting anyone to be there. But even in that darkness I knew who it was – Oh yes – despite all that shadow and with him half crouched over a large bunch of flowers, a plastic carrier bag and a big, wrapped box of something – I knew all right. He didn't even have to say anything – which, indeed, he seemed to have difficulty over – because there was no doubt at all that standing on my doorstep and letting in the cold night air was Finbar Flynn. A fleeting thought – very fleeting – was that at least it wasn't Jack. It is not Jack, I thought, it is Finbar Flynn.

'Oh no' I said – and then again, much louder 'Oh no, oh no – not you ...'

And he, no doubt with that actorly skill of the well turned phrase, replied with equal positivism 'Christ all-bloody-mighty ...' as he looked me up and down.

Thus we stood for a microparticle of a second before he added 'Your usual warm welcome, Geranium. Needless to say I am overcome with the warmth of your delight ...'

And then he had the affrontery to burst out laughing, fillings and all, though of course I could not see those in the gloom.

'Well, well ... I expected something a bit out of the ordinary – but not this –' He made a sort of teetering gesture among the flowers and packages. 'This is extraordinary. Do you always dress up like this when you're at home?' He wriggled a finger free from the various burdens and pointed at my hand, which was, of course, holding a glass. 'The usual, is it?' he said. 'My ... my Geranium – you really are quite a girl. May I come in?'

And wriggling past me, in he came.

Ecce Homo, I thought, mesmerised.

To say that the conjuring Faustus could not have been more surprised would have been to pretend. To say that Godiva on a blowy day could not have been more embarrassed would have been an understatement. And to say that I was sorry to see him would have been, to call up Byron for a moment, a masquerade of the truth. The best gifts, after all, are the ones that you don't know you want until you get them.

I switched on the light thinking it might – possibly – dispel him – but the scent of the flowers remained, like him, and while you may invent the sight of something, inventing its smell is far less easy. He was there all right.

'Shall I go in?' he said, already halfway around the door of the front room, peering as if he might find someone else in there. 'All alone, are you?'

No single female should ever acknowledge to a male whom she knows only in passing that she is alone at night in her house.

Fifth Dimension rule number one. They may, just possibly, have designs on you. You should never do it.

'Quite alone' I sang out. 'There is no-one here. Absolutely no-one. I am quite and utterly on my own.'

I followed him into the music filled room and just to be sure he had heard I added 'Nobody here. See? Not a sausage.'

'Ah' he said non-committally. Then, negotiating his baggage, he pointed from the door to the window. 'Walk from here to there' he said.

I did so.

'Straight as a die –' he said admiringly. 'Look at that. Geranium – I salute you. You can certainly hold it.'

The music soared all around us.

'Let me tell you' I said, turning to make the point more forcefully 'that I have not been drinking at all.'

Whereupon my foot got tangled in a ruffle and I fell over – right – as it were – in the second Andante ...

'Bad luck' he said. 'So have I.' And he deposited everything he was carrying on the settee before reaching out a helping hand which dignity forbade me to take.

I turned the music down. I couldn't take both it and him at the same time. There was already a pumping and hissing going on in my head as if some steam had got trapped somewhere – at least lowering the music acted as a small safety valve. Slightly calmed I said, and not very graciously 'And what are you doing here?'

'I bring you gifts ...' He gestured towards the strewn settee. 'Why?'

'Don't you like gifts?'

'I mean – why have you come?'

I don't know what I expected really. Him to fall to his knees and beat his breast and say that he had come because he could no longer stay away seemed quite a nice development but that didn't seem likely. He did have a wild look in his eye but not that kind of wild look – more of the hunted variety – and when he said 'I've come to take refuge because I've had an appalling day ...' I realised that he was very far from any such meaty declaration ... Yet ...

'I spent the morning at the airport saying goodbye to a friend who I thought might have cared enough to stay for my opening. Then I had lunch with Jimbo and some asinine film producer

155

from Texas who acts like a caricature of himself and who wants me in his next movie. And then I dried very badly in rehearsal this afternoon – which is not surprising since Jim and this Texan were sitting out there assessing the size of my biceps in case I might need intensive training for the part.'

'What part?'

He gave a little shudder and closed his eyes for a second. 'This Texan – who, I should say, is very much Born Again, wants me to play a boxer! Me!'

'You don't have to, do you?'

'No, my dear innocent flower, I do not have to ...' He prodded my shoulder with his finger. 'But when you are talking about some deal involving half a million dollars – and you have an agent like Jim who has been busting a gut to pull it off – and you like your agent – try saying no. Anyway – this evening I just walked out of a photographic session arranged by him with one of the women's glossies.'

'Oh' I said, interested. 'Which one?'

'I don't know ...' he said peevishly. 'I didn't ask. But I drew the line at being photographed in a church round the back of the studio for something that would no doubt be captioned "FF takes a brief moment out of his hectic day for spiritual solace ..." The Irish connection you see.'

'But you're from Tunbridge Wells ...'

He put his finger to his lips. 'Ssh my dear – walls have ears ...' he said mockingly.

'Well, I suppose all this is just par for the course.'

Terrific use of the language, that.

'Ye Gods' he said. 'Don't you start' and he made a magnificent gesture of appeal to my ceiling. 'All I ever wanted to do was act – preferably on the stage – and be myself the rest of the time. And now all this ...'

'Would you like a drink?' I asked. 'I've only got some vodka.'

'You mean' he said hammily, clasping his hands to his chest and falling to one knee 'that you are going to let me stay?'

For an awful moment I thought I was going to yell Geronimo and throw myself on top of him but fortunately he righted himself very quickly and the danger passed.

'I wouldn't dream of taking your life's blood from you.' He reached for a plastic bag off the settee. 'I've brought my own.' He removed a bottle of whisky.

Glass in hand he said "This is very naughty of me. I've got an eight-thirty sword practice with Aufidius tomorrow morning.'

'Who's that?'

'I thought you were gifted with a wisdom that is infinite. I'm disappointed. Aufidius is my greatest enemy. Apart, of course, from vaulting ambition.'

'Oh – in the play.'

'Of course in the play. You don't seriously think that I go round with friends called things like that, do you? I mean, even I draw the line somewhere. Why are you dressed in that wonderful gown?'

'It's my nightdress.'

'I'm sorry' he said quite seriously, looking at his watch. 'It's not very late. I had no idea you were going to bed.'

'I wasn't. I put it on to listen to the radio.'

'Naturally' he said shrugging. 'She put it on to listen to the radio – how very silly of me ...'

'Won't you sit down?' I indicated the settee.

He picked up the flowers and handed them to me. 'You'd better put these in water or gin or whatever strange females like you do with such things.'

He followed me out to the kitchen. 'You really are weird, you know. I like that. And it's not artificial, is it? I can tell artifice, there's a lot of it about in my business. But you are the genuine article. Naturally odd.'

I tried as hard as I could to look normal which was difficult in a long white nightie holding a glass of vodka in one hand and a bunch of flowers in the other.

'It's a very neat kitchen' he said. 'Where do you keep your potions?'

I filled a milk bottle with water and plonked in the flowers – I was past being able to find a vase.

'It's easy to be neat when you live on your own.'

'Not in my case it's not.' He laughed. 'Why don't you and Robin live together?'

'Because me and Robin are not –'

He held up his hand 'None of my business anyway' he said airily. 'Freesias. Lovely smell. You could stick one in your hair if you wanted. I'm quite broad minded about such things as you know ...' He picked at a piece of paint on the door. 'You and Robin are not what?'

157

'Look' I said 'I want to clear something up – about me and Robin ...'

'Which reminds me ...' He began fishing about among the swathes of white coat, that well remembered garment, and digging into the pockets of his jeans.

'Why don't you take your coat off if you're staying?'

He sauntered out to the hall and threw it over the banister.

One layer down, I thought, assessing the grey polo neck and tweedy jacket that remained, and about three to go.

While he fumbled about with his coat I went back into the front room and switched off the music – which I now did not need. He followed me in holding two white envelopes and his glass in one hand, and my postcard from Fred and Geraldine in the other.

'New York' he said. 'Isn't it just beautiful?'

'Oh yes' I agreed, staring at the picture with him. 'One of the most beautiful skylines on earth.'

'One of my favourite views' he said.

'Mine too' I replied. 'What a coincidence.'

He handed me one of the envelopes. 'Your ticket for the play. Pity the Durrells will miss it. I've got one for your Robin here as well ...'

'He really isn't my Robin. We are just friends – colleagues – that's all.'

'Well then' he said 'if it will compromise you, give me his address and I'll send it to him.'

'Don't be silly' I said, taking it and putting them both on the mantelpiece 'I see him every day. I can give it to him tomorrow. Now do – please – sit down.' I pointed at the settee.

He sat.

And immediately leapt up again.

He had landed on the last and biggest of his packages.

'I nearly forgot' he said. 'This is for you. I've got rather an excess of them. Happy Valentine's Day – an odd token of esteem, I know – but a useful one ...'

Now I realised what Rhoda meant. Just fancy – I had come far enough along my independent road to forget all about St Valentine. I looked at Finbar's agreeable face. Was it really worth giving up all that journeying for? I tore at the wrapping paper without answering.

What could it be? Something to wear? Something useful, he

had said – a wine cooler for those intimate little dinners, perhaps, or a piece of crystal to hold the future flowers?

'I'm going to get absolutely stinking tonight, Geranium – if you don't mind?'

'Be my guest ...' I pointed at his bottle and went on removing paper.

'Will you take a little ... ?'

I shook my head as the last bit of wrapping floated to the floor. I was happy enough getting drunk on him.

'Hope you like it' he said eagerly. 'It's one of the smarter ones.' I slipped my hands into the box and removed a shining chromium object. It was a toaster.

'I seem to have rather a lot of them' he said ruefully. 'They keep arriving from all over the place ...'

'Why, thank you, Finbar' I said.

Was ever fair woman won by so technological means?

'I was on a chat show a few weeks ago. Did you see it?'

'I try to avoid such things.'

Always truthful where I can be, you see.

I was certain that he showed the faintest glimmer of relief at this.

'Quite right' he said. 'They are the lowest form of life. All they really want to know about is who's fucking whom, when and how often. *Coriolanus* could have been a musical on ice for all that idiot who fronts it cared.'

'Why do it then?'

'As you said, my dear, par for the course. My agent fixed it up – dear Jim – so painstaking with my publicity.' He finished his drink and poured another and then sat there looking at me with troubled eyes. 'Geranium – do you care about money?'

'You're a fool if you don't.'

'But big money – I mean thousand and thousand of pounds.'

'No' I said, on easy, honest ground. 'As long as I can live comfortably and run my car – I am content.'

'I am content' he repeated emotionally. 'You really are a rare bird. How old are you.'

'Nearly thirty-two.'

'I'm nearly forty' he said. 'Perhaps that makes the difference. Time runs like sand from now on – there's so much I want to do – if I bring off this movie I can do so much ...' He was beginning to slur very slightly which I took as a good sign. He

159

sighed. 'But there are always things you have to give up –' he wagged his finger around as if declaiming to an audience ' – things that don't fit into the received pattern of success. Do you know what I mean, Geranium, do you know what I mean?'

I hadn't a clue but since something was required of me said 'Never mind, Finbar – the riches are not the end – it's the use you plan to make of them that counts ...'

'You're absolutely wonderful.' He patted me like a dog which made me shiver despite the intense heat of the room. 'How can you know so much and yet be so young?'

'Actually I think Napoleon said that originally. But I'm sure it's true in your case.'

'I had plans, you see, for an alternative theatre – but that's all up in the air now –' And then he burst out laughing. 'Genuinely up in the air – because I was going to do it with Ricky but he's flown off to New York. Jim got him something juicy. You can't blame him – '

'He wasn't very nice.' I said.

'No. He wasn't. But he could act like a dream. Above everything that's important.'

'You seem very depressed' I said.

'Really? I can't think why ... I mean ... it's caviar all the way now and here I am with a lovely young woman in her night-dress.' He laughed again.

'Come on, Geranium – let's have another drink.'

Some people go puce and sweat a lot when they drink heavily; some slobber, some dribble. Others become aggressive or ugly or both. But Finbar just got more and more attractive and I just became more and more seduced.

'Quote me something' he said after a while. 'Like you did once before. Something with a bit of hope to it – Eliot again if you can. I love Eliot ...' He lay back in the settee and said dreamily 'Hope, the green shoot upon the withered bough – that's what I need. Spring to follow winter ...' He sat up and looked at me before lapsing into soliloquy again. 'You alone can bring hope to me ...'

I wasn't quite sure how to proceed. Taken verbatim this was all very encouraging but he didn't seem to be pursuing the physical side very much. I thought about our lips melting into each others in a dewy embrace but as his head was about a yard away from mine, and as I'd have had to cross the dangerous

160

terrain of his knees to get to it, and still be an athlete to achieve contact, it was out of the question. He was still soliloquising away about hope and beauty and truth and his apparent belief that I could supply – or already had supplied, I'm not sure which – some or all of these. 'You have the key, you lovely girl, you have the key ...'

I decided to get moving, spurred on by my own desire.

'You look exactly like that portrait of Edmund Kean in the National when you put your chin on your hand like that.'

His eyes, glazed with romantic soliloquy, suddenly cleared and he sat bolt upright. 'Don't you want to know what the key is?'

'Oh yes' I said, rushing on, getting right into the gallop now the game was truly afoot – and deciding at that very moment that have him I would – 'Oh Finbar, everything about you interests me.'

That pleased him. We all like a bit of flattery, don't we? I was quite pleased with myself – after all, I'd never seduced anyone before. I rather preferred this side of things, this being on the attack instead of always on the offensive.

Ho, ho, me proud beauty, I thought, twirling an imaginary moustache and carving the first notch on my gold handled cane.

'Does it?' he said. 'Everything?'

I nodded.

'Not because I'm famous actor Finbar Flynn?'

'Not at all.' I tried to suggest that such things were ten a penny in my world. 'It's just that you've got a specialness about you. A presence. A gift, I suppose.' I drew a circle lightly on his bony knee wondering what to say next – my husband doesn't understand me, perhaps?

'Thank you' he said, and leaned towards me. 'And so have you.'

At last, at last we were getting somewhere.

'I find you very attractive' I said as huskily as I could. 'But not just your –' I gestured in the general direction of his body ' – but your mind. Of course that sort of voices the body's interests, doesn't it? Have another drink.'

He drank.

'Geranium' he said 'you tempt me. You are a peculiar young woman and I have no idea how to take you –'

I just about stopped myself from saying Why worry, just take

161

me ... 'And thank you for being so kind, so warm, so generous and so hos-pit-able.' He had trouble enunciating this last and peered into his empty glass. I thought he had drunk enough for a while; there was no sense in overdoing it; I didn't want him flat on his back ... I was saving that.

'Why don't you take off your jacket? It's very warm in here.' I put my hand on his knee and he did not remove it. A good sign that.

'You were always so rude to me – ' he said sadly.

'It's a bit like adolescents. Always rudest to the one they fancy the most.'

'Extraordinary.' He wiped his hand over his face. 'I think I will take my jacket off if you don't mind. It is very hot –' He stood up but this time I was ready for him and moved my chin well out of knee shot.

The jacket was consigned to its partner, the white coat.

When I returned he said 'You were going to quote something with a little hope in it for me. You know you recite very well for someone who's untrained. There's something delicious about you, Geranium – had we but world enough and time ...'

'I've got a good memory. You can be much more confident with the lines if you know you aren't going to forget them.' I gave him a very slight push and he plopped back down onto the settee. I resumed my hunched cross-leggedness at his feet. Given this troll-like position it was difficult to get a seductive pitch into my voice, but I did my best. It was either this or strip poker and I preferred poetics. A gender preference perhaps?

And so I began

> In the juvescence of the
> year

'It's juvenescence. Hah! Your memory's failed you for once.'

'No, it hasn't ... he's just shortened it for the rhythm.'

'That's cheating' he mumbled.

'Shakespeare does it all the time.'

'But –'

'Be quiet!'

Not for nothing was I an experienced schoolmistress.

> In the juvescence of the
> year
> Came Christ the tiger

162

In depraved May, dogwood and chestnut, flowering
judas
To be eaten, to be divided, to be drunk –

'Ah!' he said savagely 'To be drunk ... What's all that about
then?' I ignored him. I was desperately trying to give him a sense
of the sap rising.

'Spring' I said soothingly. 'It's all about spring – the green
shoot – just the kind of thing you've been talking about ...'

I beg the poet's forgiveness for misrepresenting him.

'Spring! That's what I need. Buds bursting and a little bit of
hope – just a teeny one – What about the April and the Lilacs
one?'

God, it was like being a New Wave disc jockey when the
punters only wanted Beatles and Rolling Stones. SingalongaEliot.
But it was still marginally better than strip poker. Anyway, I
didn't have very much to take off.

I began

> April is the cruellest month, breeding
> Lilacs out of the dead land, mixing
> Memory and desire –

I stared at him very hard and was delighted to see that he was
listening enraptured – if a little unfocused.

> ... stirring
> Dull roots with spring rain.
> Winter kept us warm, covering
> Earth in forgetful snow, feeding
> A little life with dried tubers ...

I felt a sudden deep sadness. You can't keep a shaft of pure
poetry at bay, it always finds you out. It has been around for too
long and knows us too well even if we refuse to acknowledge it.
It had certainly touched my soul – his too –

'Don't stop' he said. 'But it's so sad. Not full of the joys of
spring at all – only regrets ...'

'Perhaps spring is the saddest time. All that young life coming
on, budding out, pushing upwards, only to take that slow
inescapable journey towards certain death and decay. No – I
think winter is best. The deed is done then and nobody expects
anything anymore. Hope doesn't play its silly tricks ...'

163

'Here.' He handed me my glass and poured more whisky into each. 'You were the one who's supposed to be cheering me up, remember? I'm the one who's supposed to be miserable.'

'I think' I said 'that it might be a case of the blind leading the lame.' He put his head in his hands and rumpled his hair. Something in the way those curls pulled and sprang around his fingers brought me back into the sphere of the physical – desire was still functioning on all cylinders. I slid my untouched glass out of sight.

'There is no spring' he said into his chest.

'Of course there is.' I stroked his hair.

'Comfort' he said 'I need comfort, and a friend, and spring, spring everywhere. I need.'

I had never equated the word comfort with any erotic sense before but now the two made a partnership somewhere in my mind.

Stumbling over the hem of my nightdress and thence the toaster (Godammit, was this any way to make an impression?) I grabbed his hand and pulled him up – he came as lightly as a baby – 'I'll show you a bit of spring' I said, heaving him gently along the passage and into the kitchen. I found a torch – one's needs must when the devil drives, I didn't even know I had one that worked – 'A lovely bit of spring. This will cheer you up.' I flung open the back door. His hand felt even hotter than mine, not surprising with a polo necked sweater and eighty degrees F.

'Lovely, lovely' he said, stumbling a little down the steps. 'Just as you are being lovely ... Comfort' he called to the night 'Comfort and hope – what benefits a man if he has not this?'

'Yes, yes' I said, hurrying him along. 'Here we are.'

I stopped at the stone tub and shone the torch on the primulas. They looked slightly perkier now the weeds had gone.

'See' I said. 'Spring has sprung.'

He peered at them and then said 'So it has. Aren't they exquisite?' and he reached out to touch them, saying 'Thou shalt not lack the flower that's like thy face, pale primrose ...'

'What's that' I asked, interested.

'Cymbeline.'

'Don't know it.'

'Oh' he said, tickling at the florets with his finger. 'It's the usual mix of love and treachery. You know Shakespeare. I was Iachimo. Good part.'

164

'Love doesn't always have to be treacherous. Only in plays and books and things. In real life it can be – well – very nice ...'

It seemed odd that I should be sticking up for it.

'Love, my dear girl, is always treacherous – and always nice ...'

He stood up.

'I'm a bit cold' I said.

'Let's go in then.'

'Why don't you just put your arms around me and keep me warm?' I snuggled up to him. 'I don't want to go in yet. It's so beautiful out here.'

I prayed his inebriation would stop him actually investigating this remark which was patently untrue. It was not remotely beautiful. The night was cloudy, the air raw, the dark patch of my garden full of dim depressing shapes and all around our feet were sodden piles of weeds. We were in no starlit bower by any stretch of the imagination. I wriggled myself closer into the jumper and he put his arms around me with reasonable enthusiasm.

'You smell nice' he said.

I realised that the cold air was sobering him up a little. Never mind, I could always top him up when we went back in.

'Do you know who I was doing this with earlier this evening?' he laughed. I kept my breathing as even as possible and said gaily, if a little muffled 'No – who?'

'Marion French.'

'The actress?'

'The filmstar' he corrected.

'Is she a friend of yours?'

Breathe, wait, breathe ...

'No' he laughed. 'Never met her before. She was on this photo-session – just bosoming in.'

And relax ...

'Why was she there?'

'Her agent's pushing her for this boxing film ...'

I could feel his heart if I stayed quite still.

'... excellent box office ...'

'She's very beautiful.'

'She's a pain in the arse.'

I loved the woman.

'I wouldn't mind looking like her.'

'You could probably act her into the ground.'

165

'She's very sexy.' I snuggled nearer and tried to ignore the way our feet were slipping on the sludgy weeds.

'She's awful. She must have been wearing a ton of steel under her mink. All I could feel were these tits sticking into me like under-ripe melons.'

'Sorry' I said, backing off.

'That's all right' he said kindly. 'I can't feel yours at all.' Just about the most backhanded compliment I've ever had. He swayed a little and said 'Whoops' which was encouraging.

'Will she get the part? In the film?'

'Not a hope' he said happily. 'Clayton Junior is very Christian. He jus' caint abahde promiscooty. He wants everythin ter be goo-ood, an Christian, an 'bove bowerd. Nuthin sin-full. Right?'

'What is sin, anyway? Besides, Let those among you without it ...' I said.

'Just what I told Jimbo.' He took my head in his hands and kissed me right between the eyes. 'Are all eccentrics as perceptive as you?'

I shivered.

'Come on' he said, putting his arm round my shoulders 'it's cold and you're shivering – we should go in.' He turned and gave a neat little bow towards the primulas. 'Thank you, my dears, for your vernal display ...'

I leapt ahead of him and turned off the light in the kitchen – they have a terrible way of dispelling moods.

'Let's dance' I said back in the heat of the front room. 'Let's have a party. Eat, drink and be merry (my desperate desire was echoed by desperate creepiness) for tomorrow we –'

'Actually' he said 'I could do with something to eat.'

'Here, have a whisky.' I poured a great glug of it into his glass. 'Go on, spoil yourself. You said you were going to get stinking ...'

And while he stood there with the drink in his hand I twiddled the dial on the old steam radio.

If you look for signs you surely find them. Some thoughtful soul had chosen to play Ella Fitzgerald for their night travellers. She was crooning 'The stars fell on Alabama ... My arms wound around you tight' and we clung to each other going round and round to the music with me occasionally stopping and helping him to whisky.

166

We moved out of Alabama into a Blue Moon and I held on to his bottom which was a very nice one, and round and round we went again.

'And then suddenly I saw before me, the only one my heart could ever know ...'

'You're amazing' he whispered in my ear.

'Am I' I said softly.

'Yes' he said. 'You know all the words.'

I tickled his neck.

He wriggled his shoulders.

'Kiss me' I said. I felt really nervous – not at all like the confident temptress I fondly imagined I could be. Still, one of us had to get the thing moving, we couldn't stand there shuffling around all night. 'Finbar' I said – 'Aren't you a bit hot?' It was a silly question – heat radiated from him.

'Yes' he murmured, somewhere near my ear.

'Have a cooling drink –' I held it for him and he drank, looking over the top like an obedient child.

'Why not slip out of your sweater?'

'Are you trying to seduce me, Geranium?'

'Yes' I said firmly.

Why prevaricate?

'You're a lovely girl' he said. 'And very alluring.' And then he hiccoughed.

We slid rather ham-footedly up the stairs and I sort of propped him by the lavatory door while we joined in the struggle to remove his jumper. Roll necks are the pits when it comes to a smooth take off.

'Lovely, lovely girl' he was murmuring.

'Lovely, lovely man' I reiterated, tugging at his neck and nearly decapitating him.

Well, we got that off and successfully made it to the bedroom. I began to think that I had overdone it with the drink when he took on a new kind of dignity – he slid off his shoes and removed his socks. Then, standing up all by himself, with a snap, pull, twang – he was out of his jeans, hurling away his underpants and prone on the bed in a welter of wonderful nakedness.

And deeply and unashamedly asleep.

Me, the Archbishop of Canterbury, and the Queen. All three perfectly safe from AIDS.

I bunched in beside him as best I could, put my face close to his and opened one of his eyes with my fingers. It gave a little roll, twitched, and closed again. I ran my hand over his back but nothing stirred. He was beautifully made – perfect for his intended role as a boxer – perfect for the role I had intended him for too. I sighed, trying to get used to someone being there in bed beside me after all this time. I shall never get to sleep was just about the last conscious thought I had that night.

Chapter Five

It was a moment or two before I could place the noise. There was a beam of sunlight across my eyes which made me blink and close them again. The fretful noise was repeated, followed by a thud. I remembered, and stretched, and hoped that I didn't look too frowzy. I opened one eye and let the sunlight's force recede a little. Then I looked. What I saw was a naked man, hopping on one foot with the other hopelessly entangled in a pair of underpants, alternately making weak gestures at the scrunched up cotton and his head; he was moving like an animal in terrible pain.

'Oh God' he was uttering. 'Oh God. Oh God ...' Then, giving up the battle, he fell crumpling to the floor. He groaned again and moaned softly. 'My head ... my head ...'

'A kingdom for my head.' I giggled.

'That's not at all funny' said the muffled voice from somewhere between his knees.

A masculine foot, quite perfect since it had never had to bow to the exigencies of shoe fashion, poked its way gingerly into the leghole of its Y-fronts; its companion, still with a tiny stiletto mark faintly visible, continued to thrash about for a time until it, too, found its goal; the waistband was clutched, he stood up with another groan and the elastic twanged into place around his midriff. He stood there for some moments like an ailing Hercules, weakly triumphant. A frisson of excitement made me pat the empty space beside me.

'Come and lie down' I said, fondly imagining myself like some sloe-eyed siren.

'Where are my trousers?' he said with all the peremptory irritation that goes with a hangover. I pitied him. This was no time to try to consolidate. I put the sloe-eyed siren back into her depraved boudoir and went to help him. After all, it was mostly my fault that he was in such a state. I pulled the curtains against the brilliant sun, found his jeans and carried them across the room.

I thought about telling him how I felt. And saying 'I love you Finbar' would have been so nice – but – really – he was in no condition for it. Instead I held out his jeans. 'Now – just put your foot in there ...'

He tried and failed.

'Lean on me.'

He did.

Giving one more groan he negotiated first one leg, then the other. I pulled them to waist level but left him to do them up: why associate myself with the loss of potential?

'Thank you' he said humbly. His eyes were closed and he looked pale. I kissed his cheek. 'Coffee' he pleaded. 'I need coffee ...'

'Rubbish' I said. 'What you need is water. Gallons and gallons of it to rehydrate you.' I had a wonderfully erotic thought. 'Why not have a bath? You might feel better then ... ?'

'No time' he mumbled, making vague flapping motions at a tee-shirt. 'I'm supposed to be getting the sword fight sorted out ... Oh God, Oh God!' He held his head in his hands. 'I feel terrible.'

I stroked his temple with my finger.

'You're very sweet' he said miserably. 'I apologise for being in such a mess. God – I didn't think I'd drunk that much ...'

'I'll get you an Alka Seltzer ...' I picked up my nightdress and put it on – it seemed unlikely that there would be any reason not to – and went downstairs.

When I returned with the fizzing glass he said tersely 'How come you're so bright this morning?' He winced. 'Oh but I forgot – you're practically pickled anyway –' He made a brave attempt at a jokey smile which came out looking like Danton's death mask and touched my cheek. 'You look remarkably fresh.'

I almost confessed why, but didn't. Instead emerged a hopeful 'I think you ought to have a bath.'

'No time. Where's my sweater?' We found it on the landing, all tangled up outside the lavatory door.

'Finbar' I said 'You're not being very gallant – considering what happened last night.' I cast my eyes downward and simpered. It was not the most opportune moment to say it as he had just drained the fizzing glass.

'Oh Christ' he said, and burped.

'Better now?' I hazarded.

'No' he said. 'Worse ... Forgive me please – both for this and for last night – I should never have come here disturbing your peaceful life with my problems.'

I went and collected his shoes and socks, sighing over their abandonment, but it was too late for fond memory. I thought about hiding them under the bed but realised this was useless and took them back to him, plonking them down like a sacrifice. Then I put my arms around his waist and put my head sideways onto his chest. It was awful in there – I could hear bubblings and poppings and the complainings of many organs.

'I enjoyed it' I said. 'Don't apologise. I haven't had so much fun in a long time.'

He pushed me away a little holding on to my arms and looking down at me with concern. 'Fun?' he said. 'Have I ...' He looked up at the ceiling, back at me, and then at the ceiling again. 'Did I –' he repeated the motion as if it was some sort of neck exercise 'I mean – so far as I know – I think I remember everything quite clearly – the poems, the flowers, the dancing afterwards – there isn't something I've left out – is there?'

'Oh no' I said. 'You remember everything quite clearly. Would it matter very much if you didn't ...?'

'I don't know' he said. 'It depends what bit I might have forgotten.'

'I don't think there was very much to forget, Finbar.'

Worse luck.

'I shouldn't like to hurt you.'

'But you wouldn't.'

He held my head down into his chest and kissed the top of it. 'You're a wicked flirt, Geranium.'

'So are you.'

'Oh Jesus,' he said, squeezing his forehead as if it might wring out all the suffering, 'I must go. Really. It's about the least professional thing you can do to turn up late for rehearsals when you're at the critical stage we are.'

'I'm sorry' I said, letting him go.

'It's not your fault' he said, pinching my chin, 'I'm big enough

170

and ugly enough to take full responsibility. After all – you didn't force the drink on me, now did you?' He winced.

I confess that I shook my head.

We began plucking at his shoes and socks.

Oh the banalities of reality.

'What about the film, Finbar?'

He was struggling with his shoes as if he had never seen such objects before. I waited in respectful silence until the aliens were secured.

'Will you take it on?' He didn't look as if he could take on anything much but I felt conversation was called for. He rose up from the ground, clearly moved by his achievement.

'Oh – I shall do it of course. I was just putting myself through all this angst so that I'd feel better about succumbing to the loot.'

'It doesn't really matter what roles you do does it? I mean, someone once said that an actor is like a sculptor who carves in the snow ...'

He considered this. 'That's all right when you're talking about theatre – but film is different – it's there for all time. But no matter – I shall take it on – and behave myself and be a good boy so that Clayton Junior can Praise the Lawd fo' mah virgeen sheet. Ha-Le-Loo-Yah!' Then he put his hands back to his head and groaned once more and began negotiating the stairs.

He really was very nearly as pale as his coat but haggard and unshaven as he was, he was still the most attractive man it had ever been my misfortune to not know carnally. And I could see, when he swirled the coat about him, that he had become an actor again; he just grew into it.

'You've never seen me acting, have you?'

'Oh I've seen you all right – you're acting all the time. Go on' I said, for I knew that I had lost the moment 'you'd better get a move on.' And I pushed past him to open the door.

Sunlight flooded in making me blink. He shaded his eyes and walked out into it.

'When ... ?' I began, but he gave a little whimper against the light.

'Weeks and weeks of dull days and nature has to choose this morning to shine out – Oh well, I suppose that's justice of a sort.' He stepped over the threshold and out on to the path. He turned. 'Oh dear, oh dear Geranium – what have I done? Does forgiveness feature in your exotic world?'

171

And then, like a knife out of hell, a voice cut across the peace of the morning air.

'Joan' it said. 'Is that you?' It was Maud Montgomery, bobbing her coiffure over my fence, her eyes alight with triumph. 'I thought you'd like to know that we've caught the – er –'

She looked at Finbar Flynn, who looked back at her with a shudder and a loud groan. Her voice was difficult enough to take in robust health, but cutting into a hangover it must have been murderous.

'Oh' she screeched. 'So sorry ...'

He groaned again.

'... I had no idea you had a guest.'

'... Pox?' said Finbar vengefully.

'Pardon?'

A combination of laughter and tears jostled inside me. How could she have interrupted just at that point? But laughter won.

'... Fox' I offered quickly 'He thinks you mean fox ...'

'Clever' he said admiringly, giving me a game if groggy wink.

'No, no' she pealed so that he closed his eyes in pain. 'The – er – rat.'

'Geranium' he said 'I must go ...' And he opened the gate and swung himself out of it. I stood there in my nightie, in the sunlight, quite helpless.

He waved and then held his temples. 'I'll be in touch. Farewell.'

It seemed to me I was always saying goodbye to him after inflicting some kind of injury. No wonder he didn't seem over keen to arrange another encounter.

'Don't forget the tickets –' he called, and holding his head in his hands he began to run down the sunny road.

'Isn't he an actor?' asked Maud.

'He certainly is' I said, and slammed my door so hard that the whole house shook to its empty foundations.

Chapter Six

I did not see nor speak to Finbar Flynn during the next two weeks. On the day following the non-orgy an immense bunch of flowers arrived accompanied by a note that said simply 'Flowers for a flower. Love and apologies. F.' And then about a week after that I had a short telephone call from, of all people, little fat Jim.

'You'll be coming to the opening, my dear?'

'Oh yes' I said. 'Finbar's left me the tickets.'

'Good, good. You must forgive his not telephoning himself but it's that tricky time.'

'I understand' I said.

Oddly enough I didn't mind the lack of contact at all. For some reason we don't seem to expect famous people to act in an ordinary way. A sort of snobbishness this and just as bad, really, as Maud and Reggie's wanting to hang around with the bloods. If I had spent a night like that with an accountant or a bus driver and he had just sent a bunch of flowers he would have got very short shrift – but where Finbar was concerned it all seemed perfectly reasonable. I rather enjoyed the oddness of it. Besides, I felt wonderfully well and alive.

Some of this must have shown because Robin came up to me at school and said 'My word, Joan – you look radiant – positively brilliant with life ...' and for once the Lawrentian twang failed to irritate. After all, why shouldn't he be allowed to indulge his obsession? I was indulging mine.

I did consider not telling him that his ticket had arrived, but it would have been so unkind. Besides, he might find out one day. So I gave it to him and was rewarded by his gratitude and pleasure.

'I sent a note to the box office' he said. 'But it doesn't matter now.'

I was glad I had been honest.

'Joan' he said, clutching the ticket, 'we can go together, can't we? Maybe we could meet and have a drink first. I'd still like to talk to you – I really would. There's a lot I want to say.'

I thought, I bet there is.

'Yes, Robin' I said, we can certainly go together but I'd rather not have a session beforehand – do you mind? Let's just enjoy the event, shall we?' And he shuffled off looking a sad picture of dejection.

Rhoda came up behind me. 'Someone should put that poor sod out of his misery' she said.

'Well, it won't be me.'

'Then you shouldn't go round tempting him all the time with your golden hair and your sexy airs.'

173

I smiled, rather pleased.

'You look as if you can't wait to get your knickers off.' She winked lasciviously.

'That's a terrible thing to say.' I couldn't help smiling.

'There you go, you see. You look like a cat brought in to help out with a cream mountain.' She laughed. 'Honestly – if ever I was looking for the perfect example of the benefits of leaving home – you're it.' She wagged her finger across a pile of exercise books. 'Marge always put me off the idea – I only had to look at her to know I was better off staying put but since I've seen you, and if I'm dealing with a particularly nasty baked bean pan or a pile of masculine understains, I have to say that the temptation grows.' She nodded in the direction of Robin's exit. 'Do I gather you've rejected the advances of our resident sex symbol in favour of a superstar? – What's the secret? Is it ditching your husband or what?'

'No' I said. 'It's not ditching your husband at all.'

'Well – that's a relief' she said, half seriously. 'So what is it then?'

'It's waiting for him to ditch you ...'

And I skipped off in the same direction as Robin.

'Gather ye rosebuds' she called after me acidly. 'While you can ...'

The newspapers filled their gossip column inches with news of the proposed boxing film; they quoted ever spiralling fees and were much taken with Clayton Junior who was Born Again and not afraid to say so. He apparently saw the whole script as some kind of analogy for Christ's ministry which, true or not, produced maximum publicity. I had no doubt that Finbar would get the part: leaving aside his acting skills, he had just the right physique for playing a well-trained ex-carpenter from Nazareth in the boxing ring. At least I had got far enough to find that out. I wondered – vaguely – how on earth they planned to fit in the disciples. Twelve sparring partners, perhaps? The contract had yet to be signed, according to one tabloid viper, but I felt sure it would be despite Finbar's creeping conscience. It is one thing to reject riches when it seems unlikely you will achieve them, but quite another when you have them in your sights. Hence, of course, the rise of the SDP here.

I read Proust to get me through the two-week waiting period

174

as his enervating minutiæ helped diminish the increasingly prurient aspect of my wandering mind. What I and Finbar Flynn did after we had walked along the surf and into the sunset was really quite shocking and the trouble with imaginings is you can keep going back over them. I began to wonder if I had stumbled, by accident, into that preserve generally counted as masculine and called Lust. I did try to include some beautiful conversations in my fantasies but Joan-in-my-head was not very enthusiastic about debating the finer points of Shakespearian blank verse and I am afraid most of what went on was what they call Action. Still – it all helped to pass the time – and there was always dear old Swann if things got too much out of hand.

About a week before the opening of the play I was driving towards the school when I saw a strange sight. Robin was cycling along in front of me, minus his usual cyclist's kit and wearing a pair of jeans and a very crumpled jumper. This was so uncharacteristic of him that I overtook gently and looked in my mirror; he was even wearing sunglasses – a wimpish affectation that he usually eschewed. He seemed barely able to put one pedal in front of the other and despite all that fresh air his face looked drawn and pale.

I waited for him in the parking area. He descended from his bike very slowly and gave a small wail as his bag of books fell onto the asphalt. I picked them up for him, feeling quite worried.

'Thanks' he muttered.

If I hadn't known how he valued his health I would have suspected him of razzling; he looked as if he had come straight from a night out in some gin palace.

I was moved.

'You poor thing' I said. 'Is it 'flu?'

'Not quite' he said, putting his hand to his head.

'It's a hangover!' I crowed. 'I recognise the signs.'

He closed his eyes. 'Not so loud – please ...'

Remembering my experience I said 'I hope you didn't pass out on her, Robin.'

With considerable dignity despite his blush he said 'I wouldn't have expected such crudeness from you, Joan.'

'Oh well' I said 'I expect the Prophet of Sexuality is keeping good watch.'

175

He shot me a look of embarrassed distaste and walked off. I ran after him into the building to apologise but only the shuddering of the men's lavatory door indicated where he had gone.

Later, in the staffroom, I did manage to say I was sorry but he just hung on the edge of things, drinking cup after cup of coffee and squinting the pinks, rather the whites, of his eyes.

After a day or two of this Rhoda began teasing him mercilessly. 'Giving you a hard time, is she? Thought you'd have more stamina with all your training ...' And more of that kind of thing.

I rather missed his perching on the arm of my chair but he remained on the periphery for the rest of the week, resuming some of his fresh faced charm, but not all, and presenting a perfect picture of love's young agony. I was quite surprised when, despite all this, he said he was still coming to the theatre. 'Giving you the night off, is she?' I said, without thinking – Rhoda's gibes were horribly infectious.

'Don't you start' he said. 'It's difficult enough as it is.'

'Sorry' I said, and winked. 'But it's fun to be in love, isn't it?'

'Who says I am?' he said, looking hunted.

'Well – aren't you?'

He rubbed the back of his neck and looked uncomfortable. 'Maybe. Yes. Perhaps. I'm not really sure.'

'Won't she mind you escorting me tonight?'

I was thinking, meanly, how much I would prefer to go alone.

He looked slightly embarrassed and addressing my general direction rather than me, he said 'You still want to go then?'

'Of course I do. But you don't have to come with me. I can go by myself if it will cause you problems.' I realised as I said it that I had put it badly. He was bound to feel his pride was at stake, but I couldn't retract; still the prospect was now far less exacting since I wouldn't have to worry about keeping him at bay any more.

'I have said I will take you, and take you I will.'

'Not if you'd rather not?'

'Joan – we're going as planned. I'll be round in a taxi at seven – all right? I am looking forward to it.' He added this last through gritted teeth so I thought it best not to argue any further, and head held high, off he went.

I saw Rhoda give him an amused stare. She came over to me.

176

'Trying to make him think again?' she said. 'No chance, duckie. You're right out in the cold.'

'And that's the way I prefer it' I said. 'I function better like that.'

'I like you' she said. 'Even though you never quite come amongst us mortals. I don't blame you.' She snapped her sharp eyes above the vermilion lips and pointed at Pimmy and Marjorie who were bending their heads over a knitting pattern. 'There's your choice' she said. 'Them in their sex-starved comedy or me in my domestic tragedy. Not much of a choice, is it?' she hissed. 'Just think, dear, all this could be yours if you'd only give in ...' And she threw her twinkling black patent handbag across the room. It landed at the knitters' feet with a thud and they looked up surprised.

'Sorry' said Rhoda with a brittle little smile. 'Dropped my bag.' Even though I laughed I felt an almost imperceptible little shiver down my back, as if someone had stepped on my grave.

Omens are peculiar things. Despite this calculated high-tech age and our rationally scientific lives we still call on omens in the same way that those whom we like to call primitives do. I remember hearing the opening blurb about a space shuttle launch with the ripe American voice telling us that the sun was shining, the heavens were clear, and wasn't that a good omen? So much for the space age: you can't get more primal than requiring the sun to bestow its blessing on an event.

Well, similarly, by the time March the third arrived I failed to dismiss as ominous the lack of geraniums in bloom in the shops. At least, I say in haste, lest I go the same way as Finbar and his toasters, not in my neck of the woods. Buds they had aplenty. I even bought one of these and left it around with the central heating on full blast but it wouldn't open. I bought another and popped it in the oven on gas mark ½, but it just shrivelled up. I stuck both abused plants outside and apologised to them, particularly the one with the singed leaves. There was nothing else for it, I'd have to make do with some of the primulas – after all they had their own sentimental connotation too, though he might not exactly remember what.

I managed to sleep a little that afternoon which was just as well. But from waking at around three thirty onwards all the usual clichés about time applied. It didn't just drag, it went

177

moribund, until at some point around five o'clock I began to feel that I was the unwilling participant in some sort of experiment. But from five o'clock it began to speed up a little and I could start to make preparations at last. For tonight we would meet in Philippi.

Chapter Seven

I laid out everything I was going to wear on the bed – it was something like being a bride again – each item holding its own significance. New knickers, new tights, the pink satin shoes that had originally gone with the outfit – even the locket on its original ribbon – all in all it was rather a good thing that I hadn't found a red geranium, for it would have clashed most horribly. And alongside everything else, of course, sponged and ready, the ethereal white dress.

I washed my hair and bathed – excitement beginning to grow now: I put in plenty of Badedas and lay there in huge mountains of suds, my knees emerging like a pair of erratics from a yellow swamp: you know what they say happens after a Badedas bath, I thought, and this is most certainly full strength. It also occurred to me that the manufacturers of vodka's similar claims about their product's potential, *had* turned out to be true in my case: I added a little more Badedas, just to be sure.

And what was I thinking and feeling as I lay there in my ad-man's dream? Only, I think, that the thaw had come completely now, and how lucky I was to be blessed with a fantasy made flesh. I surrendered myself to the pleasurable prospect of me and Finbar Flynn starring in a relationship together, sank further down into the bubbles and thought engagingly of the time when we might both be happily up to our necks in this foam of seduction.

> Oh the little Ice Maiden
> Where is she?
> Soaking in the bubbles
> Of a fantasy

I warbled into the steamy air. Funny how your voice always sounds better when you are in the bath.

The primulas were cut and ready in the kitchen, hanging their surprised little heads over a glass of water. I was going to wrap them in wet cotton wool and not fix them to my hair until we were in the taxi.

Good omens followed.

I did not accidentally stick my mascara brush in my eye thereby rendering myself a walking conjunctivitis case for the rest of the night. I did not drop an earring on the bedroom carpet and crawl around looking for it for a quarter of an hour; nor, once having found it, did I then bang my head on the open drawer of the dressing table as I got up, or catch my heel in the hem of my dress with that lavish ripping sound that only those who have done it will appreciate. No – I did none of these things. I could forget the ominous lack of geranium when everything else went so well. Even my hair – subject to its own will at special preparation times – behaved perfectly. I felt I was at my best and as I sat in front of the mirror inspecting the troops, a little melty sensation tickled round my heart for I suddenly thought that while I sat here doing my toilette, so must he be sitting in his dressing room at the same time, doing similar things in readiness for his big moment. Both of us about to go on stage. I doubted there was much to choose between us for nervousness.

Downstairs I paced about, killing time which had decided to be cruel again. Those last ten minutes before Robin was due went almost as slowly as all the rest put together and I put on the Sibelius as loud as I dared to drown out all further thought.

All knowledge is loss, all achievement a giving up of one state for another: I was about to go forth into the mucky old world of human emotion again. I turned the knob higher to drown out Rhoda's brittle voice which echoed back to me with its cynical projections about rosebuds. Finbar Flynn, I thought, Oh dear, Oh dear – what have you done?

But then, in the normal form of this narrative, the doorbell went, and all such reflection was banished in a single gush of overwhelming excitement.

Robin looked magnificent.

I might pause here to suggest to all hopeful males that a bit of window dressing can do wonders for the cause. I had seem him half naked in his cycling gear, and wearing perfectly decent casual clothes, and not been overly enticed – but I have to say

179

that seeing him as he stood before me then was something else. He was wearing evening dress, a dark blue coat thrown about his shoulders with a white silk scarf (tasselled quite decorously) hanging down. His white shirt gleamed, his bow tie sat in perfect symmetry to his neck, and he had a definite air about him of being confident goods on display. We women often do this. Men seldom. They should.

If it hadn't been for Finbar's claim on my affections, I think I might well have had to reconsider.

I said 'You look wonderful.' And felt safe about doing so since his affections were now elsewhere.

'Thank you' he said stiffly. 'And so do you.'

He helped me into my old fur jacket which I had had the forethought to drench in Chanel since it had taken on my mother's Mothaks rather generously, and he sniffed the air.

'You smell nice' he said. 'Kind of musky. Very unusual.'

That's me, I thought, I am my own creation.

We sat very far away from each other in the back of the taxi and dealt only in pleasantries. He made no move to grab me and I could tell that he was on his best behaviour. As we passed Lambeth Palace I held up the primulas and a hairgrip and asked him if he would oblige me by fixing them to my head. 'Finbar likes me to wear flowers in my hair' I said.

'Does he indeed?' said Robin, and while he fumbled about he added 'You should be careful with the likes of him.'

You stick to your patch, I thought, smiling non-committally, and I shall stick to mine.

'I mean it' he said, giving the flowers and then me a critical look. 'You could end up back where you started.'

'Robin' I said, as gently as I could 'thank you for your concern – but I think I can look after myself.'

'You need to' he said darkly, and then added, rather pompously I thought 'And you should have let me look after you while you had the chance.'

'Don't be sour' I said. 'We've both got ourselves sorted out now. Let's just enjoy tonight for what it is and not get personal, eh?'

He shrugged and said that was fine by him.

'No trouble about your coming with me tonight, was there?' I asked, suddenly pricked with conscience.

180

'Absolutely none' he said. 'We understand each other perfectly.'

Bully for you, I thought. And how many times have we heard that?

We were nice and early so we went to the bar to wait. The foyer was thronged with the usual mix of blue rinsed dowagers in their sparklies and trendy rainbow hair cognoscenti: the former, most likely, being related to the latter. While I waited for Robin to come back with the drinks someone squeezed my elbow. I turned round and there was little fat Jimbo, dressed in modest evening clothes, with a man at his side of whom the very last descriptive epithet could be modesty.

Jimbo smiled up at me and took my hand.

'I'm so glad to see you here' he said. 'How are you?'

'How's Finbar, more to the point?' I laughed.

'Highly strung' he said. 'But very much looking forward to seeing you when it's all over.' And then turning to the monstrous person at his elbow he added 'Clayton – may I introduce Finbar's ladyfriend, Geranium. I must say' he turned back to me 'you look the picture of innocent loveliness, my dear – doesn't she, Clayton?'

'Sure does' said the monstrous person and he bowed low over my hand and gave it a sort of suck.

It became very difficult not to laugh out loud. On the one hand there was Jim, looking like a rotund penguin, and on the other – much more difficult for the self control – was the Clayton person who looked like a caricature of himself. He was big all over – all that Texan protein, I suppose – and he wore a maroon suit which, I had to blink a bit, was edged in rhinestones round the lapel. Oh well, at least he didn't sport a ten gallon hat.

'How do you do?' I said, extricating myself from the suck.

'And so Engerlesh.' He smiled like everybody's idea of the Cheshire cat. 'Ah hope yew are happy in Cherist, Miss Geranium?'

I nodded that I was.

'And I also hope –' His big, florid face scrutinised some of the people nearby, coming to rest on a particularly outlandish pair of punks. So far as I was concerned their outlandishness had nothing to compare with his. But he looked back at me and said 'And ah hope yewer not unaccompany-ad, Miss Geranium?' His

181

ruddy face looked genuinely worried. 'We seeyum to hayve syam verrry straynge persons heeyar.'

I smiled. 'No no – I have brought a friend to look after me –' I nodded in the general direction of the bar. 'A colleague from school.'

Jimbo smiled joyfully at Clayton. 'She's a schoolteacher' he said. 'A schoolteacher.'

'Well – that's dandy' said Clayton.

'Ah' I said, seeing Robin making his way towards us. 'Here we are. Robin – do come and meet ...'

The introductions were made. Not surprisingly Robin was rather frosty with this strange looking duo.

'Well' said Jim 'we'd best go and take our places.' And then he turned to Robin. 'We'll all be going back to my place for a little party.' He handed him a card. 'That's the address. Be sure to get this friend of yours there safely. You can skip the Green Room — they'll all be coming on to my place anyway. Say around eleven-thirty?'

Robin did not unbend one ounce. He just took the card with the briefest of nods, and pocketed it.

I had to endure another handsuck from the monstrous maroon ringmaster before the two of them toddled off.

'There' I said in triumph. 'You can come too.'

Robin did not have the air of excitement about him that I would have expected.

'Prats' he said to their disappearing backs.

'Look' I said 'you really don't have to take me. I can get there myself.'

'Certainly not' he said, throwing back his drink in one, big gulp. 'This I have to see.'

And he went back to the bar to replenish his glass. I stayed sipping mine and thinking of Finbar, somewhere in that building, preparing himself for a role that, if I had my way, would rank merely second to the one I had in store. I had even left a hot water bottle in the bed at home – just in case it was to be My place and not His.

Chapter Eight

The auditorium was low lit and filled with the usual noises. Programmes riffled, coughs brayed, and people whispered and twisted in their seats with restless expectancy. As Robin and I reached our very good position in the stalls and sat down, I realised that I was wound up tight inside, like a coil, my proximity with the stage, as it were, encouraging the possibility of a fit of the vapours. I had that rushing in my ears again and a sense of steam building up. This passion was a curious thing for it had its own life quite apart from mine. Basically it manifested itself in physical heat and energy, and I feared for the safety of the poor shuddering primulas perched on the top of my head as I sat there with all those Etna-like rumblings going on. That the object of my desire was somewhere just beyond that proscenium made absolute control impossible but I did manage enough to appear outwardly uncertifiable.

Robin was looking at the stage which was open to view. The set was sparse: just the great central gates of a city and tiers of benches flanking them, the colours and lighting giving a uniform greyness to the scene.

'That looks a bit poor' said Robin in the voice of one for whom only a straightforward proscenium and a pair of red velvet curtains would suffice.

'You won't need scenery' I whispered. 'The actors themselves will paint the stage.' At least, I thought, one will.

'There's that wine-coloured wally waving at us ...' he said. I laughed. It was rather a good description really.

'Wave back' I said. 'He's a film producer and he wants Finbar to star in one of his films for thousands of pounds. Be nice to him.'

'Hypocritical Jesus Freak' said Robin, and he began creaking around in his seat (such spaces not being designed for the athletic type) and poking and plucking at his tie.

I waved across to Clayton Junior who smiled broadly and sat down again. Robin's creaking grew louder. 'What on earth is the matter? If your collar's too tight then loosen it. They'll throw us out if you keep up all this activity.'

183

It was a terrible thought.

'Sorry' he said, jamming his knees against the seat in front, 'But there isn't much room.'

'Well, scrunch yourself up and think of England' I said tersely. More than ever I regretted coming with him. Every time I got ready to yield to the night, his pragmatic presence ruined it.

Fortunately the lights began to dim which produced the usual dramatic hush and even he stopped wriggling.

Not knowing the play it occurred to me as the citizens came on and did their scene setting bit that Coriolanus might not appear in the first half of the play at all. They kept on and on about this perfidious chap called Caius Marcus and his surplus of faults so that I despaired of Finbar's appearance. I do realise that the Elizabethans liked their plebeian choruses to set the scene but frankly, if you've got the hots for the central character, such poetic nicety can drag a little. They made countless allusions to bellies, made it quite clear they had no truck with this Caius Marcus whoever he was, made absolutely no mention of Coriolanus but many obscure ones about big toes and themselves. I found all this just a shade too abstruse and began feeling fidgety myself. Until – quite suddenly, and taking my breath away with the shock, there he was, standing above the rabble, his eyes glinting down on them, his body unmoving: Caius Marcus was Coriolanus – and Coriolanus was Finbar Flynn.

Here was great art. It mattered not at all that I did not know the play: I had only to see him as he stood there to know that he represented the Master of their Universe: Hero, Ambitious Soldier, Despoiler of the Small Minded, Potential Tyrant. He held the stage, this Finbar Flynn, and was as far removed from domesticated male as Zeus from a launderette. Beside me I even felt Robin draw in his breath and I grabbed his hand, as if I was at the dentist, and gave it a mighty squeeze. He gave a little yelp and pulled it away from me. It was no good, I was in this thing on my own.

I stared at the stage in wonder. This man, the one up there now, could not possibly have lain naked with me in my bed. This man, I thought, with the last ashes of my reason, could never have been made drunk by me. Delilah and Samson, yes – but This Man and Joan Battram? Never.

He was so close that I could have chucked my programme on

184

to the stage to attract his attention, or called his name and he would have heard. These impulses came so close to being realised that I was seriously worried. A modicum of control was imperative. I found it from somewhere and metaphorically manacled my programme throwing hand, metaphorically super-glued my bottom to my seat, and literally put my hand over my mouth in case I said Coo-ee.

'Now who's creaking?' said Robin.

A primula flower, overcome with the agitation, fell plop into my lap and I settled for methodically shredding it, He loves me, He loves me not, shred, shred, shred ...

But I never once took my eyes from the stage. Indeed, thinking back, it could have been an entirely virtuoso perform-ance. There was no-one up there except him, and the whole of *Coriolanus*, I am sorry to confess, could as well have been written in monologue.

He was bare headed when he appeared, the black curls shining oilily, the face as chiselled as stone. Staring down at the gossiping plebs he looked imperious, cruel, proud (crumbs, I thought, what was that line of Sylvia Plath's? – something about Every woman adores a fascist? – Until then I had always assumed it to be ironical ...) – And as if all this was not enough, he was wearing that same incomparable white coat. I recognised at once the gestures and style of the patio table performance – no wonder the candle holders had been so engrossed that night, and no wonder Geraldine acknowledged his mastery of the profession. If this wasn't genius then it was as near as made no difference. He was a wonderfully physical performer and I sat there watching him in the true bliss that only the most privileged of us groupies may experience. So what if I had given up the Fifth Dimension and the lonely road for him. So what? The next hour and a half was vindication enough. Even if vindication were needed. By the time the first part of the play was complete my little heart was his – ay – and happy to give it too.

Half-time would have been a more accurate description than Interval. I felt as if I had been rubbed through a sieve and then scrummed for Wales. As the house lights went up I watched everyone else in amazement – they were standing up, yawning, stretching, chattering, making their way to the bar exits apparently unscathed by the drama of the first half. I seemed to be the only one who could not move.

185

'Pretty good, eh?' said Robin, creaking to his feet. His was the kind of soulless understatement that managed to call Passchendaele a scrap.

I had completely forgotten that he existed. 'Coming for a drink and a leg stretch?'

'No thanks' I said, fumbling with the little shreds of blossom in my lap. 'I think I'll just sit here.'

He sat down again.

'So will I then.'

I stood up. 'Perhaps I will after all.'

'Make up your mind' he said, and followed me out.

Oh well, at least there was one place where even he could not follow.

I was a woman in shock as I waited in that long line of bladders, but at least it was peaceful – the silence only occasionally punctuated by the gentle whoosh of a cistern and the rustle of replaced tights. Then someone about three bladders up from me said to her friend 'Isn't he gorgeous? He could put his shoes under my bed any time he chose.' To which the friend replied 'I don't think he'd be interested in you, dear.'

Since 'dear' looked like the back end of a bus (I know, I know, that's wickedly unsisterly – but she started it –) I thought her friend had a point. Would Finbar Flynn love me when I was old and bus-like – surrounded as he was and always would be with the pick of beauty and youth? All I had was eccentricity and a modicum of good looks. What would happen when I only had eccentricity? I whirled away on my heel, forsaking the peace of a quiet sit in a cubicle: projections about the future had no place in tonight's enchantment.

And back to Robin I went.

'Everybody thinks it's a wild success' he said.

It was bad enough sounding like a character in a Noel Coward revival, without him then going on to say 'Finbar certainly seems to have got them by the short and curlies tonight ...'

So much for the influence of D. H. Lawrence on his prose patterns: I knew it was really all sham.

But this, added to the comments of that pair of routemasters in the Ladies' made me wince. Remnants of an old savagery surfacing perhaps? Protection of one's own?

I shoved my untouched glass into Robin's hand and stomped

back to my seat to wait in silence. Just as before, the influence of outsiders made me uneasy. I was better off keeping this love of mine to myself. Such joys can be dispelled by a breath. I must acknowledge it to no-one.

There was wild excitement at the end of the play. My hands hurt from clapping as the semi-naked, blood-stained anti-hero of the piece revived himself in time to lead his company back and forth across the stage to take their bows. Frankly I had been very worried by the over-enthusiastic sword fight between Coriolanus and Aufidius right at the end. Remembering my part in scuppering its rehearsal I took fright, thinking while it was going on that if he came out of it unscathed I should never eat chocolates, park on a double yellow line or transgress any morality ever again. I had buried my head in Robin's shoulder, only peeping at the end bit, and when Finbar finally lay down and died I wept real tears. I hated Aufidius and later when we were clapping and hollering our accolades and Finbar suddenly took his erstwhile combatant's hand and made him take a special bow, I am afraid that I hissed.

'Joan!' said Robin. 'Stop that. Everyone's looking.'

'Oh bugger everyone!' I yelled. 'Hurrah! Hurrah! He's done it. He's done it ...' I was bouncing up and down in my seat with bits of primula flying off in all directions – well and truly dead they were now – fittingly.

When I stopped bouncing I realised that Robin was staring at me with an expression of mingled amazement and distaste. For an instant I saw what he saw – a madwoman, leaking shrivelled petals and emotion all over the place. And because I couldn't think how to stop his stare I poked my tongue out at him. He blinked as if I had made a physical assault.

'Hurrah! Hurrah! Hurrah!' I said again, distinctly and slowly, staring at him. Then I bounced up and down a few more times, and reached up to tweak his nose ... 'And Hurrah!'

'Stop it' he said, removing my hand.

'Well. Stop staring at me like that. Whatever's the matter? Haven't you seen enthusiasm before? I bet they ra-ra-rahed in Canada over your DHL.'

He rubbed where I had tweaked.

He went on staring.

All around us the crush of the exodus began but we remained in our seats.

187

'Well?' I said, and bounced another bounce or two like a child who's been told to sit still.

'It's just that I've never see you so – um – er – um ...'

'So um – er – what?'

I shoved my face right up to his and twanged his elasticated bow-tie. I expect he was blushing though what with the moisture of joy in my eyes and the dim auditorium I couldn't see.

'So um – er – what – Robin?'

'Well – um – ' he struggled. 'So – lively.'

Is not, I paused to think, this English language of ours so rich? Here was I busting a gut with ineffable exhilaration and all he could suggest was that I was lively? But how to get the truth across?

'Oh Robin, Robin.' I took his face between my hands and squeezed his cheeks until he looked like an Epstein maquette. He flinched – not surprisingly – since the nose tweak and the bow-tie must have caused him considerable discomfort. 'Don't you realise – don't you even now realise – that I love him?'

I was going to add, And he loves me, but thought this superfluous.

And – rather as I had never witnessed someone literally reel until my own poor dear mother on the night of the *crème de menthe* incident, now for the first time I was witnessing a face that, quite literally, crumpled. Just like a punctured balloon, Robin Carstone's normally sturdy visage suddenly went pop.

'That' he said quietly, from the folds of his deflation 'is obvious.'

Despite what you think about those ladies and the buses, I am kind.

'I think' I said, looking around me at the almost empty theatre 'that we should now go and have a drink.'

You have no idea how kind.

What I wanted to do was to rush behind the scenes, storm into Finbar's dressing room and fling myself triumphantly into his arms to tʰ nk him for his performance in the only way I could think of – which is old as time itself and still the most satisfactory. But it would have been a cruel woman indeed who could desert Robin at that hour. Anyway there would be time enough for me and him at Jimbo's.

'Come on now' I said happily, helping him to his feet. 'We'll have a nice relaxing drink here and then go to the party.' And

188

with very little help on his part, I sort of lugged him into the bar. 'Brace up' I said. 'We'll just wait here until it's time to go.'

He rallied a little and took out his wallet.

'No, no' I said gaily. 'This is on me.' I plonked a resounding kiss on his cheek and half threw him into a chair.

I never promised you anything, I said to myself as I edged my way through the crowd, nothing at all – it's all your own fault with your D. H. Lawrence and your imagination – and I don't feel guilty one jot, not at all.

'Give me a triple scotch and an orange juice' I said to the man behind the bar. 'And step on it.'

I thought Robin probably needed something and since I certainly wasn't going to administer the kiss of life, this seemed the next best thing. I know, I know, it wasn't very original, but it was all I could think of for shock at the time.

Meanwhile, back at the slumped one, nothing had stirred. I put the glass into his motionless hand. Was I forever to be playing Mrs Bacchus to the men in my life?

'Thank you' he said stiffly, and drained it.

And were they always destined to cooperate?

'You can go home now if you like' I said. 'Thank you for coming.'

'Oh no' he said, getting up. 'I intend to see you safely in as requested.' And he went off to get another drink.

I sipped prissily at mine and thought that life would never be the same again. What a wonderful thing is love.

We passed the time somehow.

'And what did you think of Virgilia?' I asked.

'Who?'

'His wife in the play.'

'Very cosy' he said, cradling his glass. 'Wives' he said mournfully –

'Very cosy things.'

'Beautiful, would you say?'

'Oh yes' he said. 'Beautiful things, wives.'

'I mean in the play – Virgilia –'

'What – Oh – her – very chunky.'

'And that bit when he took Volumnia's hand.'

'Whose?'

This conversation was only marginally better than addressing an empty chair.

'Volumnia. His mother.'

'Really?' said Robin. 'Was she there?'

I was addressing an empty chair.

He was running his fingertip around the edge of the table with Archimedean intensity.

'You know, where he said —' I couldn't quite remember it 'something about the things he had forsworn to give should never be called denials ... What a beautiful moment that was ...'

'Time to go' said Robin, standing up. He wobbled slightly, but righted himself. And off we went.

I felt happy and nervous at the same time – as if I was about to be awakened or something – one of those poetical budding ladies all ready to come biddably into flower.

Because the night held an extraordinary mildness, we walked over the bridge towards the Strand, ignoring the taxis. The water was inky and calm with only the occasional silver ripple to disturb its smoothness. The sky was part cloudy, part clear and though the moon was hidden some of its light illuminated the misty edges of the haze. I didn't feel cold at all. I felt full of life and energy and would have been quite happy to walk all the way to Jimbo's flat, except that it would take too long. I was eager beyond everything to be with Finbar again.

When we were almost at the other side of the bridge Robin, who had been quite silent until then, said à propos of nothing. 'You are like a sharp little needle in my side. All the time.'

'I'm sorry' I said meekly.

'Sorry!' he yelled. 'Good God, woman! Tonight of all nights you tell me you love him!' The violence of this outburst caught a couple who were passing by and they squeaked with alarm and went scuttling away like a pair of frightened mice. I called an apology after them.

'Robin' I said. 'I think we ought to get a taxi.'

'You think' he expostulated. 'You think ... ? The trouble with you is that you don't think. You never did think. You and your freakish behaviour. Look where that's got you. And me. Christ – I even went off to Canada because of you. And look at me now!'

Fortunately a taxi was passing. I hailed it. 'Get in' I said. 'You're drunk. Come on. Get in.'

'No' he said.

190

'Robin ...' I warned.

'No.'

I opened the door and pushed him so that he folded up quite neatly in the corner of the seat.

'Where to, love?' said the driver.

'Now behave yourself' I said to Robin. 'Where's the address?'

'Shan't tell you' he giggled.

I poked his stomach. He closed his eyes and shook his head.

'Too late' he crowed as I fumbled around in his trouser pocket. 'Get your hands out of there – leave my assets alone ... they are no longer part of your territory.'

I was furious, and burning with embarrassment as the taxi driver turned round and stared at us in amusement. 'It's usually the other way round' he said drily. 'Are you really going somewhere or do you just want to fumble all night? It's all the same to me now the clock's on ...'

I found the card at last and with as much dignity as I could raise, which was not a great deal, I read out the address.

'Robin' I said 'as soon as we get there you're going home.'

'No, I'm not' he said. 'I'm going to stay. I've been invited. So there.'

At the door to the flat I said 'Well – just be a little circumspect, will you?'

'Why?' he gurgled, leaning on the doorbell so that it pealed and pealed. 'I'm not Jewish, you know ...'

Chapter Nine

Finbar came towards me with his arms outstretched, smiling, welcoming, nodding with pleasure. If he had been moving in slow motion it would have made a lovely sequence in a romantic film.

'Geranium' he said dramatically. 'So you have come.'

It was so perfectly delivered that it was all I could do to stop myself sinking to my knees and saying 'My Lord, I am come indeed.' Instead I just smiled up at him.

'And what is it to be tonight? Your heel through my other foot? A punch on the nose? Or do you intend to be kind to me in my humble moment of triumph and let me through unscathed?'

I opened my mouth to speak, but before I could think of anything to say he looked beyond my shoulder, extended a hand and said 'And Robin here too? Excellent, excellent. Come in.'

They shook hands, I could see that Robin was all tight jawed about it, and I had a momentary desire to say Two submissions or a knock out to decide the winner when, fortunately, Jim arrived on the scene and led me gently onwards into the room.

Behind me Finbar said. 'The drinks are over there in the corner. Come, I'll show you ...' and he propelled Robin away, calling over his shoulder that he would be back in a minute, that Jim should look after me and not let me out of his sight. I watched him go and thought how dreadfully attractive he looked. Just a white tee-shirt and jeans and freshly damp hair clinging to his neck – I sighed.

'Fond of him, are you?' said Jim pleasantly.

'I believe I am' I said.

'Good. That's good. Because he's very taken with you ...' For the second time I could have picked that fat little man up on his dumpy legs and kissed him.

What was odd was how ordinary everyone looked. There were one or two dickie suits and one or two extravagantly gowned women, but in the main the actors and actresses – whom I vaguely recognised from their various roles in the play – looked unremarkable. Virgilia was wearing a black jumper and sinking her teeth into a chicken leg, Aufidius had on a very ordinary shirt and jacket and was pressed up close to a large bosomed woman whom I had last seen hurling abuse at Coriolanus in a crowd scene. And Volumnia was sitting on a chair with a serviette on her lap crunching celery. The oddest person in the room, who could just be seen over the maze of heads, was Clayton Junior whose shiny face was stretched in profound laughter; I probably ranked second with my wedding dress and the primulas.

A champagne cork popped and then Finbar was back at my side again. I saw that he had left Robin with a bubbling glass, sort of propped up against the wall near the bar. Robin was staring after him looking very pink. My conscience pricked for a second – and then I forgot all about him as Finbar put his arm round my shoulders to steer me deeper into the gathering. Jim smiled up at us both, said he would see us later, and waddled off. Alone, I thought, alone at last. But I wasn't quite ready to say anything as I felt in danger of either bursting into tears, or fainting, or both.

I was saved from either calamity by Finbar's encircling arm giving me a little pull in his direction, which I needed as I seemed to be rooted to the spot, and as I arrived jerkily at his side he bent to place a kiss on my cheek. At least, it was intended for my cheek, and if I hadn't chosen that moment to look down and check that the coast was clear for my feet to follow, all would have been well. As it was I gave him a great mouthful of dead primulas. Righting myself I looked up to see him removing a stalk of dried matter from his teeth. I helped him. It was the least I could do – apart from die on the spot – which ran a close second.

'Thank you' he said graciously. 'I might have known.'

'I'm sorry' I said.

'Please don't mention it.'

He was laughing at me, quite nicely, which I supposed was better than nothing.

'Finbar' I said. 'You were magnificent.'

'I'm so glad you liked it.'

I kissed his cheek and more or less got the right spot apart from a bit of ear that didn't much matter. 'I think you're a genius.'

'Eight parts the playwright, one part the director and one part me ...' he said, but he looked pleased.

'I'm glad you liked it. It's important that you should. And I am sorry that I have neglected our –' He smiled up at those poor flowers and flicked them before putting his hand under my chin (where it sat like a piece of warm silk) '– friendship. I should have come to see you after that funny night – but things get tricky towards the end of rehearsal time.'

'Thank you for the flowers' I said.

He flicked at the top of my head again and gave me a wonderful smile that went right down into my eyes. 'On the contrary – thank you for yours ...' And then, apparently catching sight of someone, he stiffened, and bent towards me and whispered in my ear 'Are you ready for this? Here comes the yellow rose of Texas ... apologies in advance ...'

'Feeyanbarr' boomed a voice behind me.

'Clayton' he replied with amazingly convincing bonhomie 'may I introduce a very special friend of mine – Miss Geranium Um ...'

'Charmed' he said, and this time he pumped my hand with his own which was better, if more tiring, than being sucked at.

'Did you enjoy the play?' I asked.

He looked at me very solemnly from under his bushy grey brows and his eyes were reproachful. 'Ah think injoy is not the right word, Miss Geranium. Ah think that ah have bin moved tonight – Ah have touched a lil piece o' holy grahnd – Ah think this boy is blessed with the spirit ...'

His voice rose very slightly at each Ah think, until he seemed to be watching it arrive somewhere on the ceiling – staring after it like a Shaker about to Shake. But instead he returned his revelatory gaze to me and said 'Yew ever bin to Texas, Miss Geranium?'

'No' I said. 'But I'm sure it's lovely.'

'Flahrs there' he looked at my topknot 'last a sight longer than they do seem to ov'r heyar – that's f'sho ... Like t'come sometime?'

'I'd love to.'

'Fin-boy.' He patted Fin-boy's shoulder. 'Yew bring this lil lady with yew when yew come over –' He looked at me. 'Yew hold him tew it, ma'am.'

Finbar squeezed my shoulder a shade too tightly. 'Yew'd like that, honey – now wouldn't yew ...'

Texas, I thought, or Bognor on a wet Sunday in February, or anywhere really.

'Oh yays' I simpered.

I felt him begin, very slightly, to shake all over. I had the same problem. Much more of this and I'd be what my old granny used to call Rolled up on the floor ...

I plucked a fairly sobering topic out of the charged atmosphere and said 'Is the film definitely going ahead then?'

That did the trick. Finbar stopped shaking immediately.

Jim, who had been standing like a little nodding dog, swivelling his head from speaker to speaker during the last few minutes, was suddenly still.

'Yup' said Clayton. 'And Feeyanbar here is the boy.' He clapped him meatily on the back. 'Whatsay ter thayt? Have we got a deal?'

I felt Finbar go all slack. He said firmly 'We most certainly have.'

Clayton laughed delightedly.

Finbar laughed delightedly.

I laughed delightedly.

And from beneath all this delight Jim popped up his head and said 'Then it's only a matter of the contract.'

'Sure, sure –' said Clayton. 'We c'n do all that stuff tomorrer. Say mah hotel around tayn?'

Hands were shaken, mine was sucked, and with a reminder to me about visiting Texas he gave my flowers a final, regretful look, and let Jim lead him off.

'I'm sorry' Finbar said. 'That was all very insulting. But he was very keen to meet you. They can get very proprietorial, these moguls.' He let out a great sigh of relief and made a wonderfully elegant beckoning gesture to a waiter with a tray of drinks. 'I think we've earned this' he said, handing one to me and chinking his against it as he did so. 'My God but I bet Jimbo's in seventh heaven now – he's been sweating on this for a fortnight. So have I. I think that must be why it got so difficult doing the play . . .' He rubbed the back of his neck with his hand and looked rueful. 'I've never had any problems before – it just used to come naturally. Learn the lines, do the rehearsals, open the play and do the best that's in you for your audience. This time I was so conscious of that overblown oil-man and his dollars; it was a real struggle . . .'

'Finbar' I said softly 'you were really wonderful tonight – I shall never forget it.'

'I'm a shit' he said humbly. 'And what's more, I begin to understand that cynical, ambitious hero of Corioli all the better . . .'

'Well then – that explains why your performance was so good.'

'My performances are always good' he said, losing all humility.

'Well – inspired then –'

'Geranium' he said. 'Don't make me feel worse by praising me. From you I expect the heaping up of scorn, some weird physical manifestation of your displeasure – not sycophantic tribute.'

'Sycophantic tribute!' I trilled. 'You'd never get that from me.' (Unless, of course, it would improve my chances. He could have it in bucketfuls if I thought it would do that.)

'You are so genuine' he said, much moved.

I fluttered my eyelashes.

'You have no idea how easily the word sincerity trips off the tongue in this business. I sometimes wonder if there is anyone left using Truth.'

'Oh come on' I said. 'You're being over dramatic.'

And then the stupidity of my remark sank in. I had just told the heir to Olivier's throne that he was being over dramatic. It was so funny that I began laughing helplessly, and I gave him a little push so he could enjoy the joke. 'Over dramatic' I gurgled. 'Do you see –' but the laughter wouldn't stop. 'Oh go on –' I pushed him again 'You must learn to laugh at yourself if you're going to survive ...' He was staring at me, unsure of himself, I think. 'You know' I said, wiping my eyes and trying to regain some degree of restraint –

We laugh and laugh
Then cry and cry –
Then feebler laugh
And then we die ...

... Or something like that.'

'Come over here' he said suddenly, and with unexpected but rather exciting roughness (remember the fascist, girls?) he grabbed my arm and led me over to a wall that had two paintings on it: hard-edged ones from the feel of them as they poked into my back. He put his arms on either side of my head so I was trapped there – we used to call it the wolf position at parties for it always meant that heavy chat was imminent – I looked up at him hopefully but he just looked sad.

'What is it?' I asked.

He shook his head and looked away, downwards, as if he were ashamed of something.

'You're so lovely' he said. 'And I'm such a wanker.'

'No, you're not.'

'Oh yes I am. I'm only doing this film for the money – nothing more than that. It has no artistic credibility whatsoever.'

'So what? You have ...'

I counted the lashes of his eyes as he continued to stare downwards.

'You know – when I came to you that night – I was really drawn to you, you do know that ... ?'

196

'Ah yes ...' I began. 'I wanted to ask you – the key you mentioned – and all that stuff about hope and me – I got a bit confused – what exactly ... ?'

He put his hand over my mouth.

'Forget all that' he said.

Once more the carpet seemed more alluring than me.

I didn't mind if we stood like this all night, but I felt we were on the edge of something, that he wanted to make a particular statement, and I had a sad feeling that I knew what it was. And, because I was brought up that way, I thought I should help him out – make it easier for him.

'You could look at me' I said, thinking She shows more mirth that she is mistress of.

But he did not.

'Look' I said, so breezily that it deserved an Oscar 'I'm a woman of the world, you know. I do understand what a one-night stand is – even an unconsummated one. And if you don't want to – well –' I tinkled a merry laugh '– compound it – you don't – well – have to. It's just that I'm not sure what my role is here. I mean – it was lovely to be invited and I did enjoy the play ever so much and I'm flattered to have been singled out from the rest of womankind when you needed a bit of care and attention – but really –'

And then courage, as it will, deserted me. Who was this fool of a woman burbling on about it all being perfectly OK and ships that pass in the night stuff? Not me.

'Oh Finbar' I said miserably, leaning forward to kiss the curls on his downbent head. 'I'm in love with you. That's the trouble. I really am in love with you ...' Fantasy made flesh, I thought, fantasy made flesh – we all need that from time to time.

The head did not move.

'Please say something?'

He looked up as slowly as if a camera were filming an atmospheric shot of grief. And he said 'Dear Geranium. Will you marry me?'

When Jack proposed it was in the middle of an icy January night. He was in my bed and we were warm and cosy in that nice, sticky sort of way you get, when he suddenly sat up and said 'Oh my God. I've got to be at Heathrow by six and all my stuff is at the flat ...' (His flat, a mile or two up the road.) 'This can't go on, Joan' cuddle, cuddle, cuddle 'I think we should get married. Life would be easier. Much easier.'

This was true. The previous week he had hurtled out of my place at seven o'clock in the morning and driven all the way to Dover before he remembered that he hadn't got his passport. So it was a marriage proposal that had a certain inevitability and usefulness about it, with just a touch of dewy surprise.

But this one?

Just about the only thing that kept me upright and conscious was being stabbed in the back by those cruel picture frames, which had the same effect on me as picadors' prods.

'Yes' I said at once.

My father has always stressed the importance of being decisive. He always said that if one wanted to lead, one must speak first, sound positive, and then find a way of making what you said fit the bill.

He really was a loss to the armed forces.

Finbar looked at me then. Sort of suffering really. It occurred to me that this was an odd emotion to experience at a time like this, but since there are no rules for feelings it would have been arrogant to say so.

We were just about to embrace in a proper grown up way when, for some reason – perhaps a jealous Semele somewhere in the ether – I said 'Oh no! – Robin. I've forgotten all about him.'

And Finbar went all tense and broody eyed and said 'Robin? What about him?'

'Well – ' I said. 'He brought me here and I haven't spoken to him since. He was a bit out of sorts when we arrived. Perhaps I'd better ...'

We both shifted out gaze around the room and saw that he was still where he had been when we first arrived – leaning against the wall by the bar, misty eyed and glass in hand. He appeared to be talking to himself.

'My God' I said. 'He's gone mad.'

Finbar gave a little jump.

'Oh no he hasn't' I said, much relieved, for I saw a pair of corduroyed, masculine legs poking out from under the table next to him. 'Who's that?'

'Our director' said Finbar shortly.

'I think Robin ought to be got home somehow' I said, for he looked in imminent danger of collapse.

198

'Leave it to me' said Finbar, and I thought My Hero, as he strode off. Generally I have found the usefully assertive male a fiction: mine were either in the lavatory or diving under the restaurant table when required. Things seemed to be changing.

I reached out and swung another glass of champagne off a passing tray and tried to adjust myself to what had happened.

Giving that up, I just leaned there, waiting.

I could see Finbar being all oil on water with Robin, and Robin gradually going from brick red that was first induced to his more normal emotional colour of pink. Finally he seemed calm enough to let Finbar lead him out of the flat. As he passed through the door near me he turned and said 'Congratulations' with very careful and slow enunciation; then, looking even taller than he really was, he sailed onward with Finbar in his wake.

'I'd better see him into a cab' said my new fiancé.

What an odd party it became after that. We told Jim. Who passed it on to Clayton Junior. But Finbar asked that it should go no further that night. He took me to one side and said 'It will be bad enough once it's made public anyway – you might as well enjoy the last shreds of your anonymity while you can.'

'Are you happy?' I asked him.

He didn't look it.

'Are you?' he replied.

I smiled but inside I thought, I just don't know. If I looked at him or reached out and touched him and he smiled at me – which he did easily – then I was happy. But on my own with my thoughts I wasn't in touch with my true feelings at all.

But then, as I counselled myself, this was a theatrical party, these people laughing and eating and drinking all around me were actors and actresses: it was hardly the right place for emotional verity. I did say to myself, But I hardly know the man, and then I thought, So what? You never do anyway. Look at the woman who marries a mild-mannered accountant who then proceeds to break her nose the first time she buys the wrong cheese ... or the man who marries the sweet, dovelike creature who turns out to have the gentle temperament of a Fury. Considered like that it made as much sense as any other. We had chosen each other. That was enough. At least, we seemed to have chosen each other. I was very confused.

And then Finbar became the Grand Illusionist again, which

was the role I knew and liked best. He strutted around joking with people, sometimes introducing me, sometimes not – winking at me from time to time as if to say, I know this is a terrible bore, darling, but they expect it ... doing silly little dances in an expert way ... cracking jokes at which everyone roared ... posing exquisitely and using his eyes all the time to amuse, to quiz, to ogle slyly. The rumour had already spread its ripples throughout the party – Oh, not about the two of us, not that – about Finbar's success with the film. Lots of back slapping here, with covert looks in the maroon ringmaster's direction and intimate smiles that acknowledged his singular power as well as his singular awfulness. Clayton stood there beaming at the melee as if he already owned it.

At one point Finbar whispered 'The celebration, at least, is sincere. We may have the best theatre in the world ...' (Always one for the demure statement, our Finbar.) ... 'But there's not much money in it. Everyone's hoping this has opened the floodgates for them, and who –' he threw his head back and laughed joyously ' – can blame them ... mmm?'

Music came from somewhere – Jack Buchanan, Glenn Miller, that sort of thing — and suddenly Finbar grabbed my waist and began whirling me around the room – others followed so that it became more like a barn dance than a West End social. I was passed on to one of the Volscians while Finbar went off around the room with Volumnia, then I got Aufidius while he changed to the Gentlewoman attending on Virgilia – and so on. You can forget anything when you're bound up in good, physical activity. I certainly forgot I was newly engaged, and I really began to enjoy myself. Clayton, Jimbo, everybody, caught up in a grand swirling charivari of dance, and all to a dollar tune. And whenever our paths crossed I looked at Finbar, and he looked at me, and I waited for that pleasant, now scratchable, tickle to begin – but it did not. Only more music, more dancing and a sense of grand unreality.

The four of us were left, and two staff. But whoever counted staff? Jimbo, looking pleased as punch and stretched out like a little shortform on his sofa, cradled a brandy glass.

Clayton Junior occupied another, his maroon patent shoes with Gucci buckle kicked off, his jacket like a pool of dried blood at his feet. He was sleeping, purring lightly.

Finbar and I were sitting on the floor, side by side, quite limp and, I think, quite happy. He had his head turned half towards me. A good profile, I noted, and then I shivered. He turned and looked at me, and then smiled. 'Even eccentrics get tired' he said. I took the flowers, what was left of them, from my hair and put them in his hand. He closed his fingers over them and put them up to his nose.

'Madness' I said softly. 'All madness.'

From the sofa Clayton let out a long untroubled snore.

'Your place or mine? Isn't that what they say?' He leaned over and kissed me very delicately on the lips for the very first time. It was a very chaste kiss. I felt exceptionally virginal.

'My hot water bottle will be cold' was all I could think of to say.

Finbar gave a little grunt of mirth and shook his head; the curls, flattened by sweat, no longer moved.

'Trust you to say something like that.'

If someone had played 'The Party's Over' I swear I would have howled.

'Finbar' I said 'I need some thinking time. A little pause to assimilate . . .'

'Geranium' he said. 'Of course you do. Come on –' He stood up and pulled me to my feet. 'You shall have your pause. We'll get you into a cab. You can sleep on it all. Alone.'

He was a very sensitive man.

'Goodnight, Jim.' I took his hand. He looked up at me swimmily. 'Good luck with the contract tomorrow.'

'Sure' he said comfortably, and closed his eyes, joining Clayton in the bliss of sleep.

We went out into the night which was very silent and dark. There were rubbish sacks leaning their odd shapes up against the walls of the street and even the sweep of St James's was empty of traffic. The clouds had thinned from the inky velvet and the moon was an almost perfect luminous disc. It was much colder. After the hothouse of the flat I was grateful for this and took some deep, reviving breaths while Finbar ranged around looking for a taxi. It didn't take long – being so near the Ritz I suppose – and he opened the door and helped me in as if I were very fragile. But it didn't rankle. It was no piece of showman's gallantry, just kindness, and I was grateful for it. I did feel fragile, even a little lost, and I decided that this was some new plain of happiness; after the yearning, the achievement, and after the achievement the sense of loss.

'Shall I ring you tomorrow?' he said, through the open window.

I nodded.

'And don't go upsetting this good driver of yours with your impetuous ways. I warn you' he said to the man behind the wheel. 'This woman is the very devil.'

If it was meant as a piece of humour, it failed. I couldn't raise a smile and Finbar looked positively morbid. And then, just as the engine's throttle opened to move on, I clutched at his hand. It reminded me so much of the show-stealing moment in the play that I said 'Say again what you said to your mother Volumnia, because you said it so beautifully.'

I did not know then that, of all the praise to come, this was the jewel the critics would hold up tomorrow for its especial brilliance.

He said it very simply, just as he had done on the stage, holding my hand as he had held hers.

> 'Or if you'd ask, remember this before:
> The thing I have forsworn to grant may never
> Be held by you denials. Do not bid me ...'

The taxi was moving too fast. We released each other's hands.

'Which bit of Chiswick?' said the driver.

I watched and waved until we turned a corner, then I sank back into that warm, taxi smell.

I told him.

'And I am engaged to be married' I said.

'Warm tonight' hazarded the driver.

'Actually, I think it's getting colder.'

'That's right' he said cheerfully. 'Very warm.'

Chapter The Last

I was wide awake and far too restless to go to bed. The taxi passed through Hammersmith Broadway and into King Street and I looked out at the completely empty street and thought, Why not? What is the point of having two legs and no responsibilities if you don't walk when you want to? Anyway, I felt invincible. I also felt a lot of other things that walking might help to define. I wished now that I had stayed with Finbar and I was also glad that I hadn't. If you see what I mean.

One or two cars passed me and one of them slowed, but I scarcely heard the suggestions that were whispered on the air. The coldness stood like a guard around me and I walked with a nicely blanked out mind, skipping from time to time and giving the impression of a carefree soul on the wing. And so, I suppose, I was.

I was just crossing at Turnham Green traffic lights and looking up at the stars thinking, I don't want to go home, I want some company – when I remembered that Robin lived very nearby. I shall go and see him, I thought, with that single mindedness that you sometimes get. After all, he had disturbed me enough in the past. So I trotted to his road which was completely dark save for the street lamps and one illuminated ground floor window about halfway along. Luck goes with lovers, I thought, happy again, for it was his window. And it was only after I had rung the doorbell that the single-mindedness left me and I realised, like a punch in the stomach, that this was probably not a good idea. I remembered the state he was in when he was escorted from Jim's flat ... Oh no, I thought, this was not a good idea at all.

I was just creeping off back down the path when the door opened. A figure stepped into the wedge of yellow light. Robin.

'Hi!' I said creepily, giving a little half wave of my hand. 'I was just passing ...' I moved further towards the gate '... just thought I'd say Hallo ...' I had my hand on the latch now, passport to freedom – but his voice (not half as lushed as anticipated) thundered down the space between us.

'You!' he roared.

'Me' I said gamely, since the fact was undeniable.

'Come here!' he thundered.

The light in the upstairs flat went on, a curtain twitched. I released the passport to freedom and went up to the front door.

He looked llike the supporting stooge in a Dean Martin movie. Bow tie askew, collar undone, hair pushed about as if he had run drunken, despairing hands through it.

'I think I'll be on my way now ...' I trilled, giving a wide-

203

mouthed impression of a yawn. 'A bit tired. I expect you are too – dear me, is that the time ...'

He put his large hand to my jaw (shades of a previous encounter this) and hauled me through the front door – which considerably reduced my sense of invincibility. I went easily enough. It was all madness anyway. What did another weird encounter here or there signify?

'Nice place you've got here ...' I said as he pushed me into a large room to our right and closed the door. Someone had removed a dividing wall so that the space ran from the front to the back of the house in a nice proportion. He seemed to use the front as a sitting area with a couple of squashy wing armchairs either side of a gas fire and a desk by the front bay which was piled high with books. Closer inspection showed them all to be either by or about Lawrence. Naturally. There was a bed and a chest of drawers and a small pine wardrobe at the other end of the room and on a small table just where the wall had once been there was a bottle of mineral water and a glass. It was all surprisingly neat, defying my quondam conception of a man living alone.

'... Very nice place indeed ... I always thought I should get the wall at home knocked down. It does make a difference – much better space. Did you do it or was it already done?'

'The previous tenant did it' he replied in a tone that said he was prepared to play this game for a short time only.

'I always think a room with a double aspect is so much nicer ...' I said, amazed at my ability to talk like an estate agent (Maud Montgomery would have been so proud of me. I suddenly saw her at a dinner party with someone saying 'They've just dropped the bomb on Kew ...' 'Really. Very interesting. Pass the cheese ...')

'Sit down' he said.

I sat. There was no mistaking the seriousness of the command. He sat in the opposite armchair.

'That's a very nice clock' I said, looking at a really awful wall clock modelled like the sun.

'Also the previous tenant' he said. 'And it is the opposite of nice.'

'Oh I don't know' I said, thinking maybe we could keep the conversation on matters of design. 'I think it's quite jolly.'

'Perhaps' he said icily 'you would like me to give it to you for a wedding present?'

'Could I use your bathroom please?'

'No' he said.

The bounder.

'And why aren't you tucked up tight with your intended right now?' he asked.

'Not that it's any of your business – but I just wanted a little time to pause and think about things. You know –' I shrugged and gave a light-hearted laugh ' – what we women are supposed to do after being proposed to . . .'

'And how does it feel to be engaged?' He pushed his face into the space between us.

'Peculiar – odd – I don't know. You should try it. You've got a girlfriend.'

He looked so sad suddenly that a great spurt of compassion overwhelmed me. After all, I had all this happiness (the sensation of which had momentarily escaped me but I was sure it would soon be back) and he was left with nothing except, from the looks of him, a potentially king-sized hangover. I decided to claim immunity.

'I never said when we went out together tonight that you and I were anything but friends, Robin. You can't blame me for . . .'

'. . . For what?'

'Well – I mean – if you feel humiliated. I just want to say that I am very sorry.'

'Thank you very much but there's really no need to apologise.' He gave a sort of groan. 'Bloody Hell, Joan, you didn't even seem to like him when we met at the theatre and now you're going to marry him? When on earth did all that change?'

'I think when I found out that he felt the same about me'

'And when was that wonderful moment?' he said acidly, placing his finger tips together and tapping them like a dangerously goaded headmaster.

'You didn't see him on that television chat show?' I said.

'No' he said wearily. 'Get to the point.' Tap, tap, went the fingers. So I told him, sparing no detail when it came to the bit about the lovable schoolteacher in Chiswick.

'Joan.'

'Yes, Robin.'

'Poor Joan.'

'Yes, Robin?'

'There is more than one lovable teacher living in Chiswick . . .'

Odd – but interesting.

He sighed, really deeply, right from the heart. 'I shouldn't be saying this – but he –' he indicated the pile of books on the desk 'believed in absolute truth. So I will.' He looked at me sadly. 'There is also – me.'

Clarity.

'Yes Robin,' I said carefully. 'But I don't love you.'

He laughed sort of grimly. 'I know you don't.'

'Look' I said, as kindly and as coolly as I could. 'I love Finbar Flynn and he loves me. We are going to be married …' I decided to stretch the truth a shade, just for emphasis. 'And the point is that since Valentine's Day – we have been lovers –'

'Oh no' said Robin. 'The point is – you haven't.'

'Pardon?'

The silence between us was punctuated only by the hissing of the gas.

'Finbar and you are not lovers. Finbar and me' he said 'are lovers. Finbar and you have yet – as David Herbert might say – to hit the wild orgasms of love …'

Pop, pop, pop, went the gas.

As we sat there confronting each other I remember vaguely wondering whatever happened to Fidelity and deciding it was part of a bygone age. And of course, how could it be otherwise? Just as I thought that very thing, the doorbell rang.

Robin stood up. At the very least I expected him to stand on his head and turn a double summersault – but no – he just walked, quite calmly, out of the room towards the front door.

I heard the tread of his heels in the passageway.

I heard the rattle of the latch on the door.

I heard the swing of the wood from the doorjamb.

Felt the wind whistle round on the floor. And

I heard a familiar velvety voice say 'Dearest Rob. I had to come.'

Feet shuffled, bodies rustled, the doorlatch clicked shut, and two pairs of heels trod their return to the room.

I wished myself invisible. Above me Semele cackled and refused to help.

They entered together. Robin first, Finbar second. Robin looked at me before his face swivelled away, pulled by Finbar's long fingers which twined around his neck to embrace him.

What, I thought to myself, is going on? Some kind of

rehearsal? If it was it was at premiere stage for I could detect no faults in technique. And what was my recently acquired fiancé doing rooting around in Robin's mouth with his tongue?

I coughed, which seemed the only decent thing to do, and my recently acquired fiancé stopped his dental investigations. He did not, however, look round. I knew that feeling very well. It was the feeling that if you ignore something it will go away.

'I am afraid' said Robin quietly to Finbar 'that you have just illustrated a narrative I was in the middle of.'

And that doyen of attraction turned his dark, hunted eyes towards mine. He blinked once, just to be sure, and then said 'Oh Jesus' in such a ringingly tragic tone that it might be counted as his best performance to date.

Oh bugger being emancipated, I thought.

And not to be outdone, I swooned.

They sat me up in Robin's bed with a duvet wrapped around me and a cup of Bovril in my hand.

'How do you feel now?'

'Fine' I said wearily. 'Just fine. A quick cup of tea, then I'm off to the Palais.'

Someone, Robin I think, put a hand on my forehead.

'I'm not delirious' I said sourly.

Just for a moment I observed the picture we all made. Me in the duvet with my hot drink, flanked by a dark-browed Celt on one side and a fair-faced Angel on the other. It was rather like a modern travesty of some Bellini panel: 'The Madonna of the Bovril Cup and Two Sinners.'

'How could you?' I looked at Finbar who was looking at me with a suitable expression of anxiety.

'How could I not?' He shrugged. The anxiety was replaced by an attractive candid roguishness. The temptation to sling my beef extract all over him made me weak with longing.

'Look' he said 'I'm not a respectable person. I never said I was a respectable person. And I could no more behave like an accountant than you would have been interested in me if I had done ...' While I sifted my way through the convolutions of that particular gem of logic, he continued 'You more than anyone should understand that.'

'Why?'

207

He touched my face very tenderly. 'Because, my little darling, you are an eccentric yourself.'

I had to ask the inevitable question, although I was sure I knew the answer. 'Why did you ask me to marry you?'

'It just seemed the right thing to do. I hadn't planned it or anything ... I certainly didn't set out that evening to propose something as honourable as that, it just happened.'

'It was because you wanted a blind for that film man, wasn't it? You needed a woman in your life?'

'Geranium –' he said 'I had a woman in my life. You.'

'You also had him' I said, pointing with my mug in the general direction of Robin who sat there looking mortified and hungover, a combination that, quite frankly, I felt he deserved.

Robin said quietly 'If only you had been prepared to listen to me when I came back from Canada all this might not have happened.'

By now I had finished my drink. Otherwise the temptation so narrowly avoided with Finbar would certainly have won.

'I admit' said Finbar 'that you were useful in clinching that particular deal. But I can assure you that the attraction was more than functional. When I saw the two of you together at the Aldwych I was desperately torn. I wanted both of you.'

I closed my eyes. But quickly opened them again. Even this reality was preferable to my mind's eye which was showing all three of us thrashing about in what Fred's prurient newspaper readings would describe as an intimate manner ...

'What about you, Robin?' I said. 'Didn't you mind?'

'You get used to sharing' he said. 'The guy in Canada was a married man.'

Just for the teeniest fraction of a microparticle of an atom of a millisecond I thought – Hell, it might work –

'The trouble with you' said Finbar 'is that you underestimate your attractions ...'

Banish the microparticle.

Shades of Helen Gurley Brown – whom God preserve of New York, with her Every girl has something if it's only smooth elbows –

'You're good looking, intelligent, quite a character –'

'Thank you' I said. After all, he had just given me all the attributes of a first class dog.

'It would have been a good marriage, you know. We could have had some fun together ...'

'Yes' I said. 'The three of us.'

He had the grace to wince at that.

He bent and kissed my forehead. I waited for the frisson but it had understandably departed.

'And now Robin –' I said. 'Don't leave him out.'

Finbar sat up again and looked hurt. I could view his considerable attractions quite calmly now, regretfully even. I began to feel strong again, stronger than either of those two now looked. And, as I said, I am basically a kind person.

I pulled the duvet round me and sat up very straight. 'Look' I said. 'It's all right – it really is. I'm not going to say anything about all this. I don't even mind – ' I looked from sinner to sinner – it was curious how superior I felt ' – keeping up the pretence for a while. Except – ' I poked Finbar in the chest 'I am not going to Texas. I don't want to go to Texas, Texas moves me not, to Texas I will not come. Apart from that I'm available for the odd bit of propaganda.'

Finbar stared at me with the kind of radiant face that I was supposed to display had we got to the altar.

Robin said 'Would you like some more Bovril?' Which was perfectly in character.

'Why Bovril?' I asked. 'Why not tea – or coffee?'

'Because' he said, standing up and taking my mug 'it's better for you.' Considering the trauma in which I had just participated, I thought this was ever so funny.

Both Finbar and I began to shake – I could feel him through the bedclothes.

'Oh thank you' I said 'for being so concerned for my health. Yes please.'

And as soon as he was safely out of the door and chinking about in his kitchen before Finbar and I stuffed bits of duvet into our mouths and laughed and laughed and laughed.

'He'll make a better wife than me' I said.

'I'm not so sure ...' Finbar wiped his eyes. 'Oh Geranium' he said 'I do love you. I really do. In my way.'

I thought of that damn patio table and the candles and how he had sung those very words and I thought that I had not, really, been sober ever since. But I was now.

And it was good.

*

209

It must have been about six in the morning when I left Robin's flat. Snow was falling.

'We must get you a cab' they chorused.

'No need' I said. 'I love it. And anyway, I am invincible.'

The world looked so pretty again as I walked along.

A few of the houses nearby were beginning to stir, and the occasional car shooshed its way along the distant High Road.

At the end of Robin's street I turned and waved.

They were still standing on his path, two figures in the pristine snow, holding hands.

Ah, I thought, how sweet.

I remembered the two geranium pots I had left out on the patio.

They will have a shock, I thought, first the oven, then the frost.

A bit like life really.

And then I burst into tears.

I cried and cried and cried, all the way home, enjoying every minute of it. And when I turned into my street I felt so much better, so much like the person I had once been, the soul before Jack, that I began smiling as I walked up my path – the Montgomerys' clipped hedge on one side, the Durrells' rampant laurel on the other, and my little honeysuckle fondly waving in between, covered in a powdering of natural icing sugar.

I sauntered through the settling flakes, shushing them with my feet, and reached the front door. The house looked at me reproachfully. You took your time coming back, it said.

I didn't apologise, but once through the door, I did a little dance in the hall for it, just to show that all was well. Fidelity might not exist, but I did.

Then I went out to the patio and rescued the geraniums. They would always be Finbar and Robin to me.

Then I climbed the stairs to my bed.

I selected my favourite book, which is *Middlemarch*, and said 'Hallo, old friend' before snuggling down under the covers.

And I thought of that other Eliot, dear old T. S., with gratitude. Winter had certainly kept me warm.

BEGINNING